THE GREAT PEACE

or,

GET WITH THE POGROM

by,

RYAN GEORGE KITTLEMAN

exploding books

new york - san francisco

Published by
EXPLODING BOOKS
explodingbooks.com

THE GREAT PEACE

"Trust me, one had better mix in, and do like others. Sad business, this holding out against having a good time. Life is a pic-nic *en costume*, one must take a part, assume a character, stand ready in a sensible way to play the fool. To come in plain clothes, with a long face, as a wiseacre, only makes one a discomfort to himself, and a blot upon the scene."

- Herman Melville, *The Confidence-Man*

"I must soon quit the Scene..."

- Benjamin Franklin, *in a letter to George Washington*

THE ONE PART:

The Going out of Business Sale

HOW NOT TO TIE A KNOT

Rufus Wiggin elbowed his way inside Smitty's Tavern and shouted, "My best days are behind me!"

His entrance had been calculated to provoke some or any reaction by the patrons. Instead, among the rowdy din of a bar-wide brawl, he found that his proclamation went unnoticed.

Nuts, Rufus thought.

Undeterred, he forged on. After all, a flubbed beginning needn't have any bearing on the outcome of his mission. Rufus surveyed the floor, battle-pocked with a mix of blood, sweat, and beers, and hiked up his pant legs so as not to soil the bottom fringes of his trousers.

A foppish dandy to the last, Rufus always endeavored to stride in the confident and gallant manner befitting an aged Schuyler Academy gadabout and the sole heir to the Wiggin fortune. Yet he now found himself slowed by the caramel glue of dried beer that caked the floor with a high gloss shine. Hunched over, argyle ankles bared, Rufus cut a perimeter around the crowd. Diligently, he ducked, dodged, and sidestepped the mob.

What a scene, he thought.

Throngs of grown men, old men, shopworn and haggard, had taken to pounding the living piss out of each other. Dozens of them at least, though Rufus suspected there may be hundreds.

Sweating, bleeding, drooling.

Black eyes and cauliflower ears.

Bulging veins and missing teeth.

The steady onslaught of fists was interrupted only by bottles, pool cues, and beer signs. Men were fighting one against one, two against one, four against two; it was an orgy of aggression. Rufus had never seen anything so distasteful in his life.

Sure, even Rufus knew that Smitty's had a reputation for being a fuck-or-fight kind of place. Sure, it was harder than ever to find women within a two block radius of this hellhole, diminishing its patrons' options by half on a nightly basis. Nonetheless, this kind of brawling was unprecedented, even for Smitty's.

At first it made Rufus question the choice of venue for his mission. Why not do it in private? he wondered. Why give himself over to these ugly, uncaring faces?

No, he affirmed, it was already settled. This was the perfect milieu to stage his spectacle. Rufus sauntered up to the bar and summoned the dive's decrepit proprietor.

"Smitty," called Rufus nostalgically, as if they were old and beloved acquaintances, "You rusty old nail, you!"

Smitty recognized Rufus. The fancy boy, he called him. Always wearing that fruity ascot and treating his bar like the goddamn Yale Yacht Club. Smitty never forgot the hordes of pompous snobs that often accompanied Rufus, or the time that he had the nerve to order a martini in that airy cadence of his. He would rather have the dregs of the earth tear his place asunder board by board and plank by plank than have his door darkened by any more spoiled blue bloods. He pretended not to see him.

"Smitty, I say," Rufus tried again. The barkeep responded by languidly pouring himself a shot and downing it in one even draft.

"S'been happenin' mor'an more since the war started," Smitty observed coolly in the direction of Rufus, but to no one in particular.

It was true. Ever since Polo Younger seized power and the *Droit Moral* fired the first salvos of the civil war some eighteen months back, brawling had grown increasingly common. Unemployment had soared among the laboring classes as the *Droit* seized all of the factories and warehouses and converted them to live-work lofts for the city's starving artists.

With an elbow resting casually on the bar, Rufus watched a bald man with a hefty beer gut throw an even balder man with a heftier beer gut onto the pool table. There they wrestled – bellies rubbing, ass cracks exposed – until Smitty cut in.

"'Kay, nuffa dat," he said, nudging the pair from across the bar with the butt of a broomstick. "Folks'll still pay t'use dem tables." They tumbled to the floor, simultaneously kicking each other in the groin as they fell.

"Doctor Cocktail, my dear chap," Rufus persisted. "Purveyor of the alcoholic arts."

No response. Rufus had lost his patience.

"Get me a Double Basil on the rocks, you insipid prick!"

That got Smitty's attention.

"Buy ya'self a setta balls did ya?" Smitty asked, lifting the heavy drapery of wrinkles around his mouth into a parody of a smile.

"I'll – I'll mash yours to mushy peas if you don't out with the booze already," Rufus snapped, immediately wishing he had come up with something more clever.

Smitty looked down, looked up, looked left, looked right, and shrugged. "Don't got any," he said.

"It's right there, you jackanapes!" yelled Rufus, pointing indignantly at a bottle shaped like a Benedictine monk wearing a *papier-mâché* smock.

"You want it, you get it."

Smitty shrugged again. To Rufus it appeared that half a century at the helm had left the man firmly rooted to his post; were he ever to be pried away, the indentations of his size 9 Stacey Adams would surely be revealed. Rufus was convinced Smitty would die standing up.

It was a matter of practicality, Rufus supposed. With minimal strain, Smitty could reach the beer taps, the glasses, the cash register, and his trusty .45. He had claimed this imaginary tube as his domain, and it simply wasn't worth the effort to leave.

With no aid forthcoming, Rufus brushed the broken glass off the bar, climbed over until the bottle was in reach, deftly snatched it, and fell backwards onto a stool. By the time Smitty had swiveled his bulbous head, Rufus was downing a second swig. Without a shot glass to temper his intake, Rufus swallowed one generous gulp of bourbon after another, all the while observing the melee that was continuing to unfold.

Where do these animals get their stamina from? Rufus wondered. His own extemporaneous display of physicality had brought a rush he hadn't felt since his pole-vaulting days at Schuyler, but even that single jump over the bar left him winded. This fight, however, had been going on since he had arrived some twenty minutes ago, and who could tell how long before that it had started?

Rufus watched one man kick a fallen foe half a dozen times, each blow harder than the last. Another hurled pool balls across the room while ducking a barrage of darts. Their viciousness would've been a farce if they hadn't looked so adamant in carrying it out, Rufus observed to himself. Or perhaps that's what made it a farce.

At last he grew bored with the mayhem. Rufus was working up the courage to carry out what he came there to do. This is it, he thought, trying to convince himself of his righteousness. Is this it, he wondered.

Putting the bottle on the bar, (How had he already consumed half of it?), Rufus straightened his ascot, smoothed the wrinkles from his embroidered worsted blazer, and tamed his wavy helmet of hair. His hair was his greatest source of pride. Tousled in the open air of countless regattas, autumn mixers, and charity fundraisers, it was the hair of the entitled elite.

Yet let them have it! he silently raged. Let them make hay with my follicle follies! Let them have it all!

Rufus eased his way to the corner of the bar, took hold of a giant oak barrel, and rolled it with his entire frame into a small clearing among several limp and broken bodies. The barrel was held solid by iron rings and secured by square nails; it seemed sturdy enough to support Rufus' full one hundred and eighty pounds.

From his inner pocket, Rufus produced a length of rope tied at one end with a modified Multifold-Overhand knot – what is commonly known as a Hangman's Noose. From atop his oaken perch, Rufus surveyed his audience – a rowdy bunch indeed. The melee continued.

What invidious slobs, he thought. Shall I picture them in their underwear to calm my nerves? He looked again. Better not, he decided.

Clearing the film of liquor from his throat, Rufus closed his eyes and started in.

"My best days are behind me!" he shouted. "Our best days are behind us!" His voice was quivering like a freshman in front of a public speaking class. Again he thought of Schuyler.

"Art for art's sake is like taking a shit and not wiping your ass!" he pronounced. No response. He was, as they say, bombing. He reconsidered picturing the crowd in their filthy, tattered undergarments.

"Get off my barrel, ya fruit," yelled Smitty from inside his tube.

Rufus took a deep breath and tried to focus.

"Which is worse, ignorance or apathy?" he asked the crowd.

"I don't know and I don't care," quipped a faceless heckler.

"Fuck you faggot!" shouted another. A left hook to the gut sent the final syllables up his diaphragm, through his throat, and out his mouth in a muddy rainbow of vomit and what appeared to be a fruity cereal of some kind. Rufus comforted himself with the thought that the man was suffering instant divine retribution for uttering such a homophobic remark. He smiled and found his stride.

"I should be knuckle-deep, nay, elbow-deep in the hot-wet stink of new adventure! I should be feasting on the loamy loins and succulent sides of nubile temptresses." Rufus stomped his feet for added effect, hoping the barrel would continue to support him.

"Come one, come all, say I! Good ones! Bad ones! But never fat ones!" Rufus felt himself veering off-message, but he was on a roll. He gesticulated wildly as he spoke, channeling the passion of Garibaldi, and the oratorical flare of Eugene Debs.

"Why shouldn't I be conscripted into the great war of ideas, bought and sold on the marketplace of ideas? I could fight valiantly for the noble causes, defending virtue from the barbarous throngs of the disenchanted!"

And now the coup de grace.

"But alas," Rufus lamented. "I have already tried and failed. Despite being handed every opportunity to succeed, I have squandered my gifts, foreclosed my path to greatness, and pissed away a princely sum on the creature comforts of conspicuous consumption. We are at war with ourselves. May I, by this action, herald the great and everlasting peace that will be the denouement of our internal and our civil strife!"

Rufus held for applause, of which there was none. He then flung the loose end of the rope over a rafter and secured it with a Sailor's Eye Splice knot. Slowly, he slipped the noose around his head and dragged it through his prodigious coif. He held the cord briefly around his temples as he reflected upon Christ's Crown of Thorns. He had abandoned religion years ago.

How will I be remembered? he wondered. Will my death be a turning point, a catalyst in ending the war? Will I be a martyr for justice, recalled fondly as a tragic yet heroic figure?

Or will I be lumped in with every desperate nobody who ever threw himself in front of a bus?

Rufus let the noose fall over his ears and tumble to the base of his neck. He pulled the knot with both hands, tightening it around his windpipe. He swallowed hard and it tightened further, constricting his Adam's apple. It was a strong Adam's apple, a dignified...oh, forget it.

Rufus paused again to congratulate himself on the speech. It was just as he had practiced it. He went a little over-the-top perhaps when he improvised that bit about the 'barbarous throngs of the disenchanted', but on the whole the speech was delivered with exquisite erudition nonetheless.

In fact, Rufus was surprised he had been able to pull it off. He had never had an aptitude for public speaking. In the next instant the mystery was solved. As a wave of nausea rose through his body, he realized that he was wasted.

The bourbon vertigo came first; his brain felt like a thick slurry slowly churning in a cement mixer. His stomach's only remedy for the coming flood was an influx of acid and bile. His tongue longed for water, though his choked and filmy throat was already impossibly tight. His knees weakened, his legs wobbled, his barrel teetered. He tried pivoting his feet and waving his arms, but his impaired coordination only made a fall from Barrel Mount more imminent. The only thing keeping him upright was the rope around his neck.

The rope! Oh god, what have I done? he thought.

The barrel spun off-axis, oscillating elliptically.

Rufus realized he should have done more research on this whole hanging business. He could have blown his brains out, for instance, or plunged off a cliff. Also, he was fairly new to knot-tying, a hobbyist at best. What made him so sure that at this, at last, he would finally be a success? Why hadn't he considered that a poorly tied noose can cause one to die slowly of strangulation? Worse yet, didn't he know it could snap the vertebrae only partially, leaving him to dangle there like a jackass, humiliated, until Smitty decided to leave his tube and cut him down with a pair of garden shears?

The barrel tipped onto its side and rolled into a pile of bodies. Rufus had experienced this feeling once before, on a boardwalk ride during one of his family's summer pilgrimages to Maine. He felt it in the pit of his stomach. It was the law of gravity passing sentence.

A failure in life and in death, Rufus thought.

His arms flailed as he fell, a little slack the only thing keeping Rufus Wiggin – hair, Adam's apple, ascot, blazer and all – from the great unknown.

The slack vanished in an instant, tightening against its quay. Here comes the death knell! Rufus' head cocked to the side, striking its final pose. But before the rope could inflict the mortal blow, the Sailor's Eye Splice snapped, sending Rufus crashing onto the floor.

Dumbfounded, Rufus inspected the frayed end of his rope, a piece of it still tethered to the rafter.

I'm saved! he thought. By my own incompetence – Saved!

Rufus looked around for approbation, only to find that his was still only a sideshow act. The epic battle of attrition continued to be waged all around him.

Smitty fired a round into the ceiling. Chunks of moldy debris and asbestos rained onto the bar.

"Knock et'off, apes! A'show's a'startin."

The shot didn't startle Rufus, though he was surprised to hear that Smitty had successfully engaged a musical act. Noose hanging freely from his neck, he sat contentedly on the floor, clinging to the barrel like a marooned sailor. He had never been happier to be alive.

How had he ever failed to notice how beautiful Smitty's looked? he wondered.

Rufus had touched the sticky floor, and now was enjoying the feeling of adhesive tension as he pulled it back. When he nudged the unconscious body next to him, he could swear the man was smiling.

Eventually, the fight had to end. The few left standing were swaying warily, clinging to one another in a kind of macabre slow dance. Even the winners, whose haymakers had felled scores of challengers, were still losers.

"Band's a'startin. Shettup!" Smitty yelled. He transfixed his attention upon the stage.

How delightful! Rufus thought, eating a peanut from off the floor.

In all the commotion, including (but not limited to) his own deliberate/regrettable/accidental near suicide, Rufus had failed to notice a trio had begun setting up on a small riser at the opposite end of the bar. A small group of hipsters, surreptitiously checking for any signs of the *Droit Moral*, was gathering among the carnage. Even a couple of girls – comely, raven-haired, bubbly girls, so rarely seen these days – had braved the night. They were blowing kisses to the guitar player as he fiddled with a mélange of pedals and modulators.

"Well I'll be, Smitty," Rufus said, grinning madly. "Women have joined the ranks of your perennial Spartan camp."

"I start'd'a like ya when ya's gonna kill ya'self."

"Touché, chum, but that man in fact did die. Sitting before you now is Orpheus emerged, Orpheus reborn!"

Rufus took off his socks and shoes and made himself at home.

He looked on as the band finished tuning and speculated about these unlikely troubadours.

The guitarist was short and lean, his tightly coiled locks flattened down by a corduroy newsboy. His eyes were dark and remote, as if forever hitched to a star that no one could see but him. He wore a tight striped shirt; a silk neckerchief draped down his chest to his waist. Rufus admired its perfect Pratt-Shelby knot; it put his own rather pedestrian Windsor knot to shame.

Worldly Rufus had him pegged as the romantic revolutionary type, a self-styled poet with reams of verse scribbled in battered journals. Undoubtedly, he was a vain egotist to boot.

The drummer was harder to read. Shielded by a veritable barbican of kick drums, a battlement of toms and a canopy of ride, crash, and splash cymbals, he was within his fortress, hidden in plain sight. His face was covered by a mop of scraggly blond hair that looked like corn silk in the unforgiving light of Smitty's. In anticipation of the buckets of sweat that would undoubtedly leak out of him during the performance he, like most drummers, opted to go shirtless.

Finally, there was the bassist. Ah, Ashleigh! Rufus was instantly enamored, hopelessly smitten, nauseatingly drunk with love. She was all arms and legs and a shape nearly identical to the bass slung low around her neck: a wide bottom and voluptuous curves, then a lean stalk. Her sandy hair was startlingly straight and incredibly long, parted down the middle, though she was no flower child. Even the tiny t-shirt and jeans that she wore looked charmingly too big.

Rufus loved to watch a girl perform on stage. It could transform even the mousiest Jane into a goddess.

"Listen up, pricks," the guitarist growled into the mic, letting out a blast of feedback. "We're The Going out of Business Sale."

The band's faithful responded with whoops and cheers, drowning out the moans and groans of the casualties strewn about the bar.

"I love you, Kody!" screamed two girls in unison.

"This is our last show ever," he announced. "The *Droit Moral* won't have us to kick around anymore! We, and you out there, have been intimidated by their goons and harassed by their agents long enough. Many others, not as brave as us, have gone into hiding."

Rufus perked up at the tone of this polemic.

"But we're not scared, we're not hiding. We are the final relics of the late, great underground scene!"

"Fuck the Dwa!" someone shouted.

"We've been banned from every club in town," the guitarist said, scanning the deteriorating, body-strewn room. "Leaving this shithole as the site of our last stand."

Smitty raised a middle finger high towards the stage. Rufus could only drink it all in.

"Yeah, fuck you too, old man!" the guitarist yelled. "Tonight we're going down in flames! This one goes out to Polo Younger and the *Droit Moral*, it's called 'Get with the Pogrom'. 1-2-3-4..."

The drummer started in with a thunderous backbeat at the speed of a heart about to expire from a cocaine overdose. The bassist came in next, plucking out a McCartney-esque run, walking the sidewalk scale under a cloud of distortion.

The floor rumbled under Rufus' behind, causing all the broken teeth on the floor to dance and shake, like players in an old magnetic football game. Rufus plucked a rather lively incisor from the scrum and stuck it in his pocket for luck.

The guitarist bobbed his head as the rhythm section laid the foundation. He played meandering harmonics on the high end of his fretboard, the notes doubling and tripling with the help of digital delay. At the twenty-fourth measure a tom fill gave the cue. The stomp of a pedal sent his ax soaring into a dirge of minor chords.

There was something pleasantly discordant about this music, something compelling complex about the arrangements. The time signatures were odd, but changed with sharp precision. Every nook and cranny of space was filled with some morsel of sonic stuffing – a small, quiet note here, a booming bass octave there.

Rufus sat prostrate, wrapping himself in the warm sonorous blanket that enveloped the room. Closing his eyes, he found it hard to believe that these three young souls alone were capable of producing such a glorious cacophony. He yielded to rolling waves of abrasive yet otherworldly, claustrophobic yet expansive, tuneful yet atonal sounds. At last, there seemed to be no contradictions.

Just as the music threatened to implode under the weight of its own ambition, the band would pull it back from the brink. This went on and on, song after song. As far as Rufus was concerned, it could go on forever.

"It's easier to get people to dance than to think," the guitarist crooned in his reverb-drenched baritone.

The bassist sang harmony, lending high fifths and low thirds. They teamed up for rhyming quatrains with catchy hooks and dulcet riffs. Rufus took the bait, letting the band reel him out of his gloomy sea.

At a lull, he looked around himself to see if everyone else was as deeply affected.

The attendance for the show had now grown to an unlikely crowd of over two dozen, and all were equally enthralled to this melodious rapture. To call them fans wouldn't do their devotion justice. These were disciples. The largest joint Rufus had ever seen burned bright between the lips of four such disciples before the last of them kindly passed it to the band.

How fashionable this crowd is, Rufus thought. How careless of the typical *de rigueurs*! How free!

Rufus was disappointed in himself. How had these chic bohemians escaped his notice? He was supposed to be hip to these things.

He looked with envy at the brooding and contemplative guys and frisky and ebullient girls. What I would do for just a peek inside their world! Rufus thought. Little did he know what was about to transpire.

The music was building to a crescendo. The band smoothed the jagged edges of their epic fever dream into a series of gentle, sloping curves; the terrifying heights eased into mellow valleys. Each movement had been chaotic and individual, but at last the entire show was revealed as a single symphonic poem.

This music is far too refined, far too artistic, for a slovenly grog shop like Smitty's, Rufus observed. Curse the *Droit Moral* for relegating them, and their beautiful disciples, to mingle among the caste of Untouchables! Rather, they should be hoisted into the pantheon of High Art, lauded in the grandest of music halls, buttered-up by an adoring press!

Instead, they languished on a stage too small and shrinking.

HOW PUNK ROCK

The show ended with a typical Big Rock finale: the drummer wailed on every cymbal in sight, the guitarist thrashed the same chord repeatedly, and the bassist kicked on a looping pedal, put down her instrument and sipped a beer. Her final notes marched on with the band.

One of the disciples handed her a candy apple red gas can – the kind with a nozzle like a bendy straw. She passed it to the guitarist, who also kicked on his looping pedal. The drummer continued to pound away.

"We're The Going out of Business Sale," the guitarist reminded the crowd. He lifted the container above his head. "Good night."

He turned the can upside down.

Thanks to a safety feature (undoubtedly introduced after a ghastly accident and subsequent lawsuit), only a few drops leaked out. Through trial and error, the young songsmith achieved success by tilting the container to a forty-five degree angle; he was rewarded with a shower of sweet petrol. When he was properly soaked, he passed the can back to the bassist, who playfully sprayed the drummer. He didn't seem to mind. The bassist then turned the spray on herself.

Despite her best efforts, including what struck Rufus as an almost vulgar manipulation of the nozzle, she couldn't achieve the same level of immersion that her bandmate enjoyed.

As she struggled, the guitarist grew noticeably irritated, and not only because he was sopping wet with 87 unleaded slowly drying and bonding to his skin.

"You're doing it all wrong!" he snapped, not into the mic, but loud enough for all to hear.

Rufus wondered why the drummer was continuing to play.

As if to answer his mental question, the guitarist yelled, "Shut up, Satch!" but was ignored.

"Hold on, I'm getting it," the bassist interjected. She obviously was not getting it at all.

"You're not doing it right," he said, lunging for the gas can. "Let me do it."

"I'm not doing it right?" she asked. The can sprayed gasoline in his face.

He groaned. "My eyes! You bitch!" he shouted. Blindly, he grabbed at thin air in his quest for the can.

The girl dangled the can in front of his face, just out of reach. "Is it really that hard? Is it something only a misunderstood genius can do?" she mocked.

"Once again, you've proven that I'm the intellectual and you're the fucking retard!"

Finally, the drummer stopped playing.

"That's the dumbest thing I've ever heard," he said, and punctuated his quip with a rimshot.

Although Rufus was an only child, he had hosted enough parties to recognize that the pair were fighting like brother and sister.

Now that Rufus thought about it, he realized that until the finale, those two had ignored each other the entire set.

"You fucked it all up, like you always do," the guitarist whined pathetically. Rufus couldn't tell if those were real tears, or simply the gasoline burning his eyes. "Do you at least know where the fucking matches are?"

Rufus was enjoying the candid back-and-forth, and as such he didn't immediately recognize the import of their discussion. He wondered why, after effortlessly transporting him to musical nirvana, they would feel the need to insert an absurdist gag at the end? What sort of point were they trying to make? Hadn't the music said enough?

By sense of touch alone, the guitarist found a matchbook and violently ripped one out.

The implication began to dawn on Rufus. Having survived his own encounter with death less than an hour before, he believed he was currently in possession of a special sensitivity about these matters. He couldn't sit idly by while these gifted angels sent themselves back to heaven.

Rufus watched the disciples passively abet the band's luckless scheme. He noticed that those smirking little twits weren't dousing their own bodies in gasoline. Of course not! What self-respecting philistine would soil their precious plaid button-up in an act of political defiance?

"No," Rufus said. "No," rising from the floor.

For what purpose had he been saved that night? What grand luck, he reflected fondly, to be saved by one's own incompetence! Perhaps he was destined to save these musicians in return.

Even with the total bummer that was the *Droit Moral*, Rufus thought, two well-intentioned, yet embarrassingly conducted suicide attempts on the same night at the same bar could be no coincidence. What were the odds? Smitty's was a depressing place, but not that depressing. If the stage was their barrel, then Rufus decided that he must be their shoddy knot.

"Don't do it!" Rufus yelled, sprinting towards them. Like a true Schuyler alum, he threw his shoulders back and raised his chin high.

"Don't do it!" he repeated, muscling his way through the disciples. He was close enough to inhale the gasoline's pungent odor. The scent of that viscous serum of dug up and refined fossils filled his nostrils. The sensation was both intoxicating and revolting.

"Don't do it!" he shouted once more.

Surely the band must have been startled by the sight of a crazed, barefoot and drunken man with a noose around his neck running towards them. They had witnessed firsthand the level of savagery Smitty's clientele was capable of. Had one risen from the piles of bodies? Would they be mauled? Would their mutilated corpses be defiled?

The thought only hastened the guitarist's resolve to strike a match. As his eyes cleared and the approaching lunatic came into focus, his hand nervously rubbed one stick after another along the matchbook's red phosphorous stripe.

With only one remaining, the potassium chlorate finally ignited, flaring up into a bright orange cone. Ghostly wisps of sulfur swirled around it.

His neckerchief caught fire instantly, burned upward and began closing in on his throat, like a long wick blazing its way back to a pile of dynamite. In this instance, the guitarist's face was the dynamite.

It may have been the sudden, unplanned running, or the noxious fumes, or the gallon of bourbon in his belly, but just then Rufus' nausea returned. He began to think that maybe he was not their savior after all. He felt like a failure once more. Rufus realized how silly he must look running across the bar, but before he could stop and turn to leave, the *deus ex machina* came thundering out.

A concentrated torrent of barf spewed from Rufus' mouth and hit the guitarist square in the chest. The flames were quelled in one disgusting swoop. Yet Rufus' internal fire extinguisher was not yet done saving the day. He added several more coats – for safety's sake, he told himself, already taking credit for the rescue.

The guitarist did nothing but stand there in disbelief.

"How punk rock," Rufus heard the bassist say. Her devilish smile was the last thing that night he would remember.

Rufus woke up face down on a hardwood floor. This was not the Cambodian Agarwood, Hawaiian Koa, or Brazilian Rosewood that graced the Wiggin estate. No, these planks – cracked, chipped, and rapidly rotting away – were scarcely an improvement over the floor at Smitty's.

Rufus counted no less than ten splinters embedded in his arm. He determined that the pins-and-needles sensation in his leg originated from a rusty bouquet of nails protruding from the wood.

Is it better to wake fully clothed, Rufus wondered, or inexplicably nude?

Nude, always, he decided, regardless of whether it involved a romantic encounter of the illicit variety.

On this particular morning, alas, Rufus was fully clothed. Nevertheless, in his soiled garments he was reduced to a rumpled approximation of his usual dashing self. He had no idea where he was, or how he got there. He imagined the room was the type used by violent extremists to sequester kidnapped foreign journalists.

Have I been shanghaied? he wondered. He was fascinated by the possibilities of potential kidnappers.

The room gave no clues. It was a big empty space, completely unfurnished except for a brooding nature print tacked to the wall. Rufus was surprised to recognize a Thomas Cole print in this place.

There were three narrow slats to let in just enough light to rankle Rufus' polluted brain. To use the word hangover would only diminish the sheer physical malaise and mental inertia afflicting him.

He was sore.

He was thirsty. He was flatulent.

He felt sorry for his teeth for having to share space with such rank halitosis.

His day old socks gave him clammy feet.

His day old shirt gave him armpit stains.

His day old briefs gave him what is colloquially referred to as swamp ass.

With his diminished faculties preventing the formation of a better idea, Rufus decided to stay put. Who knows, maybe with a little more sleep he'd feel better, or at least somewhat less bad, than he did now. His current bedding of splinters-and-nails may have paled in comparison to the ostrich feather duvets and mulberry silk sheets of his own nest, but perhaps the thought of those distant comforts would be sufficient to lull him back to sleep. He turned over in search of a more comfortable posture, and the floor creaked loudly.

"Someone's up early," he heard a voice say from the adjoining room.

Surely it was his kidnapper! he thought. Would they videotape him reading a list of demands? A ransom note? Was it time for the first thrashing of the day? Was he to be the new Patty Hearst?

Rufus could not discern if the voice was talking to another person outside the room or to him, so he decided to respond. "I have not risen by choice," he managed to say, the clamp around his temples throbbing with each word. "This floor is insufferable." That would be all the talking for today, he decided.

"I offered you the bed," suggested a mirthful female voice. "You chose the floor."

Rufus turned again. The pile of sand that used to be his brain shifted. At the doorway was his captor. It was the bass player.

Where had she come from? Rufus wondered. He tried to express this thought, but all he could muster was,

"Where? You? Huh?"

"You're at a safe house," she said. "We have dumps like this all over the city so the *Droit Moral* can't find us."

This was more information than Rufus could possibly be expected to process.

"Us?" he asked feebly.

"Geez, guy! What's the last thing you remember?" she asked, handing him a glass of water.

"Emptying my stomach onto the fellow with the guitar," he recalled with some effort.

This produced a breezy laugh, which was a relief in the stuffy room.

"That was," she told him, "quite possibly the greatest thing I've ever seen."

"Was he upset?" Rufus asked.

"Oh yeah."

"Even though I saved his life?"

"I don't think he saw it that way."

"Ah, *c'est la vie*," Rufus sighed. "One man's poorly tied Sailor's Splice Knot is another man's barf," he added cryptically.

"If you say so."

"For the record," he continued, adjusting his ascot and managing some facsimile of an upright position, "I can actually be quite charming when I choose to be."

"Well Prince Charming, I hate to be a bad hostess, but we really gotta split."

The thought of going bipedal made Rufus shudder.

"Here," she said, extending her soft, slender, feminine hand.

Rufus offered up a feeble flapper and let her do all the work. She was deceptively strong for her size, getting his worthless ass over his worthless feet with no trouble whatsoever.

Newly upright, Rufus' first official act was to straighten his hair, which was equal parts jutting up and matted down.

"Thank you, my dear," he said, averting his mouth so as not to punish this sweet girl with a tempest of bad breath. "The name is Rufus Wiggin. It's Breton for high and noble," he said with a self-conscious wink.

"Ashleigh Victoria Spalmino," she replied. "It's Italian for butter knife."

"Nice to meet you," Rufus said, embarrassed, "For a second time I suppose. And thank you for such hospitality. I'm not accustomed to drinking with such hopeless abandon."

"Well, anyone who can knock Kody down a peg always has a place under my roof."

My God, Rufus thought in the diffuse light of the interrogation room, she is beautiful. Why did he have to meet her like this, so obviously clad in his own embarrassments? First impressions are everything. Appearances are everything. By his own fuzzy math, he currently had a double dose of nothing going for him. What had become of the suave epigrammatist who could invariably charm the pants off any woman he chose?

"You are, without question, the loveliest butter knife in the drawer," he said, feeling the old cogs warming up. "May I treat you to breakfast?"

Ashleigh blushed, waving him off with a gentle flick of the wrist.

"Well? What sayeth you?" Rufus cajoled, sensing her apprehension. "Had fate not intervened last night, we would not even be alive to enjoy the many epicurean delights that this morning could bring. We must celebrate fate!"

"Okay," Ashleigh said. She could never say no to anyone, though she always wanted to kick herself for saying yes. "But you have to do something about that breath."

ALL THINGS FRIED

"The marauders have arrived!" Rufus shouted, stomping through the diner's revolving door. "*Carpe bacon! Carpe flapjacks!*"

Ashleigh slid into a tattered vinyl booth. Yellow foam stuffing peeked through patches of duct tape. Rufus told her that he tried to frequent as many diners as his arteries could handle; he was excited because he had never been to this particular greasy spoon before.

"Feeling better?" she asked over the top of her menu.

"You must be kidding," Rufus replied. "I feel like death. At the slightest sound my head is in a blender, and even the palest shadow is like a blinding eclipse. Yet – I am elated to be alive! *Et tu, Ashleigh?*"

"I guess."

The waitress shuffled over to their table. They were her only customers that morning, and perhaps her first that month.

"Whatcha havin'?" inquired the old waitress in her sandpaper soprano.

"I do apologize," Rufus said, laying his menu aside. "My eyes hang heavy from a night of drink, my dear. Reading is out of the question. So please tell me, wise one, what do you have that's fried?"

The waitress rolled her eyes. Her sigh suggested a lifetime of disappointment.

"We got fried potatoes, fried clams, fried shrimp, chicken fried steak. Then there's the onion rings, the fish and chips, chicken tenders, jalapeno poppers, mozzarella sticks..."

"And the sausage and bacon?" asked Rufus.

"Fried," she replied impatiently. She had been in the middle of a magazine when they arrived.

"Very well. I'll take one of each," he said. Ashleigh noticed him batting his eyelashes.

"One of each?" the puzzled waitress repeated.

"One order of everything you just mentioned."

"You got it," she said, filling the ticket with shorthand for all things fried. "And for you, hon?"

"Granola with skim milk," Ashleigh answered, more to the table than the waitress.

"Is that all?" Rufus cried. "Go on, gorge! Feast!"

"And a coffee," she added politely, handing back her menu.

"Make it two coffees. And add a BLT to my order," Rufus concluded.

"Comin' right up," the waitress said, already halfway across the diner.

Ashleigh observed the strange man sitting on the other side of the Formica table. Rufus had tucked several napkins into his collar over his ascot, creating a bib as bloated as his impending meal.

Who is this guy? she wondered.

Ashleigh enjoyed observing weirdos in their natural state. She considered herself a scientist in that regard. She engaged them, studied them, poked them with sticks when it proved necessary. She once spent a week living with a subway performer known for balancing wine bottles on his head. She told people it was strictly for research purposes.

"So, I noticed you trying to hang yourself before our show," she began bluntly. "What's up with that?" She inadvertently dipped her elbow into a puddle of coffee and wiped it off casually. "Did your girlfriend," she paused, not wanting to be presumptuous, "or boyfriend, break up with you?"

"I've loved briefly and often," Rufus said, candidly. "But the fairer sex played no role in my decision."

"Well?"

"If you must know," Rufus replied, as he continued rearranging the sugar packets by color, "I've been reading this book, *All the Knots You Need to Know.*"

"Doesn't ring a bell."

"It's a highly instructive volume. I believe it does in fact discuss every knot one might ever want to use, and several more besides. I was in search of a hobby to get my mind off things."

"Are you depressed?"

"Wouldn't you agree that we're all a tad depressive?" he posed. "Yet it's true that these times have been exceptionally hard on the *bon vivant*. Normally I would stuff my calendar with all sorts of inane amusements: cocktail parties, gallery openings, costume balls, perfunctory fundraisers for obscure causes. But the war has taken it all away. It's taken my life away."

Rufus, mourning for those bygone days, sunk his chin into his bib.

"All my friends have gone into exile," he explained. "They pleaded with me to come and would have absconded with me forcibly if they could have, I am sure. But what does a man gain who abandons his home? Indeed, last night was the first time in three months that I even ventured outside."

"So you were going to kill yourself because you were bored?" Ashleigh asked skeptically.

"What better reason than boredom, loneliness, indifference? Without a teeming social schedule to mark my time, I've been left with nothing but thoughts, thoughts about a life I have done precious little with. I count politicians and titans of industry among my friends. I play euchre with the owner of the bank! One of my oldest friends has recently acquired a Double-A baseball franchise! Do you realize how long I've wanted to own a team myself? Can you imagine how fun that would be?"

"Sounds like a blast, I guess," Ashleigh said. "But aren't you a little old to be measuring your worth against your friends?"

"I'm twenty-eight," Rufus said, nervously shredding a napkin.

"And I'm sure you've accomplished something in that time, right? I take it you went to college?"

"Yes, indeed," Rufus said, perking up. "Ivy League, all the way."

"Impressive. What school?"

"All of them. A semester at Harvard, two at Brown and Cornell, three at Dartmouth, a month at Yale, summer sessions at

Princeton and Columbia, and I finished up at Penn. I probably could have skipped Columbia."

"Well how many people can say that?" Ashleigh said. While she was more confused by Rufus than ever, she was enjoying the role of pep coach. "I dropped out of art school after three weeks. You really went all the way."

"Shucks," Rufus said, blushing. "You're too sweet." He was either talking to her or to his coffee.

"But where have my journeys taken me?" Rufus pondered. "Only to my study. Tying knots, alone."

"So the knots made you do it?" she asked. She would get to the bottom of this. It appeared that Rufus might be even crazier than he seemed.

"Page after page of knots!" Rufus shouted. "I tied them all: Reef Knots, Bowlines, Flemish 8's. At last I came to the modified Multifold-Overhand knot." He paused to see if she was following. "The Hangman's Noose.

"There it was, staring up at me from the page, mocking me, reminding me."

"Reminding you of what?"

"That my best days, my footloose and fancy free days, are behind me. All thanks to Polo Younger and his cursed *Droit Moral!*"

Rufus didn't mean to slam the heel of his mug onto the table, but it happened anyway.

Ashleigh looked around the empty diner. The waitress was buried in the pages of her gossip rag. The line cook busied himself at the fryalator, preparing Rufus' tall order.

"I wouldn't say that too loud," Ashleigh whispered. "They have agents everywhere."

"I won't be intimidated by *agents*," Rufus fumed, gesturing to slam his mug again, but deciding against it. "I went to school with Polo Younger. Grades six through twelve. As our surnames share the same obscure space at the end of the alphabet, I was always forced to sit one seat in front of him. For years I longed for an Xavier between us."

Ashleigh found her interest in the conversation rekindling. "What's he like?" she asked.

"He's a clod! A snotty twit!" Rufus said dismissively. "A C-student with a passion, but not an aptitude, for the fine arts. Instead he curried favor with the administrators, and soon his tired watercolors and flaccid still-lifes were hanging all over the school. An inveterate kiss-ass! I tried to break his spirit; one might even say I lead the vanguard in the task. Sadly, no amount of ridicule could stop him from stinking up the place."

"You drove him to evil!" Ashleigh exclaimed, hoping it sounded neither too trite nor too sincere.

"I wouldn't call Polo evil, *per se*," Rufus said, as if he had never considered the thought before. "He's certainly cunning and manipulative, but mostly just banal. He's a real prick, too – that's what makes him dangerous."

The call bell inside the kitchen rang, jolting the waitress back to duty and causing Rufus to salivate as a procession of plates came parading before him. Item by item, Rufus devoured his ten-course meal, exchanging one newly cleared platter for another fresh heap of crisply battered victuals. Before long, the entire table was stacked with chipped porcelain.

Surrounded by a swelling sea of plates, Ashleigh paced herself, hoping that she could sustain her puny bowl of granola until Rufus was finished.

"You sure eat fast," she observed before crunching into an oat cluster.

"I would eat faster if only I could!" Rufus exclaimed. "If I could roll all these delectables into a ball, carve it into wedges and chomp into it like a watermelon I would never eat anything else!"

He eats like a child, Ashleigh thought. How...adorable? Does he always eat like this? she wondered. How could he stay so thin? She watched Rufus' ketchup, mustard, and mayonnaise-stained hands add another soiled napkin to his pyramid. Shiny with a fresh coat of grease, his soft features almost seemed pretty.

Ashleigh didn't buy Rufus' story. How could she? Everything about him – his clothes, his speech, his mannerisms – were gross exaggerations. Occasionally he forgot himself and spoke in modern slang. He reminded her mostly of a figure in an old political cartoon.

Could he really know Polo Younger? she wondered. It sounded like nonsense: no one knows Polo Younger. He was a mystery, a myth or a ruse. There hadn't been a confirmed sighting of Polo in years; most rumors were eventually dismissed as hoaxes. Many in the underground, herself included, were convinced he didn't exist at all.

Nonetheless, Ashleigh saw something endearing in Rufus. He was certainly eccentric, but he didn't carry himself like a charlatan and he didn't seem like a sociopath. Like finding a lone macaroni in a box of jumbo shells, he was best understood as a curio. What could be the harm in believing him?

"Now, Madame Butterknife, if I may ask you a question," Rufus ventured. He was trying to wipe his face but only managed to spread the grease more evenly across his cheeks. "Why did *you* try to kill *your*self?"

Ashleigh sighed and seemed to wither. She wondered if she should trust him.

"It would only be fair," Rufus added. "You asked the same of me, and I answered honestly."

Ashleigh let a brief silence hang in the air before answering.

"It was my brother's idea," she said. "Kody. The guitarist."

"I thought I noticed a sibling tension between you two," Rufus said. He had returned to his meal and his mouth was half-full.

"He's a year older. He's the Artist, the Golden Boy of the family. Our parents always called him the Smart One and me the Other One."

"What a horrid cross to bear," Rufus replied, punctuating his point with a sausage link. "As an only child myself, I was always evaluated solely on a pass-fail rubric."

"Don't get me wrong. Kody is ridiculously smart and he's incredibly talented. But once he gets an idea in his head..."

"Let me guess," Rufus interrupted, "You're either with him, or against him."

"Exactly. Like everyone, we've struggled through this war. Our equipment's been stolen a bunch, people won't book us anymore. It's sad, we used to draw hundreds to our shows, and now – well, what you saw, maybe a couple dozen – that was our best crowd in weeks."

"Some of them might have been double-agents," Rufus added, with no small horror at his own idea. He liked to think of the disciples as pure as snow.

"These days, the sole purpose of our band is to overthrow the *Droit Moral.* We are, or I should say we were, the best band in this shitty city. They knew it too, but we wouldn't play their game. Our music is diametrically opposed," Ashleigh said, pausing to consider whether she was using the word 'diametrically' correctly, "to everything they stand for."

"I couldn't agree more," Rufus replied with a greasy smile. "Your band is wonderful. I was, if I may, blown away."

"Well, thanks, I guess. It's kinda too little, too late. The final straw came a month ago when the music critic at the *Daily Reader* gave our album a glowing review, in open defiance of the City Art Commission. He called it a landmark, a masterpiece, and a triumph."

"Good press is hard to come by," Rufus said absentmindedly as he scraped the last strings of melted cheese from his plate.

"Next thing you know, the album was banned. The *Droit* called us – what was it? – 'degenerate bourgeoisie elitists.' They said our album was 'a self-indulgent exercise of little to no artistic merit.'"

"Yawn," Rufus said, feigning the real thing. "Socialism is such a vapid cause, so old-fashioned."

"Their thugs began seizing every copy they could find. They came to our home and took our personal copies. Then, as if that wasn't bad enough, they broke into our studio and stole the master tapes."

"Savages!" Rufus cried. A tendril of bacon was swinging from his lip.

"When we realized we had no gear, no album, no home and no place to play – well, that's when Kody came up with the idea."

"Did you ever consider a less symbolic form of protest?"

"You're one to talk," Ashleigh suggested archly.

"Touché," he conceded.

"We figured they'll probably kill us anyway, so why not beat them to it? Kody called it 'the art of dying for your art.'"

"An elegant phrase," Rufus admitted. At last his final plate was clear, and he pushed it away. His master class in gluttony was dismissed. "I'm sorry I ruined the moment," he said and, worried he had misspoken, immediately corrected himself. "I mean, I'm not sorry I ruined it, because you're a lovely girl in a terrific band." Ashleigh batted her wrist. "Still, now is the time for big statements."

"I used to think so, too," Ashleigh said, taking her last bite of granola. "Now I'm not so sure."

****

Rufus picked up the tab and joined Ashleigh outside for a post-meal cigarette.

"May we do this again?" he asked at last. "Is there a way I can reach you?"

Ashleigh looked around. She was uncomfortable in the open air and didn't answer.

"Where do you live?" he asked.

"Nowhere, really."

"Do you have a phone?" he persisted.

"Kody made me throw it in the river."

"Is this genuine?" Rufus was experiencing a rare moment of self-doubt. "Or are you trying to rid yourself of me?"

Ashleigh continued to scan the empty sidewalks and deserted streets of the city's decaying center, and at last slipped him a card.

"It's not you, I swear. I've gone underground is all, off the grid. You can write me through S.M.E.A.R."

"What should I smear?"

"Never mind. There's a drop box at 444 4th Street. No sign, just a slot. Write a note, address it to Butter Knife, and drop it in that box. Okay?"

How mysterious! Rufus thought. How romantic! He was not wholly convinced she wasn't giving him the brush-off.

"I shall be in touch post haste," he said. "Please do relay my sincerest apologizes to your brother."

"Will do."

"You're a good egg, Ashleigh Victoria Spalmino," Rufus proclaimed. "I shall wait with bated breath until our next encounter. What a beautiful day it is to be alive!" Rufus sang as he waddled stuffed and happy to the trolley stop.

"So it is," Ashleigh said. She wished she had delivered a more poetic farewell.

Rufus boarded the westbound local and took a window seat by the conductor. As the streetcar plodded along, Ashleigh watched as it receded into the glare of the midday sun. Finally, she left, almost with a skip in her step, past the boarded up storefronts, the stripped cars on cinder blocks, the gravel lots strewn with used condoms and dirty diapers, until she too was absorbed into the city's concrete folds.

Aboard the trolley, Rufus hoped they would meet again soon. Several blocks away, Ashleigh had the very same thought.

Kody sneered. "Forget it. Tell him to fuck off." He wadded up the letter and threw it at his sister.

"He wants to apologize," Ashleigh said.

"He humiliated me in front of everyone!"

Even after a week, Kody was still smarting over his plan being foiled by vomit.

"It's not like you never got loaded and pissed on my amp," replied Ashleigh, "and I forgave you."

"That's different."

"Or that time you were on mushrooms and wouldn't shut up about creative destruction or destructive creation or whatever it was, which you then demonstrated by smashing my bass with a hammer?"

"I wouldn't expect you to understand," Kody said.

"Of course you wouldn't."

"Once again, my sister takes the lunatic's side. What a shock! Like it wasn't bad enough that you whisked him away to God-knows-where to do God-knows-what before any of us could get our hands on the guy. Now you want me to break bread and pretend everything's cool?"

"You could try," Ashleigh said, before receding into silence once more.

Ashleigh and Kody were holed up at S.M.E.A.R. headquarters, the Semi-Monthly Emerging Artist Rations, putting the final touches on the Spring Quarterly, a special deluxe issue of their irregularly-published newsletter. The cramped, windowless room in a hidden corner of the fourth floor of 444 4th Street served as the very nerve center of the city's underground arts scene. Few knew of its existence, much less the schemes hatched within its walls.

In addition to his band, Kody acted as S.M.E.A.R.'s Editor-in-Chief, compiling the latest works from the circle of resistance he had organized – the painters, poets, musicians, photographers, and writers who now operated on the margins or outside of them. Kody had a sympathetic connection – a sullen-faced hipster with poor customer service skills – at a nearby copy shop; therefore Kody could publish S.M.E.A.R. and keep the artists organized around a single ideal: his own.

Ashleigh was in charge of the more tangible tasks of assembly and production. She paired paintings with poems, occasionally slipping in a drawing or two from her own portfolio. She also devised a series of ciphers that, while not difficult, were too conceptual for the *Droit's* literal-minded censors. In this way she passed along important messages and, most importantly, relayed the dates and times of upcoming events. For instance, the show at Smitty's was disguised as a simple anagram:

LIVE MUSIC:

GOOF OUTING

SUBLEASE SIN

MIGHTY TIT SNOTS

Since the *Droit Moral* had made it a crime to possess or transport unapproved art, discretion had become a necessity.

Organizing or attending an unapproved event had also been prohibited. Even first-time offenders could expect a trip to compulsory Art Re-Education, an experience few recovered from, much less discussed openly. Recidivists, it was said, were sent to a secret Art/Work Camp within the *Droit's* main compound. There were many rumors surrounding the existence of these places and what went on at them. Much like everything the *Droit* did, this ambiguity was used to conjure deep-seated fears of unbridled brutality.

After a solid hour of stuffing and stapling, Ashleigh broke the monotony by quietly unwadding Rufus' letter and reading it for the third time:

My Dearest Butter Knife,

I hope this letter finds you well. I write to extend an invitation to hors d'oeuvres and aperitifs tomorrow next, at my humble lodgings, during the eighth hour of the evening. Please invite your fellow bandmates, especially your brother; I would embrace the opportunity to apologize in person. Respondez si'l vous plait – or, if you don't please, don't. Simply take the westbound trolley to the gates of Lindsay Park at the prescribed time.

Very Truly Yours,

Rufus Redfox Wiggin

"Will you stop, already," Kody exclaimed, snatching the letter again. "No time for pompous twits. We need to finish this issue."

"When did free food and drinks become a bad thing?"

"Activism before amusement," he replied, tearing up the letter. "These zines aren't going to deliver themselves."

"Oh lord, deliver me from S.M.E.A.R.," Ashleigh protested, raising her hands in mock prayer.

Given the illicit nature of their work, Kody chose to hand-deliver each issue under the cover of night. His route took him all over the city – to galleries hidden in attics, studios in storage lockers, speakeasies tucked away in the backrooms of bodegas. With a circulation in the hundreds, deliveries could take all night.

Hoping to pique her brother's interest, Ashleigh mentioned, "Rufus said he knows Polo Younger."

"He'd say anything to get in your pants."

"He called Polo a twit," she said, trying to recall Rufus' exact words. "Or was it a clod?"

"Maybe he was talking about himself."

"But, Kody, *what if* ? Why not believe him? If it's bullshit, it's bullshit. If it's true, who knows, he might also know something or someone who can help us."

Ashleigh always resorted to invoking The Cause when other means of persuasion failed. It rarely worked, and every time it was unsuccessful, her own passion for The Cause receded more. The Cause was, and always would be, Kody's crusade.

"Say, *arguendo*," Kody said, emphasizing the deliberate courthouse Latin, "that Polo Younger is a real person. I'm skeptical, but let's say he is. If this guy Rufus actually knows him – and I want to state for the record that I think he's full of shit – then the only explanation would be that he's one of them. That's not exactly the company I wanna keep."

Secretly, Ashleigh preferred the idea of spending that time with Rufus alone. Her fascination had only grown since they parted ways. As a bonus, she knew the more she saw Rufus, the more it would annoy Kody to no end. And no one could say she didn't try.

"Oh forget it," she said at last.

"Everything must be perfect!" Rufus commanded his staff.

This once-impressive eight-man crew had, since the beginning of the war, been reduced to a motley collection of its most disloyal elements: Sylvia (the maid); Ramon (the butler); and Angelo (the cook).

"Not a speck of dust will be tolerated!" Rufus shouted from his study, where he was pacing laps.

Sylvia scowled. Ramon mumbled obscenities in multiple languages. Angelo sharpened his knives.

Rufus had no doubt his visitors would find his home impressive. His sprawling estate, which exuded the hermetic charm of a small-town museum, had survived the war intact. Nevertheless, Rufus began to stalk the halls vigilantly, centering picture frames, dusting ledges, emptying ashtrays, hiding Ramon's stash of pornography.

"That agarwood cost $10,000 a square foot! Please show some respect," Rufus barked at the maid, who struggled to drag an ancient vacuum cleaner up the spiral staircase. "Ramon, get me Spit on the phone."

Rufus knew a guy named Spit. Spit was a man who could find things. No matter how fanciful or capricious the request, no matter the obscurity of Rufus' latest passing obsession – which had included Super Red Arowanas, Mesopotamian pottery, Franco-Prussian War memorabilia, cave swift saliva nests, agarwood, Francia-era Paraguayan banknotes – Spit always delivered.

"Spit, you rapscallion, it's Rufus," he said, as Ramon held the receiver to his ear. "I have a request."

Rufus took the phone and waved off his butler.

"I'm lobbing you a softball this time. All I need is the master tapes of an album. The band is called The Going Out of Business Sale. Got it?"

"Hmmm, hmmm," Spit replied in imitation of a dial tone. "That's no softball, Rufus. That's a needle in a haystack."

"Don't confuse your metaphors, Spit. It makes you sound stupid. When have I ever asked for something that wasn't hard to come by? You think I'm just calling to chat? Get a grip, dummy."

As usual, Spit already knew all of the relevant data. "That album is the rarest of all birds," Spit said in his slow Southern drawl.

"Then it shouldn't be a problem. Wasn't it just last month that you found me the slender-billed curlew? I'm keeping it in my basement. I couldn't stand looking at it, actually. It reminded me too much of you."

"Demand is high for the album, Rufus. Things have been unpredictable since the war began, but I've really never seen anything like this. Last I heard the album, even if I could find a copy, will set you back twenty-five large. Plus my standard fee."

"Any slob can get a copy! Do you not comprehend that I want the masters, damn you?"

"If the masters weren't destroyed – which they may've been – that means going into the hornet's nest."

"Haystacks? Hornet's nests? What the hell are you talking about? This isn't some backwater cow town! Speak English!"

"You're looking at least a hundred large," Spit said. "Given the situation, I'll also have to double my fee."

"You money-grubbing hayseed son-of-a-bitch!" Rufus screamed, wishing he could strangle Spit through the phone. "What gall! Why do I even sully myself with such unscrupulous transactions?"

Spit was quite used to Rufus' temper tantrums. He coolly replied: "Do you want the tapes or not?"

"Yes. And four copies on wax, if it's not too much trouble. You're a true gentleman, Spit."

"Whatever."

A SHOW THAT NEVER ENDS

Ashleigh dug out her best dress – a cotton flower-print number that stopped just above of the knee – from the bottom of a garbage bag. It wasn't the fanciest dress, but it fit perfectly, and had an elegantly wistful look to it.

For months, Ashleigh had been living out of garbage bags: one for clothes, one for everything else. Every now and then, as she and the band moved from one refuge to another, a bag grown heavy would rip. Whenever her stuff spilled onto the sidewalk, she would hastily collect the necessities and often left much discarded. Sometimes a bum would pilfer an item or two when her back was turned. On balance, though, her meager provisions stayed the same. Some new and some old, but never any more or less.

Ashleigh had sacrificed a lot in pursuit of her brother's dream, but the routine had begun to grow old. Since Ashleigh was born, Kody had cast a long shadow over her life and she was still struggling to escape. Until recently, she chose not to fight it. It was easier to embrace a vision she didn't share, even if it felt like taking a season pass to a show that never ends.

She did admire Kody's passion, his confidence, his ideas and his talent, but never as much as he admired those qualities in himself. She saw through his bravado. She knew it was a chintzy piece of armor masking the kind of vulnerability that comes from knowing that no matter who you are or who you want to be or how much you're willing to work for it, you will never be able to fool the conspiring winds of chance. So Ashleigh assumed the role of protector, then enabler, and finally punching bag. Kody called her stupid, lazy. He dismissed songs she wrote as too simple, her artwork as too childish.

After years of coddling and unconditional ass-kissing (from their parents, from fans, from teenage girls, from himself) Kody had been inflated with airs of infallibility, and now there was little hope that he could ever live up to his own lofty expectations. He immediately blamed each of their many setbacks and failures on Ashleigh.

Where was it leading? she wondered. From one self-imposed cell to the next; she was shedding some of her things, and a little bit of herself, with every move. And for what? It was clearer than ever that Kody would never, could never, defeat the *Droit Moral*.

During the slow days, Ashleigh dreamed about the theoretically attainable but continually elusive. Ashleigh saw herself enrolled at a university far-off from the arrested decay of the city. She was even open to the idea of moving back in with her parents. At least there, surrounded by the knickknacks of her youth, she could sleep until noon. She could get stoned and raid the kitchen for endless bowls of cereal. Next to wondering where her next meal would come from, it was an attractive alternative.

The party loomed. Ashleigh put the finishing touches on her outfit. She teased and straightened, dabbed and brushed, using the reflective bottom of a scratched CD as her mirror. Slipping into a well-worn pair of ballerina flats, she twirled around for a final look.

Not bad, she thought.

Time to hit the town.

A REAL LINEBACKER BEATNIK TYPE

The evening walk to the trolley stop was harrowing and gloomy. This was a particularly sad stretch of pavement in a city accustomed to perpetual sorrow. Normally, Ashleigh's baggy clothes and Don't-Fuck-With-Me face were enough to stave off any hustlers and pimps who infested the route. Tonight, however, the catcalls trailed her every step, and there was no escaping the pervy come-ons that quickened her pace.

The harassment was standard fare – *where ya goin' girl? show me that ass! spread it open baby!* – and no body part was excluded. To make matters worse, a pesky wind was howling off the river, threatening to give the whole crowd a too-tempting glimpse of what it was shouting for.

Ashleigh found little solace in the surrounding scenery. Between the vacant lots and boarded up storefronts, all that appeared open were sad little shops selling discount phone cards and cheap electronics. On every corner, bodegas with names like "USA Mart" and "American Liquors" overcharged the locals for stale cigarettes and skunky beer.

The upper floors of apartment buildings were linked together with abandoned laundry lines that stretched from one boarding house window to the next. From the street they seemed to intersect the power lines, creating the sense that the city had been bound up in an oppressive web. Even when the sun broke through the phalanx of sooty clouds that covered the city, it seemed to shine with the dull luster of lacquered brass.

Few drivers ventured into this part of town: here and there, the steel carcass of a car, stripped even of its smallest knobs and bulbs, stood as a reminder of the prolonged deterioration. The graves of this boneyard were marked by expired parking meters tagged with gang graffiti. There was little to see, and Ashleigh had already seen it too many times, so she decided simply to stare at her feet in resignation. Piles of trash crunched underfoot like fallen autumn leaves.

"Identification please," a man said, stepping from the shadows.

Ashleigh stopped cold. The *Droit Moral* agent was twice her height and weight. In that cliché getup, he was a real linebacker beatnik type. It was too easy to look past the barrel chest and tree trunk legs and only see the beret, turtleneck, and smoke-colored skinny jeans.

Ashleigh was startled but not surprised. The *Droit Moral* had patrolmen everywhere. Peons in the power structure, they were the public face of the City Art Commission. Each one was a carbon copy, out to enforce every directive Polo Younger could dream up.

"Identification, miss," he repeated.

Ashleigh's pulse quickened. She had never been cornered in daylight like this. She cursed herself for not being more aware. She knew of others who had been snatched off the street. When they returned weeks later, they were unwilling to talk. Few were ever the same again. Some never came back at all.

Now, in the shadow of this power-hungry pissant, she was ready for anything. Fearing the worst, her first impulse was flight, as rapidly down the block as an airborne candy wrapper. Failing that, a swift kick to the balls would do.

"Nervous?" he asked.

"Only when I'm accosted in a shitty neighborhood," she said, handing the man her ID.

He held it close to his face, then at arm's length. He turned it over, turned it upside down, looking for who-knows-what. He studied it intently, curious as an illiterate with a newspaper. In the dim light, he even raised his shades; his vacant, ignorant eyes glanced alternately at Ashleigh and the card. The routine was sad. It was sadder still that this man had power. Ashleigh felt like an underage kid being grilled by a bouncer at a bar.

"Melanie Cloud? S'that you?"

"The one and only."

"Engineering major, City College?"

"Harvard on the Beverwyck, I like to say."

"What's your sign?" he asked.

"My sign? I don't know, stop sign?"

"Your astrological sign."

"Are you asking me on a date?"

He glared.

"Um...Sagittarius."

He thought he had her. "Are you sure?" he practically gloated, "It says right here – oh no, you're right."

Ashleigh was no beginner to fake IDs. She always kept one step ahead, getting a new one, an original, every few weeks. It was good enough to pass in a pinch, but too flimsy to withstand strict scrutiny. Recently they had learned that the *Droit* didn't bother students of the hard sciences. It was believed that they were intimidated by people who were inherently smart and bound to the laws of logic and reason. It was just a theory, but a good one.

"Where you off to?" he asked, still not convinced he was speaking to Melanie Cloud.

"Class."

"What class?"

"Structural Analysis."

Every new identity meant a new thoroughly researched and rehearsed back story. It was her favorite part of being an outlaw.

"Well, looks like everything's in order," he conceded, handing back her ID. "Sorry to bother you."

For some time, a raid had been unfolding on a building down the block. Now in the clear, Ashleigh turned to face the commotion, pretending not to have noticed before.

"May I ask what's going on over there?"

A line of burlap hooded hipsters, zip-tied and shackled, were being paraded out of "Uncle Sam Beer & Wine", a store whose stockroom was an underground salon and S.M.E.A.R. distribution point. Some were swearing, some were crying.

"Don't take my laptop, bro," said one, muffled by the sack.

"Please, I have sensitive skin," said another, pathetically.

One by one they were shoved onto a graffiti-covered paddy wagon (army surplus, no doubt) with a swift kick in the pants for momentum and a slap upside the head for their sorrow. A gang of uncannily identical patrolmen followed close behind, hauling crates of records, books, and paints out of old Uncle Sam's. The Nepalese proprietor made no protest.

"We got a tip about an unapproved venue conducting subversive activities," the patrolman said boastfully. "We caught six offenders and got a cache of paraphernalia off the street."

"Drug paraphernalia?" Ashleigh asked. She already knew what he actually meant.

"Art paraphernalia, ma'am," he replied, with the practiced authority of a veteran cop. "Unapproved materials, unlicensed images, the works. We even found copies of the resistance's official publication."

Ashleigh couldn't know who was in the group they busted, but with her circle ever-shrinking, odds were good that it included a friend or a comrade, even her own brother. Who was it this time? Where were they being taken? She resigned herself to not caring. It happened too often to keep track, to let herself grow attached. A few more voices would be silenced, there would be still fewer contributors to S.M.E.A.R., and it would happen again. But there would be new readers, too. More and more of the enemy's eyes trying to break Ashleigh's code. She hoped Polo Younger himself would read it. Maybe he would become inspired:

ATHEIST LOOP, THEN I ROLL.

The raid was ending. Contraband seized, outlaws busted, backs slapped, plans for dinner and drinks made, the agents peeled off in their caravan of tricked-out El Caminos. Mission accomplished.

"When will they learn?" the patrolman asked, shaking his head. "Under the leadership of our Dear Leader, the *Droit Moral* has created the first great utopia, an artopia, bar none. Anyone who accepts the word of Polo is blessed with boundless opportunity. These losers are morons to reject it."

Delivered with a thousand yard stare and unwavering in its conviction, the speech seemed as well-rehearsed as Ashleigh's back story.

"I was never one for the arts myself, no offense," she said. "But to each his own, right?"

"You should think about joining up," the man said, a lecherous look coming over his face. "Maybe we can discuss it over drinks."

"Thanks," she replied. "But I'm late for class."

IS IT WHISKEY, OR IS IT PISS?

It was a few blocks before Ashleigh's frayed nerves began to calm, but soon enough the anxiety lifted and she could hear the chorus of catcalls again. The scattered trash and the mumbling bums didn't seem so bad now. At that moment, Ashleigh spied a familiar face stumble out of a bleak row house. He was dirty and shirtless, walking with the slow deliberation of a man who had nothing to live for.

"Satch!" she yelled, realizing it was in fact a man who lived only for living.

Ashleigh had never been happier to see the drummer. After two years in a band together, she still knew little about the guy. He loved women, drugs, and drums, and he was uncommonly committed to those three pursuits. His coital conquests were many, his debauched exploits were legendary, and his backbeat was the best in town. No one else could have provided the aloof yin to Kody's temperamental yang better than Satch.

"Whatcha doin'?" she asked, resisting the urge to hug him.

"Walk of shame. You?"

"Dinner party. Wanna come?"

"Are you wearing makeup?" Satch asked. He leaned closely to inspect her face through a part in his mop. "What kind of party is it? Do I have to wear makeup too?"

Ashleigh could never tell whether the happy idiot was a role Satch liked to play, or if it just came naturally.

"Why would you have to wear to makeup?" she asked. "You're not even wearing a shirt."

Satch looked genuinely surprised by her observation.

"Shit, I left it at Annie's," he said. He paused a moment to debate whether to go back. "Fuck it. This isn't some black tie event is it?"

"I don't know if they'll even let you on the trolley bare-chested. Geez, Satch, where are your shoes? There are needles all over the sidewalk."

Ashleigh was right again. In fact, only a ratty pair of cargo shorts shielded the world's prying eyes from the full immensity of Satch's nakedness.

"I swear I wore sandals today," he said, inspecting the tan line between his filthy toes. "It kinda looks like I'm wearing sandals though, doesn't it?"

"That's disgusting," Ashleigh said. Silhouettes of sandals had been etched onto his feet by a combination of sun and dirt.

"I guess I left those at Annie's, too."

"Who's Annie?" she asked, eager to gain some insight into Satch's sordid private life.

"Just the girl I just spent the last six hours giving it to," he said, boastfully.

"Also disgusting," Ashleigh said. Already she had gained too much insight into Satch's private life.

"You know Annie! She was at the show the other night – dark hair, shortish?"

"That doesn't narrow it down."

"She's the one I was finger-banging in the bathroom when you walked in to clean the puke off your face."

"And that was Kody," Ashleigh said. She thought she knew how a teacher with a slow student must feel.

"Oh yeah, I always get you two confused. I have this thing with brothers and sisters," Satch said as he aired out his pits in the warm breeze.

"How? Actually, never mind."

"Anyway, that's Annie. Sweet girl, killer rack."

"Sounds like a real keeper," Ashleigh said. She wanted to punch his bicep playfully, but somehow she connected with the dewy crevice of his armpit.

"Hey," Satch laughed. There was nowhere on Satch that she could wipe her wet knuckles, so she rubbed them with her dress.

"Anyway," Satch continued, "What's Kody up to tonight? Suffering for his art I take it?"

"He never misses a day."

"That guy can be a real drag sometimes, man. He needs to lighten up."

"It'll never happen," she said plainly, and realized it was true.

Satch decided to change the subject. "Who's throwing this rager we're going to?" he asked, rubbing his hands together and licking his lips like he did before devouring a plate of chicken wings.

"Remember that guy who puked on Kody?" she asked. She was unsure how well Satch remembered that night, if he remembered it at all.

"No shit! How could I forget?" he said, the memory lighting up his face. "That guy's great, man. Our best show ever, by far. Hey, remember when Kody pretended to light himself on fire and that dude yuked all over him? Bad ass!"

He wound up to give Ashleigh a high-five, but she left him hanging.

"You're kidding, right?"

"About what?" Satch wondered.

"That wasn't staged. Kody intended to, and succeeded in, lighting himself on fire."

"You mean you guys were serious about all that?"

Satch had a very selective memory. Often the things he did recall were hazy, or flat out wrong.

"You agreed to it, too," Ashleigh reminded him.

"When?" he asked, turning his face up to think, his eyes rolling into the back of his head. "Oh, probably the night I did all those whippets."

"That could've been any night, Satch," she joked.

"Very likely. You should have been there, Ash. Annie had this nitrous tank right next to her bed, and we huffed that shit all day long. I was seeing stars, man. Stars and boobs and vag. I imagine that's what heaven is like.

"When the tank was cashed, we unhooked the fridge and huffed the Freon. I'm not sure, but I think I may have died briefly. Maybe it was heaven, after all."

"You lead such a hard life," Ashleigh teased. Part of her wished she could indulge in the kind of free-wheeling hedonism that Satch enjoyed.

"Tell me about it," he replied. He had the fatigue of a mill worker coming off the third shift. "I need a drink."

Satch stopped in front of an overflowing dumpster and peered inside.

"Hello? Anyone in there?" he called, not wanting to disturb someone's abode. "I slept in a dumpster once," he explained. "Not bad. Smelled like shit though."

"Go figure."

Satch plunged shoulder-deep into the bin, stirring up glass bottles, aluminum cans, plastic bags, cardboard boxes, the usual, but no treasure. So he immersed himself further, head first, feet off the ground, both arms in, swimming through the rubbish. It took some digging but he eventually resurfaced with a whiskey bottle covered in a snotty, seaweed-like substance that they hoped was wilted spinach. Two fingers of a brownish-yellow swill sloshed around inside. A cigarette butt was marinating at the surface.

"Now it's time to play America's favorite game show," Satch announced in his best emcee voice, "Is it whiskey, or is it piss?"

"Piss," Ashleigh ventured, confident in her answer.

Satch tilted his head and raised a doubting eyebrow.

"I say whiskey, and let me remind you, this isn't my first time consuming trash."

"I still say piss," she said.

Satch unscrewed the cap and plugged his nose, not wanting an errant molecule of pee-smell to ruin the game. Quickly, bravely, he tossed back an unapologetic gulp. The effects were immediate and unequivocal — face-twisting, body-shivering, finger-twitching, snot-running repulsion. His organs seemed to liquefy before Ashleigh's eyes, though the Freon may have played a part in that.

"Half whiskey," he choked. "Half piss."

In between convulsions, Satch expelled the slimiest loogie Ashleigh had ever seen. It looked like a jellyfish had washed up on the sidewalk. Living, breathing, dancing, free at last.

"Let's call it a draw."

Rufus crossed three more names off the guest list. These were outright rejections. Dozens of invitations had been returned undelivered, no forwarding address provided.

The only confirmed guests were Jay Hudson Hamilton, the septuagenarian novelist, and Marie St. Alban, the equally loopy and wrinkled painter. The party would be strictly D-list, and Rufus knew it.

Rufus had been hoping to impress Ashleigh that night with one of his infamous soirees – if and when she ever showed up. Now he feared she would walk in, see the sad fading stars he called guests and the sad nursing home he called a party, and walk out.

This is a disaster, he thought. I should call the whole thing off.

Before the war, Rufus' parties were legendary. He was the hottest host in town: even invited guests were regularly turned away, escorted off the grounds in protest while they lobbed a litany of threats. This was Rufus' show, and no member of the *beau monde* was exempt. No amount of bribery, flattery, or seduction could change his mind.

Better luck next week, he'd tell them. Now off you go.

The line of limos could stretch for miles. Illuminated by the flashbulbs of the paparazzi, guests inched towards the gates while, as Rufus remembered it, a mob of reporters clamored to get an exclusive scoop on the swinging scene inside. While stodgy intellectuals and square business men were unavoidable, Rufus would cordon off the entire east wing as an anything-goes pleasure suite. It was an idyllic place where every conversation was thought-provoking, every quip side-splitting, every kiss fever-inducing.

Thinking about Jay Hudson Hamilton and Marie St. Alban, Rufus lamented. *My best days are behind me.*

Rufus checked in with his cook, who was staring vacantly into a simmering saucepan. Like a stale loaf of bread, Angelo was crusty in parts, doughy in others and covered in a thin layer of flour. The apron he wore resembled a perpetual crime scene, pocked with bloody hand prints, curly hairs, dried semen and linty fibers. It was a sanguinary mess of clues to a mystery that Rufus had no interest in solving.

The sight of his boss snapped Angelo out of his sauce. He immediately began sharpening knives, his favorite pastime.

"Bums," Rufus exclaimed, throwing up his arms. "I'm surrounded by idle and indolent bums!"

"Ya really wanna start in wid'dat right now?" Angelo asked. He picked a gleaming blade out of the rack and ran it along the steel sharpener.

"Murderous bums to boot! I swear Angelo, if you weren't such a genius at the deep fryer, I would have rid myself of you years ago!" Rufus had absent-mindedly picked up a paring knife and now he was punctuating his points by jabbing it at Angelo.

"Sorry chap," Rufus said, returning the knife to its sheath. "I've been terribly stressed."

"Ain't we all," said the cook, drawn back to the saucepan's hypnotic bubbles. "What's da headcount fer dinner?"

"No dinner, you halfwit!" Rufus screamed, reaching for the knife again. "Only appetizers! Please don't tell me you're cooking dinner. Please. Don't."

"Only apps boss, 'swhat I meant." said Angelo. He was cleaning under his fingernails with the tomato knife.

"You disgust me," Rufus scowled. "Headcount's between four and six, plate for ten. Have it ready in an hour." He turned and left the kitchen.

A VEXATIOUS NOODLE-SCRATCHER

To get to Lindsay Park, take the westbound local to the end of the line. The route begins near the industrial waterfront in the east, where the *Droit* had established its stronghold. After weaving through the shabby business district (known for the weed-like proliferation of 99¢ Stores), the trolley ambles through the moth-eaten section of downtown called the Gut; it was here that Ashleigh and Satch boarded. Even in the Flats, a barren wasteland where nothing, not even buildings, will grow, the trolley makes a quick stop before curving into the plebeian suburbs of New Urbania. At last it comes to the terminus, the place that Rufus called home. This forty-five minute tour of Hell will cost you two bucks, off-peak.

Lindsay Park was once known as the People's Pastures. It used to be public space, a popular weekend getaway for families that couldn't afford a real vacation. A small grove of trees and the poorly maintained garden was the nearest approximation of 'nature' one could get to by trolley. The park boasted two oft-peed-in pools, a carousel of headless horses, and a basketball hoop with a bent rim.

Laden with memories of many a mediocre summer here, Rufus' father, Alistair Wiggin, bribed an official at the Parks Department and was allowed to buy it part and parcel. He immediately bulldozed any remaining traces of amusement. Young Rufus insisted on keeping the lifeguard's chair, but it was removed a year later after Rufus broke his arm pretending to be King Kong.

Alistair himself designed the house that replaced the park. It showcased a jumble of disparate styles, including Adirondack Rustic, Dutch Colonial, Mission Revival, Neo-Byzantine and Brutalism. Alistair had no formal training in architecture and possessed only a tenuous grasp of aesthetics. He dubbed his new style Wigginian Modern, naturally.

The critics went crazy; for years after it was built, "Alistair's Asshat" was the butt of every cheap and easy joke they made. The nearest thing to praise came from a *News of the Weird* correspondent, who called it a 'vexatious noodle-scratcher'. Alistair took it as a compliment, of course.

When the old man died, the title to the only house in town with its own private trolley stop descended directly to Rufus, in fee simple. It should be noted that at the time, his mother was still alive.

****

"Humble lodgings, my ass," Ashleigh said. She was unsure of how to get through the wrought iron gates, an imposing palisade Alistair had erected to keep out the wayward day trippers who were unaware that Lindsay Park was shuttered permanently.

Get lost deadbeats, he'd say, shaking his fist. Go piss in someone else's pool!

"I'm cold and I have to pee," Satch complained, scanning the area by the light of dusk and shivering in the wind.

"I think we could scale it," Ashleigh suggested.

Satch emptied his bladder onto a hydrangea bush and looked up. "Sorry Ash, but a rusty spike up the ass sounds like a bad idea."

"Come on, Satch! Couldn't you wait until we got inside?"

"It's not good etiquette to enter a stranger's home and beeline it to the bathroom. He'll think I'm some kind of jerk."

"And peeing in his driveway is somehow better?"

"I've done much worse things in driveways, believe me."

Ashleigh groaned. "This better be the last time I see your dick tonight," she warned, knowing it was always a possibility with Satch.

"It would be irresponsible of me to promise that, Ash. But as long as this house isn't haunted, I think I'll be fine. The little guy tends to come out when I'm scared."

An eerie static echoed up from the hedges. Startled, Satch shook out the final drops onto his foot.

"Haunted. I knew it," he said, hurrying back to Ashleigh's side.

Rufus' voice emerged through the static. "They're here, you ingrates!" Ashleigh smiled at the sound of his voice. "Why haven't you buzzed them in yet? What incompetence! I expect you all to have your bags packed by morning. Yes, you too Angelo! And don't think that means you can leave the kitchen tonight, do you hear me? Don't point that knife at me! Don't you point that knife at me! I swear on my father's ghost it will end with you in ribbons!"

The line went dead. Satch nervously adjusted his shorts.

"I think I'm gonna bail," he said. Ashleigh hooked a finger through a belt loop to prevent his escape.

The gates bzzzzzzzzzed and creaked open, powered by the same motor that once animated the headless horses of Lindsay Park.

"If anything happens to us tonight, just know that I always loved you, Ash," Satch proclaimed.

Ashleigh turned to look him in the eyes. "Please don't embarrass me, Satch."

Ashleigh dragged Satch by his shorts up a steep footpath that meandered through a grove of willows. As they approached the top, the towers of Rufus' private playland came into view. It was bold, it was audacious, it was stunningly hideous.

The front porch was built of unfinished split logs (Adirondack Rustic), which jutted out to form the mansion's giant chin. A granite fireplace bisected the gambrel roof (Dutch Colonial), the eaves of which were rounded in a bell shape. It appeared as if a flapper's cloche was floating over the porch; this probably inspired the headwear allusion in "Alistair's Asshat," though that's only a guess.

Identical in scale, the east and west wings adjoined the main quarters at sharp forty-five degree angles. Each wing had an arcaded corridor with pier arches (Mission Revival) on the ground floor, while cold symmetrical cubes of concrete (Brutalism) were stacked above. Finally, each of these drab institutional slabs were brightened up by a hemispherical dome (Neo-Byzantine) painted with colorful frescoes.

The mansion's scale of eclecticism was matched only by the breathtaking scope of Alistair's commitment. No expense was spared in the construction; no corners were cut and every detail was seen to; only the finest materials were used. Taken individually, each section could have been considered a masterpiece of hubristic design. Yet the haphazard integration had created a circle with no center, a parhelion with no sun.

"What is it?" asked Satch, scratching his head.

"I guess it's a house," Ashleigh replied.

"It looks like several houses."

"Maybe it is," Ashleigh said, not surprised that such a strange man would bed down in equally strange accommodations.

"Wanna play a game and see how much stuff we can steal?"

"Be good, Satch. Not tonight."

Rufus emerged from under the brim of the asshat. "You made it!" he exclaimed, hopping over the moat to greet his guests. Not wanting to look too formal, he had chosen to wear his customary ascot and blazer, though he did wear new cufflinks for the occasion.

"I apologize for the wait," he said, kissing Ashleigh on the cheek. "Ashleigh Victoria, you look stunning! You are a hot knife through the butter of my heart." Rufus turned to Satch and immediately noticed his lack of attire.

"I don't believe we've been formally introduced," he said, extending his hand. "I'm Rufus Wiggin, and you, if I recall correctly, are the drummer."

Satch answered Rufus' handshake with a big bear hug, lifting his slight-framed host a foot off the ground.

"You betcha! The name's Satch. They call me Satch the Catch, quick with the Snatch Blast."

"No one calls him that," Ashleigh corrected.

"A frisky one, aren't you?" wheezed Rufus, his lungs crushed in the embrace. "It's a pleasure to make your acquaintance."

"You don't know 'em 'til you hug 'em, that's what I say," said Satch, depositing Rufus back on solid ground.

Rufus straightened his jacket and looked around. "Where's your brother?" he asked. He had been anticipating a reunion of the night fate called them all to Smitty's, (and secretly hoping for an impromptu performance).

"He had a previous engagement," Ashleigh said, preferring not to disclose Kody's adamant refusal to attend, "but he sends his best."

"Previous engagement my ass!" said Satch. "All that kid does is whack it and cry, like a little masturbating baby. If he were here, he'd already be up in the bathroom with a box of tissues and a tube of lotion. Sobbing away, jerking away. Am I right, Ash? That's no way to party. Am I right, Rufus? C'mon, give it up!"

Satch wound up and delivered the highest high-five in history. Startled, Rufus raised his hand just in time for a direct hit; the sound of their flesh slapping together echoed across the grounds. Rufus couldn't remember the last time he'd given or received such a salutation.

"That's certainly no way to live," Rufus said, unsure of how to take Satch's remark. His palm stung pleasantly.

"Ready to get fucked up tonight, my man?" Satch asked. He had already begun polishing off a six pack in his head. "How's the Freon level of your fridge?"

THE TYRANNY OF SOCKS AND SHOES

Alistair's influence was not so strongly felt inside the home. The decorators he hired had given it that subdued, old-money elegance. A bit stale, perhaps, but classy. The walls were each trimmed with cornices of Georgian molding; for every three beige walls, one was a burgundy accent. The vaulted ceilings were embossed with copper tiles and supporting unwieldy Bohemian Crystal chandeliers.

Ceiling to floor, every square foot seemed to be covered with art, tracing the arc of European culture from classical antiquity to the Renaissance, through the Baroque period and the developments of Realism, Impressionism and Modernism, all the way into to Abstract Expressionism and Postmodernism. Ashleigh recognized many of the works. Satch was more enthralled with the hardwood floors.

"Nice wood, Wig."

"Thank you, Satch. You have an eye for quality lumber. It's agarwood, the best there is."

"I hope I don't sound stupid," Ashleigh interjected. "But is that a *real* Botticelli?"

"Of course," Rufus said, stopping to admire the chubby cherub resting on a cloud. "I don't bother with prints, anyone can get those."

Rufus led them to the parlor, where the other guests sat drinking martinis and smoking long cigarettes from long cigarette holders. One was an old troll of a man with a pumpkin-shaped head, while the other resembled a mummy in an evening gown.

Rufus held his breath hoping his guests would mingle. These fresh-faced upstarts won't recognize these antiques any more than I could call a dinosaur by its Christian name, he worried.

Ashleigh smiled politely at the other guests while keeping herself a safe distance away. She settled into the thick upholstery of a Louis XIV chair, and soon became entranced with the fleurs-de-lis of the flock wallpaper.

Satch plopped down on the couch between the mummy and troll, using the coffee table as an ottoman. His blackened tootsies wiggled in plain view like worms in a mud puddle. The elderly bookends observed him as if he were the half-naked ambassador of an aboriginal tribe.

The whole tableau made Rufus uneasy. He decided alcohol was the only way to soothe the social tension.

"Would you two care for a martini?" he asked.

"Boy, would I!" said Satch, enthusiastically. "I need to catch up to these old sots."

"And you, Ashleigh?" Rufus asked.

She nodded, turning her attention back to a Winslow Homer etching she had discovered.

"You guys got a cig I can bum?" Satch asked the mummy and the troll, admiring the sheer length of their cigarettes.

"I believe you should seek a pair of shoes before a cigarette, son," came the reply from the pumpkin-headed man.

"No way, pops. My feet have sole, man. Get it?"

Everyone got it. Rufus cringed and began slurping at his martini.

"The way I see it," Satch explained. "Why should my feet continue to suffer under the tyranny of socks and shoes?"

The troll slapped his knee, expelling a crusty laugh.

"By George, did you hear that Marie?" he said, leaning around Satch to speak to the mummy. "The tyranny of socks and shoes, brilliant!"

"I'm known for my brilliance," Satch added.

"What an oppressive yolk to toil under!" the troll exclaimed. "I gave up on socks years ago, those prude Victorian coverings." He turned to Satch. "Don't you agree?"

"Totally," said Satch.

"I never did away with shoes altogether as you have, though I did resolve never to tie another pair again." He demonstrated his conviction by hiking up his pants, revealing a pair of slip-on loafers and bare ankles.

"That's the spirit, champ," Satch said, placing his feet side-by-side with the loafers. "You're half-way to freedom, my friend."

"Rufus," asked the mummy. "Who is this charming brute?"

Rufus realized that he had been so consumed with the thought of social calamity that he'd forgotten to introduce everyone. Now Satch beat him to the punch.

"I'm Satch, they call me Satch the Natch," he said, stirring his drink with a bandaged digit. "I play drums. And over there is Ashleigh. She plays bass."

SOMETHING EDGY

After the party had consumed two rounds of drinks, the butler presented Angelo's finished creations. The cook, true to Rufus' orders, stayed sequestered in the kitchen. Away from the guests.

The savory "appetizers" included a tender Lamb Osso Bucco with a fragrant Saffron Risotto, a hearty Boeuf à la Niçoise, and a Ragout of Morels that was irresistible. There were sweet options, too, including a rich Vanilla Semifreddo with a Rhubarb Compote, as well as pleasantly tart nectarine financiers.

Rufus forgot his anger at Angelo and stuffed himself. Between bites, he would put down his plate and pace the parlor, pondering a way to rescue his party from impending failure. Comfortably reclined, Satch balanced a mountain of food on his belly and ate. Ashleigh maintained a tidy plate, each portion carefully segregated. The mummy and troll opted for extra helpings of alcohol and nicotine instead.

"My compliments to the chef!" Satch proclaimed, waving a lamb shank. "Off with his head!"

Rufus kept his eye on Angelo through the kitchen door, making sure he didn't lunge for the knives. Thankfully, he hadn't heard Satch's comment.

"Loosen up, Rufus. Re-laax," Satch said, reading Ashleigh's mind. While she still found Rufus' reckless gorging adorable, interspersed with his neurotic pacing it was making her uncomfortable.

"My apologies to all," Rufus said, taking a seat. "My anxiety is getting the best of me." He addressed Ashleigh and Satch. "This get-together probably pales in comparison to the sort of soiree you're used to."

"Partying in cold warehouses with a shitty sound system and no plumbing?" Satch scoffed, dismissing the notion with a flourish of his fork. "Been there, man. I'll take this spread any day."

"You're welcome to come see for yourself," Ashleigh said, speaking mainly to the smallest Richard Serra sculpture she had ever seen, which was on the coffee table beside her. "But they're not as great as you think."

"I'd love to," Rufus said, ruefully. "But I doubt I'd be accepted. I'm afraid I'm not cut from the same cloth as your merry band of mavericks."

"You probably would have to lose the get-up," Satch suggested, himself a partisan against the tyranny of clothes altogether.

"Probably the hair, too," Ashleigh added.

"My hair is sacrosanct!" Rufus snapped. "But perhaps a new wardrobe is in order. Something...edgier? Yes!" Rufus jumped back to his feet. "Ramon, get Spit on the horn!"

The butler appeared carrying a marble phone on a velvet-lined platter. It looked extremely heavy; fortunately, it was a wireless. Ramon dialed Spit's number for the third time that day, and held the receiver to Rufus' ear.

"Spit, it's Rufus," he said to the muffled voice on the other end. "What do you mean, hold on? What could you possibly be doing that is more important than this? No, I will not hold."

Rufus continued ranting at the phone and shook his head at his guests.

"Of course I'm still here you dope! Listen Spit, I need a new wardrobe, and not the usual frippery you bring me. I want something *mod*, something *edgy*. Yes, I did just say mod, what's it to you? No, I will not hold again! Who do you think you are, the grand goddamn pontiff? Get me the clothes and goodbye." Rufus slammed the phone, causing Ramon to stagger backwards.

"I have a guy who finds me things," Rufus explained. "He's can be as useful as he is useless."

"What else can he get?" Satch asked, leadingly. His head was swimming with ideas.

"Why, anything you'd like," Rufus responded.

"Drugs?" Satch ventured. Women and drums were next on his list.

"Ramon, where the hell did you go? Get Spit back on the line."

Satch liked where this conversation was going. He jotted down a list of psychotropics just in case his expertise was needed. The butler returned, and the whole elaborate routine was repeated.

"Spit, it's Rufus again. What do you mean you knew it was me? What the hell is that supposed to mean? You're a psychic now are you? Then tell me why I'm calling? Exactly, you don't know. You're right, it could be anything. Don't jump to conclusions Spit, it's ignorant and unbecoming. Here's the deal, I want drugs, on the double. I don't care what kinds! Any kind! All kinds!"

As the conversation closed, Rufus seemed determined to add injury to insult. "I'm entertaining guests, that's why. Why weren't you invited? Because you're an obnoxious bore! Goodbye."

Everyone was put off by Rufus' tantrum. Ashleigh found it bratty and demeaning, and too much like her brother's behavior. Still, she wondered how she would act if given the power to have anything she wanted since birth.

An awkward silence hung in the air. Satch broke the tension by letting out a hearty belch, signaling his approval at the end of the meal.

"How about another cig?" he asked the troll, who was happy to oblige.

"You're too kind," said Satch. He lit up and leaned in. "Now if I can get your name, we can really get down to business."

Nuts, Rufus thought. He never even finished the introductions. What a disaster.

A DISTINGUISHED MAN OF ARTS & LETTERS
(OR, THE GRAND BREASTS OF YORE)

The mummy was named Marie St. Alban, while the pumpkin head called himself Jay Hudson Hamilton. When Satch heard this, he flung his plate across the room.

"Jay Hamilton, the writer?" he asked, beaming.

"You're not trying to put the moves on me, are you?"

"Oh man oh man. I'm a huge fan, Mr. Hamilton, and I mean *huge*," Satch said, measuring the size of his admiration with his hands. "I wrote an English paper on you in school and got an F."

Hamilton smirked. "Academia has been slow to warm up to me. I blame jealousy."

The unlikely recognition between two of his guests lifted Rufus' spirits, pulling him back from the brink of total dejection. He shouldn't have been all that surprised. After all, Jay Hudson Hamilton was a distinguished man of Arts & Letters.

"*Double-Stuffin' Miss Muffin? Jammed Up and Jelly Tight?* Classics," Satch gushed. "I used to pound my meat like no tomorrow to your books. My dick in one hand, a paperback in the other, day in and day out."

"That must have been exhausting," Marie St. Alban suggested.

"Oh, it was. Then I read *Sedimentary Cock* about this nympho-," Satch paused, "I'm sorry, Ma'am, I hope you don't mind my language."

"Oh, by all means continue," Marie St. Alban assured him.

"This nympho-geologist who brings dinosaur bones back to life and fucks 'em. I never knew science could be so interesting."

"Yes, Jay," St. Alban joked. "That one was so tender."

"And the words, man! The words!" added Satch. He hadn't noticed her tone.

"Yes, yes. I'm very proud," replied the humbled author.

"And who could forget *Der Pissfist!*" Satch exclaimed, mentally running through Hamilton's catalog as fast as he could. "That book changed my life, man. The scene where Pissfist has to fuck a leaf blower to save his family, but ends up getting his dick ripped off? That shit still gives me nightmares. Then, when the doctors grafted a blowtorch to his crotch so he could exact revenge, the whole time I'm thinking, is that real? Can they do that? Shit man, give me a torch-dick!"

This seemed to be Hamilton's cue to don the cap of raconteur. "Let me tell you the tale about how *Der Pissfist* came to be," he said.

"Not this old story again," begged St. Alban, affecting indifference.

"I wrote it when I was living in a Chinatown opium den called the Lusty Button. It was a real swinging joint," he began.

"That explains the first two chapters," Satch interjected.

"I was twenty years old and all piss and vinegar. I suppose that's right around your age," he said to Satch, who nodded in agreement. At that moment he would've agreed with anything Hamilton said. "In the morning, I'd go down to the docks and try to seduce the new arrivals as they got off the boat."

"Any luck?"

Hamilton chuckled. "Let's just say I learned many secrets of the Orient."

Satch winked. "I'll bet."

"He learned how to say 'crabs' in five languages," cracked St. Alban.

"In the afternoon, I would write, write, write," Hamilton continued. "At nightfall, when I couldn't stand another clack of the typewriter, I would drink absinthe and write poems for whores until I got lucky or pissed myself or both."

"Far out," said Satch. This confirmed his long-held belief that he was born in the wrong era.

"Then one night I was in this gangbang. This one was a real filth-fest: hairy backs, flabby flesh, you name it. And wouldn't you know it, the creep next to me was an editor in Germany. Herr Pubes, I called him. He was looking for material and we got to talking. We ended up with an outline right then and there, in that sea of limbs, as our privates plowed the same soil."

"Germans love that twisted shit," Satch said knowingly.

"You bet your ass they do! They went gangbusters for *Pissfist*; it was a bestseller in no time. We began to make plans to bring it stateside."

"Just like Pissfist's triumphant return from the land of the one-eyed monster!" Satch pointed out.

"Precisely! I've drawn that very parallel myself, haven't I, Marie?" Hamilton said in praise his star pupil. "So my American publisher, the same bastards who told me there was no market for this

filth months before, now were happy to release it, even under the original title. They said it was for lack of a good English translation."

"I think the title says it all," said Satch.

"Next thing you know, I'm the cock-of-the-walk. I was the toast of the literati. They called me the Polymath of Porn! The Orson Welles of Smut!"

"And just like Orson, you've aged into a pompous whale," St. Alban joked. Jay Hudson Hamilton waved her off.

"Everything was cool until those joyboys in Washington caught a downwind whiff of the shit I was flinging. One day I was just shooting the breeze with the guys at the stag theater, minding my own business, and these pigs arrest me on obscenity charges. They said I was a threat to the country's moral fiber. Can you believe it? I told them that fiber's used to cleanse the bowels and that the country is constipated."

"Killjoys," said Satch.

"Puritans," added St. Alban.

"I couldn't make bail because I had gambled away all my royalties playing Chinese baccarat."

"I could never get the hang of Chinese baccarat," Rufus interjected, chiming in for the first time.

"So I made the jailhouse scene for a while. Finally the deadbeats at my publisher ponied up enough dough for a lawyer. He was such an asshole I thought I was going to have to represent myself. Then the trial judge read the first chapter of *Pissfist* and said I ought to be locked up for life."

"Prude," said Satch. He was ready to track down the old judge and leave a steaming surprise on his lawn.

"I didn't care. I was guilty! The book *is* obscene! But no, my publisher's lawyer has to go and find all these critics and writers to testify that Pissfist is the new Odysseus, the new Ahab!"

"He's *waaay* more bad ass than those stiffs," objected Satch.

"That's what I said. The judge agreed. Guilty on all counts! I applauded the verdict as they led me away in shackles."

"Is that when you wrote *Locked Away, Feelin' Gay*?" Satch asked, hoping he had the chronology right.

"Yup, that and two others: *Penile Colony* and *ChainGangBang*. Not my favorite work, too much man-on-man, if I may be frank. Anyway, my lawyer kept filing motions and appeals, or whatever it is they do. We'll get you out of there, he said. Forget it, I told him, the bin ain't so bad. Of course he didn't listen."

"Typical lawyer," Rufus said. "Did you know that Spit went to law school? Useless."

"After we lost the first appeal, I wrote a letter of thanks to each of the three judges in which I lovingly compared their wrinkled genitals to the nocturnal bloom of the Kadupal flower."

"How sweet," said St. Alban.

"More time passed. Finally I got a letter saying the Supreme Court was going to hear my case and I nearly shit myself." He teetered uncomfortably on his buttocks for effect. "I was relieved. I thought, at last we can put this whole silly matter to rest. Lock me up and throw away the key!"

"Then what?" Ashleigh asked, feeling she should contribute something despite feeling completely unengaged by the conversation.

Hamilton shook his head. "They up and decide that my book, 'though lascivious, is a major literary achievement, possessing serious artistic merit.' Their words, not mine. That's bullshit, son. I should know, I wrote those words."

"They still study the case in law schools," St. Alban added. "They call it the Hamilton Test."

"If that's what they're studying, then no wonder things are such a mess," Hamilton said. "Long story short, they sprung me, *Pissfist* was released, a wave of ass-kissing ensued, and the publicity made me rich and famous. The end."

Satch applauded enthusiastically.

"Think of all the artists you helped," Ashleigh said, trying to glean a lesson from the story. "You helped liberate self-expression."

"Yeah, yeah, yeah," Hamilton said, dismissively. "I was called Hero of the First Amendment and all that, but I never wanted any of it. Leave me alone and let me write my dirty stories! I don't give a flying fuck about the First Amendment."

"Fuck the First Amendment!" Satch cried, looking ready to deliver another high-five.

"I've spent the rest of my career trying to get arrested again, but thanks to the Goddamned Supreme Court you can write whatever you want these days. No matter how obscene I get, no matter how outrageous I try to be, the critics keep dishing out handjobs."

"What a sad story," Satch said.

"Don't worry Jay," said St. Alban, her cold hand caressing the liver spots on his wrist. "History will remember you as the wanton degenerate that you are."

"I sure hope so," he replied, rubbing her thigh. "I would hate to think my life's work has been in vain."

Ashleigh felt the need to change the subject. "Given your experience," she asked, "what do you think of what the *Droit Moral*'s been up to?"

"What in the hell's a *Dwa Morale*?" Hamilton asked.

"You know, Jay," St. Alban said, pushing away his creeping hand. "That silly band of Trotskyites who bombed the museum last year."

"Never heard of them," he shrugged. "They sound like a bunch of French pussies to me."

"Hear, hear," said Rufus.

Jay Hudson Hamilton turned to his young protégé. "Let me ask you something, Satch."

"You can ask me anything, Mr. Hamilton."

"As a drummer, do you ever fantasize about hiding a supple little groupie in your bass drum to service you on stage?"

"Old news, man. April 12th, our show at Monomania. Remember that, Ash?"

"Seriously, Satch?" Ashleigh said, grossed-out but not totally surprised.

"She was in there the whole set and both encores. I think I accidentally kneed her in the face a few times."

"Now that's entertainment!" exclaimed Hamilton.

"How come no one told me?" Ashleigh wondered.

"I just thought everyone knew," Satch replied. "I figured that's why the crowd was cheering."

"I'd like to ask you something else," Hamilton said, his gravelly voice taking on an even creepier inflection. "What scares you the most sexually?"

Without hesitation, Satch replied: "Banana boobs."

"Banana boobs?" Hamilton repeated, afraid he was beginning to go senile.

"Think back to the '70s, old man. It was before my time, but whenever I've seen naked ladies from that era, their boobs look different. Haven't you noticed? They're long and curvy, yet pointy, like a saxophone."

"Or like bananas!" Hamilton exclaimed. "Yes, yes. How could I forget?"

"Lindsay Wagner in *Two People*? Cybill Shepard in *The Last Picture Show*?"

"Banana boobs," Hamilton realized.

"They turn me on because, well, they're boobs," Satch explained. "And yet they're extinct, which scares me. It'd be like fucking a dodo."

"Where have they gone?" Hamilton asked, trying to find them in his mind. "Who or what is to blame for their demise?"

"Nature?" St. Alban proposed.

"Advances in brasserie technology?" Rufus ventured.

"It saddens me, Jay," Satch said. "It is a true tragedy that I'll never get my paws on a pair of those Cavendish Creamers."

Hamilton joined in. "Plantain Palookas!" he howled.

"Manzano Milkjugs!" yelled Rufus, never missing an opportunity to turn an alliterative phrase.

"In all seriousness, Satch," Hamilton said, gravely. "Banana boobs are scary, but deliciously intoxicating I assure you. I promise to search high and low, near and far, to find you a pair."

"I would never be able repay such a generous gift," Satch said with more sincerity than Ashleigh had ever heard him utter.

"Perhaps, somewhere in the Pacific," Hamilton speculated, "there's an island untouched by modern man, teeming with those grand breasts of yore."

"We can take a banana-boob-boat there!" said Satch.

"To the banana-boob-republic!" Hamilton rejoined. His mind had already set sail to that exotic isle. "Ha-Ha! Young man, I do believe I've found the premise for my next book."

Noticing that Marie St. Alban was as thoroughly disinterested in the boys' conversation as she was, Ashleigh worked up the courage to break the ice.

"How do you know Rufus?" she asked.

"Between you and me," St. Alban said, leaning her creaky skeleton forward to speak confidentially, "I was his father's mistress. I was also Rufus' art teacher, but that was really besides the point. Do you suppose Rufus' intentions tonight are honorable? If he's anything like old Alistair in the sack, it could be the death of me. Did you know his father?"

Shocked, Ashleigh could only manage a "No."

"I'm telling you, that man could go for hours. Rufus looks just like him too, but I don't think he'd go for an old bag like me. Though I could see you two making whoopie tonight. I can sense these things. You're just his type. But maybe, if you don't mind, I can corner Rufus and slip him inside me before he knows what's going on. A girl can dream can't she? The thought of bagging two generations of Wiggins makes my nether regions tingle."

"Yikes," said Ashleigh.

"And you, my dear?" St. Alban asked.

"Well, I've never..." Ashleigh stuttered.

"I mean, how do you know Rufus?"

"Oh. Well, um, he puked on my brother. Then he bought me breakfast."

"Like father, like son," St. Alban said with a slight grin.

Desperately hoping for another change of subject, Ashleigh recalled a nugget from her childhood.

"You're not the same Marie St. Alban who did the Highway Project, are you?" she asked. She doubted there was more than one.

The mummy suddenly became animated. An ossified smile cracked through her pancake makeup. She shifted her bones to face Ashleigh directly.

"That was me, in a former life," she said with some effort. "It must be years since I've been recognized. How refreshing!"

Rufus was finally at ease. His guests were not only interacting, they were hitting it off! He sat back, ordered another drink, and congratulated himself on his brilliant job matchmaking.

"My parents took me and my brother to see it when I was six," Ashleigh said. "It was the first time I took a trip for art."

Ashleigh's first exhibit turned out to be St. Alban's last. Fifteen years ago, the artist known for her extra-large installations was commissioned to paint twenty-seven one-mile-long canvasses, which were displayed as one long piece along the northbound side of Highway 27. City officials hoped the project would enliven a doleful drive and distract out-of-town commuters from the infinite blight the city was known for.

The Project was done in an Op Art style. Each canvas depicted a nearly identical image of a blurred automobile. The only way the image made sense was driving alongside it. On the northbound side it appeared that a speeding car was racing you, while on the southbound side it seemed that a vehicle in the distance was perpetually flying past.

Given the moribund state of public art at the time, the installation was universally lauded for its ambition. Today, it would probably look rather dated, but in fact it was its popularity that proved to be its downfall. Drivers began paying too much attention to the unfurling flipbook of images and too little attention to the road. Accidents, both large and small, rose dramatically.

A month after opening, its run was abruptly ended after a paranoid drunk driver decided to drag race, then evade, the stationary image. An epic pileup and the destruction of all but one canvas was the result. So much for that.

"Are you working on anything now?" Ashleigh asked, recalling the wonder she felt watching St. Alban's roadster speed alongside the family minivan, and the fascination she experienced viewing the same thing in reverse.

"I quit painting shortly after the Highway Project went up quite literally in flames. To be honest, though, I was glad it happened. The visual arts are old hat. For the last fifteen years I've been pioneering an exciting and wholly-original new art form."

"Oh yeah?" Ashleigh asked, eager to hear how this maverick of modern art was now spending her days. "What is it?"

"Danceramics," the maverick of modern art said proudly.

She seemed to expect to be bowled over with adulation. Yet Ashleigh's blank look seemed to beg for further explanation.

"Danceramics is the performance of choreographed gyrations around a spinning potter's wheel," St. Alban explained, making dramatic hand movements as she spoke.

"Uh-huh," said Ashleigh.

"The idea is to let the dancing, not the hands, dictate the shape that the pottery takes. It's a transformative experience to behold. Like jazz, it is powerfully moving for the audience and performer alike."

"Uh-huh," said Ashleigh.

"That sounds absolutely riveting," Rufus cut in, winking at Ashleigh. "You'll have to favor us with a performance tonight."

DANCERAMICS

After the fifth round of drinks, Marie St. Alban was ready to introduce her audience to the wonders of Danceramics. Unafraid to show a little skin, she disrobed with the whole room watching. She exchanged her evening gown for an equally unflattering silver unitard that she carried in her oversized purse for just such occasions.

"Talk about a hard-off," Satch whispered to Ashleigh.

Hamilton teased, "You look like a skeleton wrapped in tin foil." This sent him into a phlegmy laughing fit, which was followed by a dry coughing fit.

Rufus was searching the basement for a potter's wheel. Although he had no recollection of ever owning one, he knew that in the bowels of Alistair's Asshat anything was possible. Two generations worth of capricious hoardings had been accumulating in those unkempt catacombs for decades.

Lo and behold, under a mated pair of Queen Alexandra Birdwing butterflies mounted to a dusty plaque, he found one. It was standing beside a hand-powered loom with a piece of yarn still threaded in its loop. Rufus had never seen these industrial relics before, and he couldn't guess when they had last been used.

Had his father gone through a handicrafts phase? he wondered. Might these tools hold some historical or sentimental value? Or, he considered, did a clairvoyant vision hip old Alistair to the burgeoning tour-de-force that was sure to be Danceramics, leading him to stockpile this equipment here in anticipation of the day it would be needed?

With considerable grunting, Rufus carried the unwieldy machine upstairs and set it down in the breakfast nook. Marie St. Alban frowned at the poor condition of his ersatz offering.

"Is this the best potter's wheel you have?" she asked.

"Yes, Marie," said Rufus, struggling to catch his breath. "I do not keep all manner and variety of ceramics equipment at my disposal in case an impromptu dance recital occurs."

"*Danceramics* recital," she corrected.

"Make me a new ashtray, Marie!" exclaimed Hamilton. "Mine's getting full."

"I need music!" St. Alban demanded. She was in full performance mode.

"But – the record player is in the attic," Rufus panted.

"I need *live* music," said the surprisingly bossy tinfoil mummy.

Hamilton scoffed. "Prima donna."

"These two are musicians," she said of Ashleigh and Satch. "Find them some instruments, Rufus."

Rufus descended into the basement for a second time, and returned with the first two instruments he found. He handed the tabla to Satch, and the ukulele to Ashleigh. St. Alban's involuntary orchestra was now assembled and she was ready for her big performance.

Satch flicked the drum's goatskin head. It emitted a warm, low tone.

"Taut as a drum," he said, thinking that it was the wittiest thing he'd said all night.

Ashleigh fiddled with the ukulele's rusty pegbox, desperately trying to tune its four nylon strings. Her first strum produced an open chord that made the whole room cringe. After a few adjustments, she tried again. This time she produced a sound only slightly more melodious.

"That's the best I can do," she said. "Hope you like the key of D."

"Very well," St. Alban sighed. "Dim the lights."

Hamilton was growing impatient. "On with the damn show already!"

Rufus dimmed the chandelier and lit two candles to illuminate the proscenium. St. Alban stood head bowed with her back to her audience. The obelisk of her shadow climbed up the wall.

Satch slapped the center of the drum with his left hand while tapping out a melody along the rim with his right. The beat was mid-tempo, in perfect 4/4 time.

Still struggling to properly hold the tiny instrument, Ashleigh began with a few uneasy notes. Working around the fretboard's many dead spots, she finally found her groove, recasting Brahms Lullaby in the spirit of a Hawaiian luau.

Rufus plugged in the wheel. Its motor creaked alive in noisy fits of vibration. The band tried to drown it out by playing louder. The motor chugged on, occasionally belching plumes of oily vapor.

"Hurry up, Marie!" Hamilton yelled over the racket. "We'll all be asphyxiated!"

Nevertheless, St. Alban was calm, cool, composed. She lifted her arms and waved them wildly. Her saggy arm fat flapped in waves.

"Ready for takeoff," Hamilton whispered to Satch, drumming mellowly beside him.

It's been said that writing about music is like dancing about architecture. In that same spirit, it must be said that writing about Danceramics is like pantomiming about glass-blowing. While not a totally useless pursuit in itself, it can be tough to do the subject justice.

The routine began with a series of adagios, knee bends, and forward thrusts around the four corners of the table. St. Alban produced a slimy lump of clay from her purse and held it high above her head, as if making an offering to the chandelier. Her movements had a fragile intensity.

BOOM! She slammed the clay onto the batterboard and the whole machine shook. The hypnotic revolutions of the wheel made Rufus dizzy and Hamilton sweat. Suddenly, St. Alban executed a sharp *brisé* from one corner of the table to the next. With each landing, she stabbed her thumbs into the clay.

Next, she wound up and delivered a grand battement. She kicked up her leg and grinded her toes into the lump until her ankles were speckled with slime. She transitioned with clay-covered jazz hands, followed by a series of stiff shoulder shimmies lacking both rhythm and sensuality.

St. Alban made the clay her bitch. She cursed it, she fondled it, she slapped it. She blew it a kiss and winked.

It was the least erotic thing Rufus had ever seen.

She shook from her tennis elbows down to her arthritic knees, much to the delight of her bewildered audience. For the grand finale, she made a surprisingly agile leap onto the coffee table and stalked the clay on all fours, like a cat ready to pounce.

Anticipating the climax, Ashleigh and Satch upped the tempo. Everyone was captivated as Marie St. Alban doubled over, arched into a back bridge, fan-kicked her body into a perfect semicircle and finally, with unflappable determination, lowered her face into the clay, burrowing it deep inside the malleable mass. Only her hair was left exposed.

Growing bored and wanting dessert, Rufus walked to the socket and pulled the plug.

Ever the performer, St. Alban held her 180 degree pose as the clay slowly ceased rotating around the contours of her face. Ashleigh and Satch rang out their final notes before joining Hamilton in a round of applause.

"Bravo," said Ashleigh.

"We'll put her face in the kiln!" joked Hamilton.

Rufus poked her in the ribcage. "Alright, Marie, show's over."

The tinfoil mummy wouldn't budge, so he poked again. And again.

"That was lovely. Really, Marie, we all loved it." Rufus said. "Now please get down from there."

Despite his best efforts, the arch held as strong as a Roman aqueduct. Rufus couldn't tell if she was normally that stiff, or if this was rigor mortis. When he extracted her face from the soup bowl she'd created, it proved to be the latter.

With a look of tranquil terror, Marie St. Alban left this world. Her death mask was both comedic and tragic.

"She's a goner," said Hamilton. He lit another cigarette.

"So it appears," Rufus said flatly. Ashleigh rushed over to help extricate the body.

"This is part of the act, right?" Satch asked.

"She's dead, Satch!" Ashleigh yelled, trying to figure out the best way to lift the body off the wheel.

"Yeah right," Satch scoffed. "She was alive just a minute ago."

"Now we really can throw her in the kiln!" Hamilton shouted.

Rufus wrapped his arms around St. Alban's torso, which was the crest of the arch. This placed her dead, gaping, clay-covered mouth uncomfortably close to his crotch.

"That's it, Rufus," Hamilton said. "Sixty-nine the old crow!"

Locking her arms around St. Alban's spindly upper thighs, Ashleigh found herself in an equally precarious position. Rufus counted to three and they lifted. They weren't surprised that the body was light, but in fact it seemed lighter than humanly possible.

Their exertion brought Ashleigh and Rufus nose-to-nose. All night they had been avoiding eye contact with each other, so it's hard to say whether at that moment it was the alcohol, or Hamilton's sleazy pheromones, or the garden of Renaissance nudes above the sofa that did it. But right then and there, they parted lips and kissed.

Had it been a quick peck the incident may have been written off, but they really went at it. Open mouths, darting tongues, swapping spit, flicking molars, probing wisdom teeth – all the while hugging the limbs of the departed.

"Me next!" Satch cheered. "Let's make it a four-way!"

"Marie would be so proud," Hamilton said, holding back a tear.

Neither Ashleigh nor Rufus would have imagined their first kiss like this, at the moment of the final performance of Marie St. Alban – painter of large canvasses and pioneer of Danceramics – dying doing what she loved.

The art of dying for your art, Rufus thought.

After they fired the soup bowl, they placed it with the body in a spare closet on the second floor. On her side, Marie St. Alban resembled a gangly letter "C" molded out of rolls of tinfoil.

Ashleigh, Rufus, Hamilton, and Satch stood inside the open closet door. Among the boxed winter clothes and forgotten laundry, they held vigil.

"Rest in peace, Marie. I never thought I'd outlive you," said Hamilton, in a rare touched moment. "Or anyone, for that matter."

"Should we say some nice words about her?" Satch asked.

"She hated nice words," Hamilton said. "Oh, how she hated them!"

"What should we do?" Ashleigh asked. She was holding Rufus' hand.

Satch turned to Hamilton. "What would she want?" he asked.

"The Irish have a fine way of conducting their wakes," suggested Hamilton. "We're halfway to blotto-town already, and I'm sure Marie would want us to finish the trip."

With solemn airs, Satch said, "I second that."

Rufus wasted no time. He dropped Ashleigh's hand and shouted, "Ramon! Another round of drinks! For Marie!"

The butler, only casually acknowledging the dead woman's presence, obliged. "Mr. Wiggin," he added, "you have a visitor."

"Nuts," Rufus said. He grabbed the tray of drinks from Ramon and slammed the closet door behind him, interring them all in St. Alban's tomb. Rufus distributed the glasses among the mourners.

"To Marie," he toasted.

"To Marie," the choir refrained, each taking a drink.

Ramon's voice came through the closet door. "Mr. Wiggin, your visitor."

"Curses, Ramon," Rufus shouted back, "Can't you see that we're honoring the dead in here! And why hasn't this laundry been done yet?"

"That's Sylvia's job," said Ramon.

"Unacceptable. Who's at the door?"

"It's Mr. Spit, Mr. Wiggin."

Rufus flung open the door as dramatically as he had closed it.

"Tell him to wait. Whatever you do – which, knowing you, will be very little – do not, I repeat, do not let him inside!"

Rufus went to greet the mysterious and inopportunely timed Mr. Spit. The others left the closet and walked out to the stairway. They huddled together around the balcony.

"Spit, great to see you!" hollered Rufus in his most disingenuous voice. "Do you have my things? No, you can't come in. Why? I have guests I don't want you to disturb! Furthermore, you are poorly dressed and smell like wet dog hair. If you will not have some respect for yourself, than at least have some respect for others. What does the rain have anything to do with it? If you were so concerned about staying dry, you should've worn a mack. Is this everything?

Where are the tapes? Why not? What am I paying you for then? You're not stepping foot inside this house until you get those tapes. Got it? "Now, look, I have another request. I need you to get rid of a dead body."

ONE HUNDRED AND EIGHTY POUNDS
OF PRIMED EXPLOSIVES

Spit came through. Once Marie St. Alban's body had been whisked off to the great pottery studio in the sky, the party reconvened in the parlor. Rufus began to sort through his latest acquisitions.

"Satch, these are for you," he said. In his hand were sandwich bags full of green buds, white powder, and assorted pills. "I trust you know what to do with these."

"No worries, Wig," Satch replied, quickly separating the drugs into tidy piles on the coffee table.

"Green mountains next to white mountains always remind me of Vermont and New Hampshire," Hamilton noted.

"Ashleigh, my dear," Rufus said, "this is for you." He handed her a copy of The Going Out of Business Sale's *Get with the Pogrom* on vinyl. "I also have copies for Satch, your brother, and myself."

While Satch was too busy playing pharmacist to notice, Ashleigh lit up like a neon sign. "This is incredible!" she said.

"What's incredible?" asked Satch. He had carved out four hefty lines of white powder. Rufus handed him another copy of the album.

"Far out, man," Satch said appreciatively. "I can put the drugs on it."

"What do you got there?" Hamilton asked. He wondered if Rufus had any presents for him.

"Well, I think I see some valium, ecstasy, xany bars, somas," Satch listed off absentmindedly as he twisted a joint.

"The album, I mean."

"Oh, that's our band. It's me, Ashleigh, and her brother Kody."

"You guys any good?"

"We were the fuckin' best, man."

"This isn't that fruity peace and love shit that Rufus listens to, is it?"

"No way, dude."

Rufus interjected. "For the record, Jay, I have excellent taste in music."

Ashleigh was curious. "Where did you find these?" she asked.

"As I told you before," Rufus answered suavely, "I have a guy who finds things for me."

"You mean that guy at the door?" she asked.

Rufus nodded thoughtfully. "He's a pain in the behind and thoroughly incompetent, but unfortunately he's the best there is."

Rufus pored over the album art, which seemed to depict a fascist state as seen by Terry Gilliam. He traced his finger along an ominous cartoon jackboot. Laces pulled tight, soles spiked, it was poised to crush a crowd of demonstrators.

"Kody drew that," Ashleigh pointed out. "He rejected the one I did."

"That guy's a dick," Satch added parenthetically.

There was a photo on the back. Ashleigh and Satch were dangling from the limbs of an oak tree while Kody, buried up to his neck in autumn leaves, sat against the trunk, brooding pensively into the camera. Rufus tried to place the tree. There were so few left in this scorched city. Yet he could only picture his own private grove. He realized it had been planted to shield him – and from what? The very folks he now welcomed into his home? The picture only reminded him of the life he hadn't lived.

Tomorrow I will climb a tree, he decided.

"That picture was taken in my parent's backyard," Ashleigh said, breaking his reverie. "Isn't that funny?"

"It looks lovely," Rufus said. He imagined climbing tomorrow's tree with her, snapping branches on the way up, pitching acorns at squirrels.

Satch lit the joint, took a long drag, and passed it along. "Have you ever listened to it, Ash?" he asked.

"Well, I mean, we spent a whole two weeks recording, mixing, and mastering it. So, only like a million times."

"Not me, man," Satch said. "I think I destroyed my copy trying to turn it into a ninja star."

Dumbfounded, Ashleigh asked, "Don't you remember recording it?"

"Shit man, that was around the time I had that squeezy bottle of liquid acid. The only thing I remember for sure was being underwater with six arms."

"A Satchopus!" Hamilton coughed.

"Every time I whipped an arm, it made a drum sound. One would be a cymbal, another a snare, and so on. It felt a little weird at first but, you know, natural. I remember thinking: how am I breathing underwater? Why am I moving so slow? But it was cool. There were all these lights, and a mermaid, and a seahorse with dark curly hair playing a trident like a guitar."

"That explains a lot," Ashleigh realized.

"But then the seahorse started yelling a lot. He made me repeat the same thing over and over, which was a bummer dude 'cause we had really been jamming. So I crawled into this big clam shell until he went away."

"Satch spent five hours in that bass drum," Ashleigh added.

"I don't know what happened. It seemed like years later, and suddenly I'm back on solid ground, but I'm still dragging these six arms behind me. I couldn't breathe. But the walls were breathing, so I tried to suck on them and get some air. It didn't work."

"I saw him do it," Ashleigh said.

"The streets were real nasty, man. The buildings looked ready to collapse, and the sidewalks were littered with corpses. The seahorse told me they were only sleeping, but I knew they were dead. And the eyes, eyes in every window, but the trolls on the street had no eyes. They looked so tired of living. I was getting really scared. When the seahorse handed me this waxy circle and said 'you made this', I realized it wasn't done. I couldn't defend myself with it. So I took a blade and finished it. I don't remember anything after that."

"A twelve-inch ninja star! What a frightening armament!" said Hamilton. "You could decapitate someone with that!"

"I think that's what I was going for," Satch said. "But at some point I started feeling normal again and when Kody said, 'what the fuck did you do to your album?' I said, 'what album?'"

"I am happy to inform you, Satch," Rufus said, "that your album is in fact real, and my guy is working on getting your master tapes back as we speak."

"Really?" Ashleigh asked. She looked at Rufus. She was flattered that a stranger would go to such lengths for a fellow stranger. "I was told they were destroyed."

"The *Droit Moral* doesn't destroy anything," Rufus said. "They steal, they trade, they horde, they sell, but they never destroy."

"Kody is going to be so excited!" she said. Still, she was glad the angry seahorse had decided not to come along.

"He's missing one hell of a party," Satch said, rubbing a thumbprint of coke along his gums.

"Rufus always throws the best parties," Hamilton said. He knew how the hours could melt away inside the east wing pleasure suite. "He's a legend."

"You should've been here before the war," Rufus added. "It was excess excessively taken to excess."

For the moment, Ashleigh was only interested in the present. "What else did you get?" she asked, rummaging through the bags Spit had brought.

"A whole new wardrobe," he said, "for a whole new me."

Satch had finished setting up the table. "Get while the getting's good, losers," he proclaimed, as if calling the others to supper.

"Me first!" shouted Hamilton. He was brandishing a silver tube engraved with his initials.

"Sorry, Hamilton," Rufus objected. "I cannot handle another death tonight."

"Get bent, Wiggin," Hamilton replied. "I've been blowing rails and thumbing gummers since your father was humping errand girls on the factory floor. Trust a pro's nose. May I, Satch?"

Satch deferred. Hamilton hunched over and adeptly inhaled a line through the tube. His labored snort sounded like a broken kazoo.

"Hot dog!" he cried, passing the tube to Satch. "That's the ticket!"

Satch accepted the offer graciously. "Mr. Hamilton, I'd be honored to use your fancy coke straw," he said, before making quick work of the rail. He pinched his nose and tilted his head back to let the drip run down his throat. It tasted like aspirin and kitchen cleaner.

Despite his lavish bashes, Rufus himself hadn't bothered with cocaine since college. He remembered a twenty minute high: the first five were spent debating its quality; the next ten engaging in passionate, unstructured expositions; and the final five repeatedly losing his train of thought. Typically, the rest of the evening was spent trying to find more coke, in a vain attempt to recapture the initial rush.

He looked at Satch's lovingly prepared display and thought, Why not? Rufus' philosophy believed more in reward than in risk;

rarely, if ever, had it failed to end in a good time. And so, up the chute it went.

Ashleigh and Rufus took their bumps together. Then they joined Hamilton and Satch in filling the parlor with cigarette smoke.

Rufus felt euphoria bubble inside his belly. Synapses popped, his body flooded with serotonin. His palms became clammy, the tips of his fingers tingled with white heat. His sweat glands kicked in, moistening his armpits, his temples, and the backs of his knees.

"Great shit, Wig," Satch said.

"I second that," said Hamilton. "Normally the white lady has me running for the can. Not this stuff. I'm talking about coke shits, of course."

"We understand, Jay," Rufus said.

Ashleigh hopped from one painting to the next, taking cursory glances at works of the masters. Her body would not allow her brain to focus. Satch began playing the tabla again, pounding out St. Alban's dirge at twice the speed. Hamilton smiled and swayed to the beat.

"I am going to try on my new clothes," Rufus said, feeling the drug's first wave of phantom power.

"Let me see," Ashleigh said, immediately abandoning a seascape by John Marin.

Spit had gone all over town to assemble a new wardrobe for Rufus. He picked over every underground thrift store and vintage shop in search of new tees made to look like old tees, cowboy shirts with pearl snaps, checkered button-ups, corduroy bell bottoms, black denim jeans, and several variations on the zip-up hoodie.

"What's this?" Ashleigh said, holding up a shirt that read: *Dildon't*.

"Hey!" Hamilton exclaimed, "that's from one of my books! I didn't approve that! Who are the bastards that made it? I'll see them hanged by their testes and I'll shake them down myself. Rufus, get your toady on the horn. I'm going to get my cut."

"There's no need for that, Jay," Rufus said.

"Wait, wait. I know this," said Satch. Hoping to jog his addled brain, he wailed harder on the drums. "Hold on, hold on."

Tap, tap, tap. Tap, tap, tap.

"Dildos and Dildon'ts. First published in the short-story collection *A Hard Man is Good to Find*, and reprinted in the anthology *Jay Hamilton, Man of the Peephole*." Satch shouted to the beat. He jumped to his feet, tucked the drum under his arm and performed a celebratory march.

"Very good, Satch," Hamilton said. He was honestly impressed and a little disturbed.

Wiggling out of his gabardine trousers, Rufus asked, "Who says drugs are bad for you?"

"This calls for another line!" yelled Hamilton.

Rufus felt very unencumbered without his pants on. Kneeling in his boxers, he ingested a row.

"Here, try this on," Ashleigh suggested, her nostrils still burning from the coke.

Off came the embroidered worsted blazer (stinking like cigarettes and martini olives), the Egyptian cotton shirt (mired in a bog of perspiration), the Russian reindeer leather shoes, the Moxon Huddersfield socks, and the cashmere ascot (slightly chewed).

Save for his herringbone-weaved skivvies, Rufus was bare to the world. He felt liberated, sexy; five foot ten, one hundred and eighty pounds of primed explosives. He still had the body of Schuyler's star pole-vaulter (give or take a slight amount of pooch around the belly).

"Now I see why you've forsaken clothes, Satch," Rufus said, flexing his quadriceps.

"It's not that I've forsaken them," Satch corrected. "Usually I just forget them places."

"I feel so free. Bestial even!" Rufus growled, collecting his old clothes. "I'll never wear these rags again! I have nothing to lose but my chains!"

"You have nothing to lose but your shorts, bro," Satch opined.

The new Rufus modeled several outfits for his guests. At last he decided on a flannel lumberjack shirt and a pair of evergreen-colored jeans.

"Well?" he asked. "How do I look?"

"You look like a hundred bucks," said Hamilton.

"You look like one of us," said Satch with a grin.

One of us? Rufus thought with delight. One of us! He had cast off the heavy stone that was his old life, had shed the layers of pretension and tradition. Was this his true self? He pictured himself at hip, underground parties, dancing with Ashleigh to funky breakbeats, blowing everyone's mind with his heavy discourse. He pictured himself as the Buddha, abandoning his life of privilege for a chance to rub elbows with the All Knowing. At the moment, he was not thinking about the war.

"You're not really gonna throw out your old clothes, are you?" Satch asked, knocking Rufus out of his ecclesiastical reverie.

"Of course I am!" he replied. "They're relics of the damned!"

Satch averted his eyes and asked shyly, "Can I have them? I'm getting cold."

"Be my guest," offered Rufus.

Satch put down the smoldering joint and put on the Egyptian cotton shirt, gabardine trousers, Moxon Huddersfield socks, embroidered worsted blazer, and Russian reindeer shoes. The clothes were slightly too small.

He struggled to tie the ascot. "How do I work this thing?" he asked.

"It couldn't be simpler," Rufus said condescendingly. He never wanted to tie another ascot again. "Pull the right side down, six inches lower than the left, cross it over, wrap it around twice, and pull it through the loop at your neck. Then, drape it over, fan it out, and voila, your ascot is tied."

"Like this?" Satch asked. He had managed a rough approximation.

Ashleigh went back to the table for another bump. "Looking sharp, Satch," she said.

Satch modeled his new duds, striking poses based on a London Fog catalog he saw once.

"Ramon!" Satch ordered, in imitation of Rufus. "Another round of drinks!"

"Obey the man, Ramon," urged Rufus. "He who hath the blazer rules the roost!"

"Damn right he does," said Satch, as he stomped into the kitchen. "Angelo, make me some nachos!"

Rufus tried to warn him off. "I wouldn't do that if I were you."

"What do you mean you can't make them?" Satch yelled from the kitchen. He sounded more like Rufus than ever. "Cut tortillas into triangles, fry them, top with cheese, sour cream, and guacamole. Is that so hard? Idiots, I say, all idiots!"

"Uh-oh," Rufus sighed.

"Woah. Calm down, bro." They could hear Satch pleading through the door. The ego of Satch-cum-Rufus had quickly deflated. "C'mon, dude, put down the knife. It was only a joke."

Rufus went to the kitchen to rescue Satch. "Angelo doesn't take well to jokes," he told him.

"But seriously, Angelo," he added. "A plate of nachos *tout de suite!*"

Ashleigh eyed her host with concern. "You're kind of mean to your help, Rufus," she observed.

"It's very unlike me," he replied. He knew it was a lie. He could hear Ramon laughing in the other room. "But I have very exacting standards. Especially tonight. I wanted everything to be perfect, since I know you're used to raging, radical shindigs and such."

"Not really, dude," Satch reiterated.

"Didn't we already go over this?" Ashleigh asked.

"Quit apologizing, man," Satch demanded. "This is way better than most of the shit-shows we call parties. Usually I just get blackout drunk and wind up sleeping with a real pig."

"Story of my life," Hamilton mused.

Rufus decided to change the subject. "How would everyone feel about a nice bottle of wine?" he asked.

"Sounds splendid," Satch said, reviving Rufus' airs.

Ashleigh followed Rufus into the catacombs of his home. They tread cautiously, forging a tortuous path through the randomly piled heaps of bric-a-brac. A trail map would have been helpful: despite several attempts to organize the mess, it had been many years since there was an unimpeded route to the wine cellar.

"What is it you do exactly?" Ashleigh asked. "I mean, how do you afford this big crazy house and all this stuff?"

"It's not what I do," Rufus explained. "It's what my father did. He made a killing in textiles on the Karachi Stock Exchange around the time of partition. I simply spend my life spending his fortune."

"Where is he now?" she asked as she petted a stuffed peacock.

"Dead. My mother, too. It's only me here now," said Rufus. He forgot to mention the help.

Having already dealt with death enough for one night, Ashleigh said simply, "I'm sorry."

"And what of your parents?" Rufus asked, stepping over a fallen didgeridoo.

"Alive and well. Dad's a schoolteacher, mom's a nurse."

"How nice that sounds," he replied. He had always wondered what having normal parents was like.

"It's okay."

"I swear that one day I'll rid myself of all this," Rufus avowed. "Divest my holdings, as my father would say. It simply is too much of a burden."

"Was your father powerful?" Ashleigh asked.

Rufus chuckled. "Old Alistair had his ways and his means."

"Are *you* powerful?" Ashleigh asked, honeying her voice with a hint of intrigue. She decided she should steer the conversation away from parents, dead or otherwise.

"How do you mean?" Rufus asked, propping himself casually against a rickety ping-pong table.

"How come you're the only rich guy left in town? How come you got to keep your money, your house, your art collection, when no else has?"

Rufus smiled.

"Polo Younger and I have an understanding," he explained. "A gentleman's agreement if you will."

Ashleigh wondered, "What kind of agreement?"

"An insurance policy, of sorts. I have something the *Droit Moral* wants very badly, something that would cause substantial embarrassment. I have agreed to keep the items in question secret as long as I can retain the lifestyle I'm accustomed to living."

"What's the secret?" Ashleigh asked. She was not really expecting an answer.

"If I told you – well, I'm sure you know."

"It wouldn't be a secret. Yeah, I get it."

Rufus scanned the piles attentively. "Let me show you something," he said. He then disappeared behind a mountain of wicker chairs. He unstacked and restacked boxes, tossed papers over his shoulder, made new piles, and finally reappeared holding a dusty yearbook. He thumbed through the pages of his past: football games, dances, the production of *Meet Me in Saint Louis*, teachers he liked, teachers he disliked, teachers he hated. He recalled the inside jokes and the things that seemed so important at the time, when the future was bright and in the distance.

"This is me," Rufus said. He pointed out a portrait of himself. He had smaller bags under the eyes, smoother skin, and the shit eating grin of a kid who had the world around his finger. Activities: Pole Vaulting 1,2,3,4.

"Pole vaulting, huh?"

"Have you tried it?"

"Nope," Ashleigh replied.

"It's unlike anything else," Rufus affirmed. "I'm sure it sounds silly, but it truly is a transcendent experience."

"You're starting to sound like Marie," Ashleigh joked.

"Where else can you harness your speed, your strength, your style, your technique to launch yourself into the air? Man's first attempt to reach the stars, with nothing but a stick. A stick! You can look like a fool when things go wrong, but when you plant the pole just right, and it bends, and the sheer force shoots you up like a rocket with your feet above your head, you are not competing in a sport. It's about acceptance and control, grace and sublimity, and giving gravity a big up yours – always knowing a big fat cushion will be there to break your fall."

"Sounds fun."

"Anyway, here's Polo," Rufus said, moving his finger to the next picture. "Stinking up the page, as usual."

The printed list of Polo Younger's accomplishments had been amended in blue handwriting: student chair of the art department; captain of the debate team; dateless to prom; mercilessly mocked; chronic bed wetter. He had chosen the quote, "I'll show you all."

"He is real," Ashleigh uttered.

"Sadly, he is," Rufus replied.

"Not much of a looker is he?"

"This picture flatters him. You should see him in person: a hideous little creature who may as well have hooves. I drew on the horns, of course. This swastika on his forehead was added by someone else, but the rest is very much him."

Ashleigh wanted to learn more. "Tell me something about him," she asked eagerly.

"I'd rather not waste my breath," Rufus pouted.

Ashleigh got Rufus to look her in the eye. She smiled. "Then tell something else instead."

"Like what?"

"Like anything."

"That request is sorely lacking in specificity," Rufus replied.

"Just give me any nugget of useless information," she said, taking a step closer.

Rufus blurted out the first thing that came to mind. "Did you know that the cashew is not actually a nut, but a seed?"

He realized that it was a dumb thing to say.

Ashleigh took another step closer, until Rufus was sandwiched between herself and the ping-pong table.

"What else?"

"Did you know that there are no commercial cashew growers in the U.S.?"

Rufus wished he could think of some non-cashew-related trivia.

"Anything else?" she asked. She grinned coyly and pushed Rufus onto the table tennis court. Its legs began to buckle under the weight of her newfound avidity.

Rufus was thinking that the resin of the cashew apple is used to make industrial solvents. Instead of mentioning this, he answered by kissing her neck, licking her ear lobe, sucking her bottom lip. Ashleigh pulled the old ping-pong net off the table and wrapped it around him like a shawl. She ran her hands firmly across the flannel newly covering the length of his back. Rufus hiked up the flower print dress Ashleigh wore to impress him, and his fingers read her freckled thighs like Braille, inspiring more little bumps to rise across her smooth flesh with every pass of his confident hands.

With backs arched and legs akimbo (Rufus thought briefly of poor Marie), they brought the aria of squeaking hinges to an ecstatic pitch. They hadn't noticed that the table was shedding screws with every thrust. It wobbled ominously.

For the lonely table, which had already spent too many years unenjoyed, the burden proved too much. First the screws popped out, then the brackets sprang loose, and at last the legs folded in on themselves.

The table imploded with a THWACK! THWACK! BA-BOOM!, collapsing inward at center court. Ashleigh and Rufus were contorted into a pretzel, stranded in the pitched recess among the valley of debris. A cloud of dust rose up around them, dancing in midair before settling back down.

Ashleigh and Rufus began to laugh. They laughed until their sides hurt and tears streamed down their cheeks. They laughed at how much they were laughing. They laughed at how they were laughing. They exhausted themselves with laughing.

Soon, the raucous peals subsided into a smattering of giggles, which in turn gave way to a long sigh and low breathing. Ashleigh and Rufus had drifted to sleep. Cradled in the V of the broken table, they spent their forty winks in each other's arms.

POCKET SALAD

Over the course of the night the table had settled into a flatter arrangement, and Ashleigh and Rufus had spread themselves over this makeshift pallet as they slept. The next morning, they awoke to the sound of a lawnmower. Is it better to wake fully clothed, Rufus wondered, or inexplicably nude?

Nude, always, he decided. Especially when it involved a romantic encounter of the illicit variety.

Wiping the gunk from his eyes, Rufus raised the question, "Who in God's name would be mowing the lawn right now?"

"Satch," groaned Ashleigh, half-asleep.

After a night in the dungeon, their retinas instinctively shrank from the bright morning light streaming into the parlor. Then they saw the wreckage of the party: spilled drinks, broken glasses, a half-eaten plate of nachos, countless empty bottles, a mound of cigarette butts inadequately contained by the ashtray, empty sandwich bags.

"Looks like we missed the after-party," Ashleigh said, taking a swig from an abandoned bottle of beer.

"So it appears," Rufus said. He wet his finger and ran it along the dusty coffee table, using the last sprinkles of cocaine to numb his gums.

On the floor, beside the ukulele (which now had three broken strings), they found a manuscript stained with water rings. The top sheet identified it as *The Banana-Boob Republic, a novel by Jay Hudson*

Hamilton and Satch "The Natch" Hardy. Its pages had already been extensively edited with red ink.

They walked outside towards the sound of the mower, where they discovered Satch at the helm, cutting obtuse shapes and patterns into the grass. A cigarette dangled from his grin, and the lapels of Rufus' blazer were covered with ashes.

Satch waved at Ashleigh and Rufus. He was distracted long enough to accidentally level a row of hedges as the mower pursued its path unflaggingly into the brush.

"G'morning freaks!" he said. He was dripping with sweat. "What a party, huh guys?"

Rufus surveyed the hatchet-job Satch had done on his erstwhile lawn. "Taking the old mower out for a tour?" he asked.

"Couldn't sleep."

"Where's Hamilton?" Rufus asked, fearing the worst.

"Over there," said Satch. As he disentangled himself from the shrubbery, he pointed to the Bentley in the driveway. It was overturned; its underbelly was exposed to the sky like a dead cockroach.

The car was totaled. Ashleigh and Rufus rushed over to the wreck while Satch played hopscotch along the trail of skid marks. He had a faint recollection of driving last night, but couldn't remember how or why they crashed. The only thing he could recall clearly was waking up, stiff but mostly unhurt, on the cracked windshield.

"Where are the keys?" Rufus asked in a panic.

Satch patted himself down and turned his pockets inside out. Clumps of lettuce, tomato, and croutons spilled onto the driveway, quickly coalescing into a complete Caesar salad. Satch completed the meal by adding a small amount of gooey dressing and a pinch of shredded parmesan.

"Couldn't tell ya," said Satch. He put a piece of roughage in his mouth. "Don't ask about the salad."

Rufus crouched down and found Hamilton as comfortably cradled inside the roof as he and Ashleigh had been in the wreckage of the ping pong table. There were pools of broken glass all around, and a litter of stray dogs molested Hamilton mercilessly, gnawing his arm, humping his leg, peeing in his ear. Two puppies licked at a rivulet of blood that had crusted around his lips.

Rufus pried open the door. An avalanche of beer bottles, mingled with some feces (canine and human) poured out.

"Rise and shine, Jay!" Rufus shouted. The pumpkin-shaped head only groaned. "What have you done to my Bentley? To whom do these dogs belong? I've warned you about animals before!"

Hamilton swept some glass away with the side of his hand and used a headrest to pull himself upright. One by one, he picked up the cantankerous canines and tossed them into the driveway, kicking at those who tried to get back inside. Most opted to sup on the salad in the driveway.

"He gave birth to a litter," Ashleigh laughed.

"Hey, lady, I'm no dog-fucker," Hamilton said as Ashleigh and Rufus each took a leg and dragged him from the wreck. The smell suggested nothing so much as a tequila-and-piss casserole being pulled from an oven where it had been sitting cold for a couple days.

Ashleigh, concerned mostly about the dogs, asked, "How did this happen?"

"Mmm," Hamilton replied. He had dozed off again.

Rufus shouted, "Wake up!" He gave Jay a couple slaps on the face and asked Satch, "What happened?"

"Don't ask me," Satch replied.

"Okay, okay," Hamilton croaked, beginning to rally. "Satch and I were working on our humdinger of a novel. This one is sure to be a classic. Satch said I should run for public office."

Satch, fighting over a crouton with a cocker spaniel, merely replied, "If you say so."

"I countered that I couldn't even be elected dog-catcher in this town," Hamilton recalled.

"That's right!" Satch interrupted. His face lit up as the conversation came back to him. "And I said, maybe you're an awesome dog-catcher. The people won't know until you try it."

"So, in the spirit of inquiry," Hamilton said, "we borrowed your Bentley."

Rufus' face had turned red. "You morons!" he screamed.

"But wait until you hear how many dogs we caught!" Satch argued. "We were fucking awesome!"

"I doubt there's a stray pooch left in New Urbania," added Hamilton.

"Calm down, Rufus," Ashleigh said, petting what could have been a collie-lab mix. "Miraculously, everyone's okay, and that's what matters. It's only a car."

"It's only a fucking Bentley!" yelled Rufus. His voice echoed across the grounds. Joylessly he spun the wheels, whitewall tires and all, around and around, while he ignored a boxer placidly chewing on his jeans.

Ashleigh played with the collar of his new shirt. "That sounds like the old Rufus talking," she said.

"You're right," he said. Rufus sighed, wanting to believe his own words. "The old Rufus died, and with him went his sleek, amazing, beautiful, expensive car."

"That's the 'tude, dude," Satch said. "Will some pocket salad cheer you up?"

"Sure," said Rufus. He took a handful of greens from the blacktop, but his eyes were still glued to his beloved Bentley.

"Didn't I tell you, Satch?" Hamilton asked. "No one throws a party like Rufus Wiggin."

THE OTHER PART:

Wiggin Out

HALF-HORSE, HALF-ALLIGATOR, ALL-MAN

The party had teased Rufus with the promise of a bold new life; nevertheless, in the weeks that followed, not much changed. In his anger over the Bentley he forgot to climb that tree. Despite the stylish new threads that he wore with ardent pride, the new Rufus acted a lot like the old Rufus. He may have looked different, but he didn't feel different.

The war continued. The only news he received was of Smitty's passing. The death came suddenly, but surprised no one. Just as Rufus predicted, he was found standing up, stiff as a one of his drinks inside his imaginary tube. In his final moments, Smitty had scribbled his will onto a cocktail napkin containing only two requests: that his bar be demolished with him inside; and that Rufus receive the oak barrel.

Flattered by Smitty's cruel joke from beyond the grave, Rufus accepted the bittersweet bequest even though the barrel's utilitarian design clashed with the interior motif of his home. Rufus began to lock himself in his study, and sit on it for hours at a time, staring at the only thing in the world that truly spoke to him.

The Great Peace by Pierre Blanc wasn't the most famous of Rufus' paintings. It wasn't the most valuable. It certainly wasn't the most attractive. It had been included in a lot of early American landscapes he had snatched up cheap at an auction. From a critical viewpoint, the painting was a disaster: the perspective didn't make sense, the proportions were poor, the palette pedestrian, the strokes shaky and uncertain. It was reasonable that Blanc died penniless and forgotten.

Despite the painting's shortcomings, Rufus was drawn to the subject matter, an enduring tale from a bygone era. The scene depicted the raging Cahoos Falls shortly after the great Huron mystic Deganawida rowed his canoe over the cliff. According to legend, Deganawida was fed up with the never-ending conflict among the people of the region and sought an end to it with a single foolhardy act that would prove his spiritual purity and physical prowess. So he disappeared into the mists of the Cahoos Falls. Some Mohawks, who had scorned Deganawida's attempts to unify the tribes, were still peering over the edge for signs of him. Yet others, who had begun to turn around, revealed amazement behind their stoic expressions as Deganawida himself emerged into the painting from the nearby woods. Whether or not this event really happened, Deganawida is credited with ending centuries of conflict practically single-handedly. It was he who first imagined the Iroquois Confederacy, an accord that marked one of human history's great leaps forward.

The Cahoos that Rufus knew didn't look anything like Blanc's gracelessly tranquil vision of the area. Depending on who you ask, white settlers either fulfilled or debunked Deganawida's vision when they cleared the dense forest around the falls to establish the gloomy city that Rufus now called home. The waterfall was plugged up and diverted, its power harnessed to run the mills that fueled the city's first and only industrial boom. Twice a year, the industrialists and the power company were magnanimous enough to let the falls flow freely. Families would make a day of it.

Rufus liked to picture himself inside the painting. Sometimes he became the noble mystic, fit and muscular, an expression reconciled to sadness fixed on a face that was somehow half-horse, half-alligator, all man. Sometimes Rufus preferred to become a warbler or starling, his wings transparent against the clear, unpolluted skies. Sometimes he imagined bathing in the frothy mists at the bottom of the falls before they had been poisoned by centuries of pollution. Sometimes he couldn't see himself in the picture at all.

Eventually, Rufus would start to think about Ashleigh. He hadn't heard from her since the party. Each of the letters he duly delivered to the S.M.E.A.R. mail slot had gone unanswered. To Rufus this probably meant that she had been captured by the *Droit Moral*. The only other possibility he could imagine was that she had been so unimpressed by Rufus' juvenile haughtiness that she decided never to see him again. Both scenarios depressed him considerably.

Short on plans and long on time, Rufus' mind became an obsessive incubator where he hatched every conceivable scheme to win her back. His initial instinct was to dip back into that well of unlimited capital and simply buy her affection. He'd taken this route with all of his previous amorous conquests. All that it had left him with in the end was a diverse collection of ornate baubles, rejected gifts, once vogue trinkets from every era – nothing that resonated with the timelessness of love.

Ashleigh had been won over temporarily when he gave her a copy of her album, but ultimately he had no more to show for it than a record spinning forlorn and lonesome on his turntable. Even that cherished crick in his neck, earned by a night on the ping-pong table, had begun to fade. He was losing the memory of her warm flesh yearning for his touch, taut like the surface of a basketball.

As he thought about Ashleigh, Rufus realized that his old solutions didn't work. The thought grew larger and larger, until it metastasized and brought about a larger recognition. Soon, it was a familiar refrain that echoed through every room of his house. He could not solve this problem with money.

But what can I do? Rufus wondered. He only knew the way of the wallet. And what's more, he thought, it's big statements that are needed right now! (That breakfast conversation with Ashleigh now seemed to have occurred ages ago.) But what? What could he afford to do without money?

Polo Younger certainly knew how to make big statements. After graduating from Schuyler without honors he was turned down by every art school, worth its salt or otherwise. Undeterred, he toiled in obscurity for several years, making connections and building up a reservoir of favors owed. Eventually Polo talked to the right guy, some (purse) strings were pulled, and suddenly the City Art Commission had a new Chairman. It had always been considered a mostly ceremonial office for which no oversight was necessary. Polo promptly instituted an old-fashioned spoils system. The sad bureaucrats who had run the commission for years were made to feel tragically unhip and were urged to defer graciously to this new rising star. Polo had carte blanche to dole out grants to his cronies, other talentless, self-proclaimed geniuses whom Polo had seduced with his visions of a new world order. He issued a sweeping proclamation effectively claiming every public wall in the city as his own.

Polo became known for his hands-on approach, tirelessly promoting his artists and curating their exhibits. Yet each show was passed over by critics and ignored by the public. Polo placed the blame solely on the myopia of the established art scene.

Although he was far wealthier than Rufus would ever be, Polo fashioned himself into a champion of the dispossessed in all their marginalized forms. Street art, graffiti art, urban art, outsider art, ignorant art, folk art, primitive art, spontaneous and improvised art were the true arts of the people, he claimed, and he claimed them as his own. 'Fringe is in!' became his rallying cry.

His true genius was for corruption. The city was practically run on its shady dealings and backroom politics, so it didn't take long for Polo to bribe, blackmail, and extort municipal government employees of every level into yielding ever more power to him; they were overworked and didn't typically want it anyway. Everything from education to zoning to basic social services soon fell into the purview of the City Art Commission; Polo reinvested their respective budgets into his elaborate patronage pyramid scheme.

The Commission's bimonthly newsletter had been a droll publication read mostly by elderly shut-ins who never got off the mailing list. Polo expanded it into a weekly broadside and renamed it the *Droit Moral* ; eventually he had commissioned so much gibberish that it became the city's most widely distributed daily newspaper. With the vitriolic style of socialist manifestos and liberation theology, the *Droit Moral* treated readers to glowing profiles of 'authentic' artists, exultations of the Dear Leader's unparalleled aesthetic sensibilities, and polemics against enemies real and imagined.

The propaganda attracted legions of starving artists to Polo's organization. Some of them embraced his vision of a utopian dictatorship of the artistic proletariat, but most were sold simply on the idea of free housing, free supplies, and a coveted solo exhibition.

After the mayor refused Polo's repeated calls to resign, the Art Commission seceded from city government. They organized under the title of their broadsheet, the *Droit Moral*, and refused to cede power. The name was taken from a fancy French legal term that describes the right of artists to control their own work. In this case, it referred to the right of Polo Younger to control it.

By snubbing the city government, the *Droit Moral* cultivated airs of exclusivity. Paradoxically, membership swelled with new recruits who wanted to feel like they belonged to a secret special club; in fact, its influence was derived solely from the sheer number of people who wanted to join. Charles Ponzi would have been proud. When membership seemed to plateau, Polo simply declared on the front page of his newsletter that joining was now compulsory; few were brave enough (or stupid enough) to ostracize themselves publicly by challenging him.

At last Polo could focus on what were his primary targets all along: the galleries and museums who shunned him, and the snobbish elite who patronized them. As with any good class struggle, the old ways were out:

Classicism? Gone.

Romanticism? Adios.

Impressionism? Forget it.

Even most Modern Art was dismissed for not being modern enough.

The pitch was simple: make a mandatory donation to the *Droit Moral* and pledge your undying allegiance or face the consequences. Some paid up, others fled, and the rest thought he was full of shit. Polo had a thuggish gang of primitive painters seize their assets, ransack their holdings, and beat up their principles.

The Fine Arts Museum was the last holdout. Eighteen months ago, they got theirs when, during the 75th anniversary gala of that vaunted institution (an event whose invitation Rufus had graciously declined), Polo Younger ordered his misguided youth to firebomb the place. Thus the war began. From that day forward the message was clear: No one fucks with the *Droit Moral*.

The mayor, the most powerful elected officer in the city, was backed by a prostrate police force, an apathetic federal government, and lagging public support. He was hanging on to his power by a thread.

THE GUTTERS OF HEAVEN

Hamilton and Satch never quite left the party. Eventually they slept, though fitfully, as their bodies wrestled against the onslaught of toxins. When they woke, they took over Rufus' library to work on their novel.

Rufus' own mood was less than festive, and the company didn't comfort him much. Some nights he would just linger outside the library door listening to the bacchanalian currents of mad laughter and harebrained ideas and the ever clacking typewriter. They would go at it all night long; eventually, their snoring would be heard rustling whatever pages of their emerging masterpiece they were currently using as a pillow. Rufus was afraid to peek inside their hermitage. Better, he thought, to stay happily ignorant of the destruction they were doubtlessly wreaking.

On one particular morning, however, curiosity combined with boredom inspired Rufus to check in on his resident scribes. When he entered the library, he was surprised only by the magnitude of the destruction. "How goes the wordsmithing, gentlemen?" he asked.

"Swimmingly," said Hamilton, as he took a red pen to a poorly-placed pronoun.

"We're sticking it right up the dickhole of the printed page," said Satch.

"Hot dog!" said Hamilton. "Where did you find this kid, Rufus? Surely it was the gutters of heaven!"

It would be an understatement to say it looked like a bomb had gone off inside the library. For no apparent reason, Rufus' collection of first editions had been dispersed around the room, tossed everywhere but the bookshelf. Bindings had been broken, covers stained with fluids unknown, flyleaves inscribed with crudely-drawn penises, corners dog-eared, passages highlighted with markers, pages ripped out to make filters for spliffs. Plates of rotting food had been scattered everywhere, even wedged on top of rows of books. The mirror, which had been taken down and was now leaning against the wall, was caked with powdery residue. There were burn holes in the curtains and the carpet. A mix of B.O., foot stink, sexual frustration, and sequestered excess made the room smell like a seedy Turkish nightclub. At least the beer bottles had been piled into a landfill in the corner.

"When can I read it?" Rufus asked. He hoped, at least, that this process of creative annihilation was yielding an intangible tidiness somewhere.

"Soon, very soon," said Hamilton, who was again hunched over the typewriter. "There are still a few plot holes we need to address."

"What if the explorers," Satch proposed, as he paced around the room, "when questioned by the village elders about their intentions, say 'We *cum* in peace'. Get it? C-u-m in peace? Then they go, 'We are here to deliver your wives and daughters to the promised land' – when they know full well the Banana-Boob Republic *is* the promised land! The ol' switcheroo, see?"

Rufus wondered how Deganawida would have reacted to the novel's pervy protagonists uttering such statements. Surely they would've ended up strapped to a raft and sent over the Cahoos.

"Brilliant," said Hamilton, typing as fast as his sausage fingers allowed. "See, Rufus, their ultimate goal is to capture the women of the island and take them back to civilization so the boobs of the Earth can be re-shaped in their image. So it makes sense that they have to gain the trust of the chief, for his daughter has the fairest pair of all!"

"Exactly!" bellowed Satch, high-fiving his partner. "Or, maybe they should just poison all the men on the island and become the presiding kings of the great republic, ruling with a tender touch and iron wangs!"

"I'm telling you, Rufus," Hamilton said. "This boy is a goddamn genius."

"If you liked that, I've been thinking about something even better," Satch continued. "I'm not happy with the opening line. Let's change it to, 'My breast days are behind me!'"

"I couldn't have written it better myself," Hamilton said with pride.

Rufus had nothing to add to this orgiastic narrative, so he left the scribes to frolic in their fantasy world, pondering plunder aplenty. He slunk back to his study to pass the time atop his barrel.

My breast days are behind me, Rufus thought. He smiled.

Rufus had gone out for another mopey walk about the grounds. As he returned to his study in the same dejected state, a familiar whine emerged from the room. "More like the Great Piece of Shit if you ask me," it said.

The voice was unmistakable. After all, that same nasally, know-it-all twang had assaulted the back of Rufus' head for years at Schuyler Academy. He exhaled glumly, barely mustering the interest to face his most unwelcome guest.

"Well, Polo, no one asked you."

"It's like the tomb of the unknown artist in here," Polo mocked, looking scornfully around the room. "Rufus the Doofus still keeping the flame, at least as long as his passion holds."

"Don't you have an appointment to scare children that you should be getting to?"

"Oh Rufus, Rufus the Doofus. Remember how we used to call you Rufus the Doofus?" said Polo.

"I don't remember anyone calling me that. You didn't even call me that. My nicknames for you, on the other hand – Lulu, Dodo, Pupu Bunghole – those stuck."

"Why must we dwell on high school? It was such a long time ago."

"Why, Polo, don't you want to recall being an annoying sycophant with no friends, who cracked his knuckles every five seconds and tattled on everyone? Shouldn't we think fondly on the time you busted us for drinking in the parking lot? Can't we discuss the fact you were always peering over my shoulder trying to copy my homework, knowing full well I copied mine from our valedictorian Quincy Quill – my friend by the way – making what should have been a foolproof plan obvious to the teacher. I will concede that all those art shows you tried inviting me to are too terrible to recall. Still, if you could remember what I told you ten years ago, I wouldn't have to tell you again now: piss off."

Polo tried to remain unflustered. "If we must stay on the topic of high school," he said, "did you hear what became of our former art teacher?"

"Let's first discuss how you got into my house," Rufus replied.

"The window was unlocked," Polo explained, smearing his finger along the spotless pane.

Rufus muttered. "Stupid Ramon."

"Apparently poor Marie St. Alban died in some freak gymnastics accident," Polo said. He was closely examining the odd ceramic soup bowl on Rufus' desk. "They found her floating in the public pool."

Freak Danceramics accident, Rufus thought. Polo never could get anything right, even though he probably already knew the truth. Rufus lied anyway.

"Not Marie," he said. "I'm heartbroken."

Few people ever saw Polo Younger in person. Fewer still would recognize the face behind the absurd Cao Cao opera mask he always wore. The expression on the mask was creepy but, since Polo was afflicted with what only could be described as douche-face, Rufus believed it was ultimately a good idea.

Polo's massive forehead extended from his tragically receded hairline down to the center of his face, so there was little room for his other features. His eyes were narrow, squinty, and spaced too far apart. His nose was long and protruding with a giant bump on its ridgeline. The posture of his mouth was fixed somewhere between smirk and scowl. His acne-scarred skin resembled a relief map of Appalachia.

"Can we have this reunion some other time, Polo? I'm obviously very busy."

"On the contrary, you don't seem busy at all," Polo observed. He settled into a rocking chair. "I'm the one spending valuable time to see you."

"Well, aren't you the big deal," Rufus said. He was looking around the room for something to busy himself with.

Polo attempted another approach. "I see you're trying out a new look. Very...young."

"You should try it," Rufus suggested. "Contribute to the cause of art and rid the world of those ghastly sweats."

Polo's fashion sense was as confounding as his face. His favorite garments were velvet smoking jackets and billowy sweatpants that had elastic bands around the ankles. He saw no contradiction in wearing these articles together. Today, Polo was in business casual: a red jacket with black lapels, matched with a pair of gray sweats.

"I'm very active," Polo said. "And I enjoy the comfort."

"And you look like an imbecile. Seriously, it's a wonder that anyone takes you seriously."

"Oh my, how that must irk you! Rufus the Doofus should know better than anyone that it's not the clothes that make the man, otherwise you'd be king of the world I suppose."

"Who says I'm not?" said Rufus. He smiled.

Polo ignored him. "I, on the other hand, am the feared and revered leader of a great and terrible revolution. Sweatpants or no sweatpants."

"Your revolution," Rufus avowed, "is nothing more than a shakedown racket cloaked in flimsy ideology!"

At last, he was squaring off with his old nemesis! All those arguments Rufus had imagined bombarding Polo with were about to be aired!

****

Polo reclined in Rufus' rocking chair and cracked his knuckles. "Is vindicating the rights of artists flimsy, as you say?"

"Everything you do is flimsy," Rufus replied. His ire was up: a drop of his spit landed on Polo's cheek.

Polo wiped his face with disdain. "All throughout history," he began, "from the King's Court to modern day, the most complex and vital part of our culture, though often produced by the most sensitive and vulnerable of its citizens, has been subjugated, coddled, controlled, and disposed of by the bourgeoisie."

"So the richest person in the city," Rufus replied, pacing the study, "dripping with gold, our very own Napoleon in sweats, will rectify the situation by taking charge of the most complex and vital part of our culture himself! Unable to prevail on his own merits, he has assumed the pose of moral philosopher, proclaiming that what's right is what's good and what's wrong is what's bad. This poor soul doesn't understand that there is no qualitative value if you don't have aesthetic judgment."

"Aesthetics is nothing but the study of beauty," pronounced Polo. He rose to confront Rufus and thrust his bumpy nose within a foot of Rufus' face. "Beauty carries no weight with me."

"Obviously," Rufus said and averted his eyes.

"The only worth is the work that goes into something. Once you see art as nothing more than the purest act of production, something that literally embodies the labor expended to realize its creation, you will realize the so-called beauty of the end result is incidental, worthless by comparison." Polo fell back into the chair feeling victorious; the chair rocked violently.

"I'm not talking about worth, idiot, I'm talking about beauty. Beauty is more than just the prettiest things. Even the grotesque and the abhorrent can be beautiful. Even you, supposedly."

"Be that as it may," Polo harrumphed, "aesthetics will never be anything more than a way to make the message more appealing."

Rufus claimed his perch on the barrel. "If aesthetics is irrelevant, as you claim, then why bother with art in the first place? Don't you confuse your message when you start making claims about the qualities of good and bad art? Aren't you defeating your own argument?"

"Hardly," said Polo condescendingly. "Singularity of purpose, clarity of vision, attention to the fleeting and overlooked – these are qualities that can be measured discretely and analyzed with impartial formulas, without subjective speculation about ideals."

"Ah, impartial formulas, the crutch of the mediocre," sneered Rufus. "At best a person can make guidelines, but art has no place for rules."

"Rules are the only law we have!" Polo yelled, tipping himself off balance. "There are laws of nature, and then there are laws of art. My humble job is to discern and codify these laws."

Rufus stared at Polo, wondering if he really believed anything he was saying. "You can't enforce the immutable laws of nature. No one can hold me liable for using gravity without permission," Rufus explained. He sprang from the barrel and jumped up and down to prove his point. "Nature metes out its own justice regardless of what man decides. The same is true for art."

"Ah-ha!" exclaimed Polo. "But is a law that's never enforced really a law? Society will never accept these laws voluntarily, so we must create a new civil framework to impose them. Otherwise nothing will ever change!"

For years, Rufus had looked forward to letting loose on Polo, but he found he was already growing bored. "Who said things needed changing other than you, Polo? Have you made people more civil? Can art be improved by decree?"

"I believe I've already proven that," said Polo with the flick of a wrist.

"And now what? A grading system?"

"I'm working on it," Polo said.

"Of course you are," Rufus sighed. "The supreme gatekeeper of the city! But a gatekeeper is nothing but a gatekeeper. Build a gate in any arbitrary spot and a gatekeeper will diligently prevent anyone from passing through it."

"Well, if artists are going to act like they're the judge and jury of their peers anyway, we might as well rely on the arbitrary," Polo pouted.

"You put too much stock in the opinion of the masses, Polo. It doesn't matter what the people, brainwashed or not, think. Art is an inherently selfish act."

"What's selfish about creating something larger than yourself and sharing it with the world?" Polo whined.

Rufus wearily leaned the side of his face against his hand. "Only a megalomaniac would describe the way you've forced your ideas upon the world as sharing," he argued. "Anyone with an ax to grind because someone, somewhere didn't get it suddenly becomes so *sharing*. Get over it, man. Most ideas shouldn't be shared."

"I agree, the ideas of most are worthless. That's why there must be someone to enforce the proper rules for doing things," Polo replied smugly. "Only then will art truly reflect equality."

Rufus spoke in measured tones. "Equality does not mean that five carpenters building five cabinets will all produce the same cabinet, no matter how specific the guidelines. Each cabinet will betray the talent and skill of its builder, and some will be better than others. Equality means they are all still carpenters, free to pursue carpentry as they see fit."

"And yet the division of labor brings them no closer to owning the means of production!" Polo shouted.

Rufus could not decide if Polo had actually been listening to him. He simply replied, "Who cares? The division of labor requires competition, so the good has at least some chance of rising to the top."

Polo insisted that "a system based in competition and driven by profit can only keep us alienated."

Rufus thought about Smitty and Marie St. Alban and his father and his mother and the Going Out of Business Sale and Ashleigh. "Life keeps us alienated. Alienation comes from the fact that every person is singular, and will never conform to a mass ideal," Rufus reasoned. He paused a moment to consider his thoughts. "And so art must be singular. It strives in any way it can to express that singularity. Pictures may be combined with words, words combined with music, music combined with dance, dance combined with ceramics..."

Polo interjected. "What was that last one?"

"Never mind. My point is that art means something different to everyone. Some don't value it at all. Art can be infinite, but in the end it's still only a transfiguration of the self."

"But what if that transfiguration is full of anger and despair?" For the moment, Polo had practically assumed the mien of a supplicant.

Rufus looked Polo right in the eye. "Then that person should seek professional counseling, Polo," he insisted. "Or, I suppose he could pin his hopes on a conniving little man of boundless wealth who manipulates the ignorant and needy, appeals to hatred and fear, and rallies against an oppression that never existed. That seems to work sometimes."

Polo now seemed ready to hasten the conversation's end. "I'm sorry, Rufus, but art isn't going to save itself."

Rufus, however, was beginning to revive. "Save it from what? Art requires sincerity," Rufus said with airs of sincerity, "and a system based on heroic myth and false nature won't save anything. If anything could be a threat to art, it's that."

"If there's any insincerity in the *Droit Moral*," Polo replied primly, as if he were absolutely shocked by the implication, "it's simply a relic of the direction things were taking before we came along."

"Laying the blame on the previous administration? The great outsider is now officially an insider. I no longer care what you do, Polo. The bigger your movement becomes, the sooner you think you've won, the sooner you'll fail. Hegel, Kuhn, Sir Isaac Newton – they all say that every thesis spawns its own antithesis. See, Polo, even geniuses agree: you're a loser. All you can do is hasten the process."

"Fair enough," Polo nodded, "but you're assuming there's an organized resistance that simply doesn't exist."

"I beg to differ," retorted Rufus. He recalled the stylish disciples of The Going out of Business Sale.

"I know of no one but a boy with an insignificant band and an insignificant magazine, and obviously he is delusional. My agents told me about what happened at Smitty's, of course. Quite funny. It's like you're making my point for me. And have you considered that Kody Spalmino may already be on my payroll? Wouldn't I be clever, giving people the illusion of choice, an enemy to get them riled up against? Let them suffer for their art, if you can even call it that. It only makes me look the better."

"Suffering for your art is nonsense," Rufus exclaimed. He had his own point to make now. "Art for art's sake is like taking a shit and not wiping your ass! Where's the joy in that? It's evacuation without catharsis!"

"It's funny to hear that from a person without a single creative bone in his body."

Rufus was feeling punch-drunk. "If you think that's funny," he shouted as he unlocked a desk drawer and pulled out a leather attaché, "Behold! Conclusive proof that it's better to be a refined admirer of art than a hapless creator of it!"

"That's what brings me here actually," Polo conceded.

Rufus looked over the most powerful man in the city triumphantly. "It's about time we dispense with the unpleasantries," he said. "I could go on debating you all day, but frankly, you annoy me insufferably."

Polo dispensed with the unpleasantries. "It so happens that the other day that toady, Spit, was poking his nose around my office. He said he was looking for some master tapes by The Going Out of Business Sale."

"Who?" said Rufus, feigning indifference.

"He wouldn't tell me who he was working for, but given your predilection for rubbish, and the kind of girl you tend to go for, and the fact that you're the only one who still has that much money, I had a pretty good idea that the anonymous buyer was Rufus Wiggin. So, as a courtesy from old one Schuyler chum to another, I decided to drop the tapes off in person."

Polo produced a reel of two-inch tape and laid it on the desk.

"I appreciate the gesture, Polo, but I refuse to pay you a cent. As I imagine you're already aware."

"This isn't going to be a cash transaction, Rufus."

Rufus tapped the attaché. "Do you really think I'm going to give you these?"

"I'm sure I can offer you more than they're worth."

"They're worth plenty. Quite rare, you know; in fact, I would say these are the very crown jewel of my art collection. By my count, I'm the largest holder of early Polo Younger works in the world."

"You're a lucky man," Polo muttered. It didn't come out the way he intended.

It had been a high-minded pursuit, more or less. Rufus had torn down piece after piece of Polo's art from the walls at Schuyler Academy, "to protect impressionable young minds," he had claimed. He had kept them tucked away in the catacombs of Alistair's Asshat. It amused him to look at them occasionally.

"And still you're content to judge talent by the doodlings of a teenager?" Polo asked. His eyes had become fixed on the portfolio.

"Yes," answered Rufus, hopping up and unclasping the attaché. "Yes I am. You do yourself an injustice to call these doodles, Polo. They are the early earnest efforts of an ungifted hack, and they were undertaken with august seriousness."

Rufus dumped a pile of drawings onto the desk. Dozens of pictures of all sizes, yellowed with age and wilting at the corners, poured out. Rufus enthusiastically sorted through charcoals on paper, watercolors on newsprint, collages on cork board, acrylics on canvas, oils on wood and more. The subject matter ranged from dolphins to spaceships.

"Take a look at this one," Rufus said, holding up a crayon-on-cardboard sketch of a man holding a flower. "Did you ever get the hang of drawing hands, or do they still come out looking like lumpy mashed potatoes?"

Polo slowly reached for the pile in front of him, but before he could grab anything, Rufus slapped his fingers.

"I love this one," he said, holding up a crude self-portrait of Polo. "Shall we call it *Portrait of the Artist as a Young Antelope?*" He chuckled, casting the portrait aside and turning his attention to a banal still life.

"Is this a bowl of oranges?" he asked. "Or a graveyard of grapes?"

"It's apples," Polo said quietly.

"So it is," Rufus said, reexamining the piece upside down. "So it is."

Trembling, Polo snatched it from his hands. "Do you think these give you any power over me?"

"That's not really the point," Rufus said. "Sure, if I ever released them, it would go far in deflating your mystique. My real goal, however, is to teach a class called Art Isn't For Everyone, or maybe write a monograph. That way I could do a real service to mankind, using your works to encourage other misguided souls to take up more useful trades, like plumbing or elevator repair."

"They mean nothing, you smug piece of shit!" Polo screamed.

Rufus crossed his arms smugly. "Then why do you want them back so badly?" he asked

Polo was beet red. "Don't flatter yourself! Do you think I've left you alone all this time because you have some kind of power over me? I could have my men in here in a second to run you out for good."

"Please, Polo, tell me. Why have you 'left me alone?'"

Polo calmed suddenly, his eyes narrowed, and his voice grew detached. He seemed to be reciting a speech that he had been rehearsing for years.

"Is it because you're creative? No! Is it because you're somehow valuable or indispensable? No! Is it because you are a threat? On all counts, No!"

Wound up and juiced on adrenaline, Rufus felt like Polo had just shoved him in the chest. Alone, unloved, his only companions incompetent help and deviant novelists, he had had enough of Polo Younger and didn't feel like sticking around for the part of the show where Polo takes out all of his insecurities on Rufus. Rufus remembered how Polo would flick boogers into his magnificent mane during class and his blood began to boil. The whites of his eyes flared caustically, his body twitched with nervous rage. A sleeping tiger was waking.

"Don't you know, Rufus the Doofus? I keep you around as a sad relic," Polo said. As a rhetorical flourish, he had turned his back on Rufus while he prepared to deliver the *coup de grace*. "I relish watching the great Rufus Wiggin, that vainglorious gallivanter, floundering in the rising tide. It gives me joy to see his tower crumbling, his island adrift."

In some way, Polo Younger could be blamed for everything that had gone wrong in Rufus' life. He found himself reaching for St. Alban's soup bowl. It was heavy and smooth, imbued with the final breaths of a once-great artist. As he gripped the rim, his knuckles turned peppermint shades of red and white.

"Gone are all your friends, all your women, all your parties," Polo laughed. "The tables have turned."

Rufus was all too familiar with his own flaws and he knew that in this strange new order he was a lost soul, but no one had the right to abuse him in his home, and he certainly was not going to take such treatment from Polo Younger.

"All you're holding onto is something that doesn't even exist anymore." Polo had reached his conclusion, so he turned around to deliver his dramatic finale. "No power, no influence."

Before Polo could continue, Rufus lifted the soup bowl high above his head, as though making an offering to the spirit of Marie St. Alban, and brought it down with all his might. The bowl shattered over Polo's skull, and together they fell to the floor.

****

Rufus stood over Polo's unconscious body, feeling powerful but scared. He stripped Polo of his sweatpants and smoking jacket, leaving the Dear Leader in his tighty whiteys. Rufus then retrieved some spare rope and his copy of *All the Knots You Need to Know*. He settled on page 8: the classic slipknot was sturdy and hard to screw up. Rufus secured Polo to a Shaker chair and then called: "Ramon! Fetch me the gasoline from the garage! Hurry! I'll have none of your usually tarrying!"

Then he called for Angelo.

The cook entered the study with a paring knife in his hand; his apron had enough blood on it to revive a gunshot victim.

"Angelo, stab this man," Rufus ordered.

Angelo looked at Rufus, then at the body, then at Rufus again, and shrugged. "You got it, boss!" he exclaimed, used to strange requests from Rufus and glad to be doing something he enjoyed for a change.

A single deft jab just under the ribs brought Polo screaming back to life. He struggled to free himself. Suddenly, his blurry, concussed eyes saw a man approaching with a gas can, another man with a bloody knife, and Rufus in front, smiling victoriously.

"You'll always be one seat behind me, Polo."

Rufus took the can and slowly tilted it precisely at a 45 degree angle; the gas flowed freely. He flung the fuel around with a freewheeling expressiveness – a splash here, a splash there – until the entire room was doused.

As Polo, quivering and crying, watched Rufus seal his fate with every spritz, he must have realized how gravely he had underestimated his rival.

Was he creative? Very.

Was he valuable? Absolutely.

Was he a threat? No doubt about it.

In that instant, Rufus figured out how to defeat Polo Younger. Not to outspend him, or to over-think him, but to become him. After all, a cult of personality is simply a tool for a powerful leader, and the fact that this particular leader was a mysterious recluse suggested certain possibilities to Rufus. If no one ever saw Polo, Polo could be anyone, Rufus realized. Polo could be Rufus. Rufus could be Polo.

Rufus cackled dramatically as he tossed the can aside. Polo sobbed harder.

CREATIVE DESTRUCTION

Rufus, Hamilton, and Satch boarded an idle trolley at Lindsay Park station and watched as the conflagration consumed Alistair's Asshat.

The east wing collapsed under the weight of the Brutalist slabs. Farewell, Pleasure Suite. Smoke billowed through the cracked domes, their frescoes melting into a colorful shapeless splotch. Goodbye, Library. The blaze swallowed much of the gambrel roof, fiery fingers clawing through the dormers, flicking bursts of shattered glass into the sky. Goodbye Asshat.

The house caved inward, reminding Rufus of a certain ping-pong table that was now surely a pile of ash. As the flames continued to spread, the house imploded further into its own smoldering morass. Creative destruction? Destructive Creation?

Rufus looked on with blank detachment as he watched his father pass away for a second time. Alistair's life and all it bought vanished in the plumes, while his son, evermore an orphan, saw his world upended once more. Rufus managed to load a few random artifacts into his barrel and roll it onto the tram. Everything else was history.

The barrel, the rope, the self-immolation. It seemed as though the motifs of his life had finally revealed themselves to Rufus, suggesting at once a deeper significance. He knew for certain that the night at Smitty's was no fluke. He had been saved, and he had saved others. Yet now there was a new dimension, and its implications were murkier and more difficult to discern.

"You ever kill a man, Jay?" Rufus asked, watching the porch logs splinter and disintegrate.

Hamilton and Satch had gone for a stroll to smoke a joint before Polo arrived and by the time they had returned the house had begun to smolder. Rufus' staff had already retreated to a safe distance to enjoy the spectacle, but Satch heroically braved the inferno to rescue the banana boob manuscript.

"Once, and the bastard deserved it," Hamilton answered with conviction.

Rufus tried to have the same confidence. "So did he," he said.

"Where are we going?" asked Satch, nervously clutching his manuscript against his hopelessly wrinkled blazer.

Rufus turned to him. "We're going to see the mayor."

A HIGHLY-SCULPTED TURD

City Hall was a stately edifice, a reminder of the salad days when it seemed like the city would grow forever. Designed by H.H. Richardson during his Romanesque period, the granite building featured dueling 200-foot clock towers, each with a 60-bell carillon, connected by an imposing row of rusticated columns. As the city entered its long, slow decline, this downtown leviathan began to serve less as a proud symbol of prosperity than as an unwanted reminder of a time that no longer existed.

Many of its mullioned windows had been shattered by rocks. Molding had been chipped away, the carillons silenced. The brown granite surface, which had once provided a dignified and majestic aura, had faded. The building now resembled a highly-sculpted turd.

Across from City Hall, Academy Park had become the city's fastest growing neighborhood. It was popular among transients, shanty town enthusiasts, and the underworld merchants who catered to their needs. So many funds had been diverted, first to be used by the City Art Commission and then to fight the *Droit Moral*, that social services had been paralyzed. The only businesses flourishing in the area were pawn shops and bail bondsmen.

Three men and a barrel got off at Civic Center station and made the short, distressing walk through Academy Park. On the steps of City Hall a line of policemen, firemen, garbage men, and librarians had gathered to protest.

"No pay, no work! No pay, no work!" they chanted.

"Finally, a semblance of sanity in this backwards city," Rufus said, hoisting the barrel onto his shoulder.

Hamilton and Satch stayed outside to enjoy the demonstration, while Rufus slipped through a ribcage of civil servants and into the heart of municipal government.

Any traces of grandeur had long been gutted from the interior of the building through a series of ad hoc renovations. The marble floors had been carpeted over with a thin, well-trod shag, soiled with the dirt of a thousand heels. The vast open spaces designed to foster the lively debates democracy demands had been partitioned into a monotonous maze of plywood cubicles. To save on heating costs, the vaulted ceilings had been artificially lowered with a grid of cheap foam tiles, and the Baccarat crystal sconces replaced with buzzing yellow fluorescent bulbs that cast a dismal pall over everything.

The silence was spooky. Rufus was amazed at the utter lack of activity inside the building. Most doors were locked and every office appeared to be empty. It was a ghost town presided over by a snoozing security guard.

Rufus ducked into a bathroom and removed Polo's jacket and sweats from the barrel. Both garments smelled like onions and pickle brine. The jacket was too big and the pants left Rufus' ankles exposed, as though he were wearing a Polo Younger Halloween costume. He completed the ensemble by tying on the Cao Cao mask, which too smelled of pickles. The white porcelain mask had been decorated with heavy eyebrows, expressive lashes, and cheeky whiskers in black acrylic paint.

The namesake of the Cao Cao mask was a brutal warlord who ruled the Eastern Han Dynasty during the Three Kingdoms era. These masks are used in traditional Chinese opera to symbolize deceit and treachery. Rufus found the mask very empowering.

In his first appearance as Polo Younger, Rufus strode out of the bathroom and ambled down the long corridor towards the mayor's office. At the door, a bored teenager played secretary, passing the time by building a toy soldier with pencils and chewing gum. She did not seem impressed by the masked man approaching her.

"I'm here to see the Mayor," Rufus announced confidently.

"Your name?" she asked as she affixed arms to the soldier.

"Polo Younger," he replied.

"Oh."

She suddenly looked up, startled. She fidgeted in her seat and snapped off the soldier's eraser head accidentally. Trying not to stare but staring anyway, she picked up the phone conspicuously and whispered into the handset.

"The mayor will see you," she said, still whispering.

Rufus could feel her eyes following him as he disappeared behind the office door.

THE CHAPTER IN WHICH
RUFUS MEETS WITH THE MAYOR

The mayor was a squeamish man, prone to nervous tics. Whenever he spoke, he compulsively jammed a thumb into his ear.

"Mr. Younger, I – er, that is, what brings you, um – I mean..."

Rufus pulled off the stinky mask and revealed himself. "Spit, it's me!"

"Rufus? What the fuck?" said Spit. Relieved but wary, he asked, "Are you trying to give me a heart attack?"

"Though I have wished you dead on numerous occasions," Rufus admitted, "not today. In fact, I have something very important to tell you."

Spittoon Shyne had lived an all-American life: the son of a tobacco farmer, he moved to the city to make a name for himself. He took a job at the municipal golf course, and soon became known among the city's bigwigs and power brokers as the most effective (that is, flattering) caddy they had ever used. It was only when, in a rare, unguarded moment, Spit let himself demolish a prominent politician on the back nine one evening, winning by twelve strokes, that he began the rapid political ascent that had culminated in his election as the city's 44th mayor. Rumor had it that the politico was so impressed that he offered to become Spit's booster, though it may have been that he never wanted to see Spit at the golf course ever again.

Candidate Shyne ran on a lesser-of-two-evils platform. His campaign slogan was 'Less of more of the same.' By a slim margin, the voters decided that his opponent, the incumbent currently serving prison time for corruption, was indeed the greater of two evils. Now, Mayor Spit was having a rough go of it.

Spit had spent most of his tenure as a wartime executive. Practically from day one, Polo had denounced the election as illegitimate, the mayor a tool of powerful interests. Since Spit was in fact an uninspiring leader, an ineffective communicator, and a poor tactician, the charges were hard to shake, and people swarmed to Polo's side. With the government effectively shut down, he had begun to moonlight as an acquirer of rare goods to make ends meet.

"Something's come up, something important," Rufus said. "I need your help."

"I told you already I can't get you anything while I'm at work," Spit whined.

"This is bigger than your principles!" Rufus exclaimed.

"What now, Rufus? A 1933 Double Eagle? The Pearl Carpet of Baroda for your home?"

"Spit, if you would just let me speak you would already know that I burned my home down this morning."

"Burned?"

"With Polo Younger inside!" Rufus added excitedly.

"Inside?"

Rufus assumed a victor's pose. "Polo Younger is dead!" he shouted.

"Oh no, oh god, oh my god no," Spit stuttered. He twisted his thumb forcefully around inside his ear. "They're going to blame me. I'm a dead man."

"Quit being so dramatic! This is no time for your ridiculous paranoid ravings!"

"You don't know how it is, Rufus," Spit said, shoulder twitching. "Whatever's going on, I don't think I want to help. Besides, you're awfully mean to me."

"For which I apologize," Rufus replied, not actually sorry at all. "But for now we need to put the subject of your incompetence aside and do something about this."

"Do something about what?"

"How's your relationship with the *Daily Reader?*" Rufus posed.

Spit replied pitifully. "They're the only friends I have left."

"Good. Get them to print this story. I, Rufus Wiggin, have barely survived an encounter with the *Droit Moral*, earning their eternal enmity. After a violent confrontation, in which I valiantly and heroically fended off Polo's frankly untoward advances, my house was destroyed by the sheer force of his obnoxiousness. My current whereabouts are unknown, but I'm presumed to be either dead or in exile."

"What about Polo?"

"Can't you let me finish? As I was saying, with Polo rotting in hell and everyone thinking I'm gone, yours truly will play the role of Dear Leader in his absence."

"That's the worst idea I've ever heard," Spit said. He was now sucking on the thumb that had been in his ear.

"You haven't even heard the best part yet!" Rufus cried. "Just picture this expose on the front page of the *Daily Reader*: Secrets of the Wiggin Estate Revealed – Polo Younger is a Fraud!"

Rufus reached into the barrel and dug out the attaché. He scattered a dozen Polo Younger originals across the mayor's desk.

"I can see it now, a big front page spread," Rufus continued. He lowered his pitch to indicate he was speaking in the voice of a newspaper. "'Before he fled, Wiggin leaked an exclusive cache of artwork by Polo Younger, proving that no good wimp is a talentless hack once and for all! The rest of the pictures Younger didn't want you to see, page A3.'"

"Wow, these are really bad," Spit said, as he rummaged through the drawings. "Do you know how much you could get for these?"

"What would you know about art?"

"I found you half of your collection, Rufus."

"Irrelevant. Once Polo is thoroughly discredited, and I'm properly lionized, you and Polo Younger – that is, me – will sign a peace treaty," Rufus exclaimed, adding, with a graceful bow, "ending the war!"

"It'll never work," Spit replied. "What if they find out you're an imposter?"

"I can assure you that won't happen."

"How can you be so sure?" asked Spit anxiously. His thumb had returned to his ear.

"Get it through your thick skull, dummy. No one ever sees him or talks to him. It couldn't be easier."

"Won't his men be suspicious if he disappears only to return to sign a peace treaty?"

"I've thought of that. That is why I'm going to return to Polo's daily business as if nothing extraordinary has happened."

"You?" asked Spit skeptically. "As Polo? All day, every day?"

"Yes! Obviously! Haven't you been paying attention to anything I've said? I will be Polo. I already am Polo! Do you think I would choose to wear this silly get-up?"

"How does the barrel fit in?" Spit asked, indicating the corner where Rufus had set it down. "Is that Polo's too?"

"It most certainly is not," Rufus scoffed. "It's mine, and mine alone. It nearly killed me once, but now it holds all of my worldly possessions."

"I'm doomed!" Spit screamed. "You're going to save us? We're all doomed!"

"Would you shut up and listen," Rufus said. He pinched his nose and affected a nasally whine. "From this day forth, I hereby decree that all chops shall be of the mutton variety, and all mustaches, for those wear them, must be groomed in the handlebar fashion."

"Holy shit, you're a dead ringer."

"I have been far too familiar with that voice for a long time," Rufus boasted.

"But what if they ask why you're always plugging your nose?"

"Goddamn it, Spit! I'll rig something in the mask or something! Do I ask why you always have your thumb in your ear or your head up your ass?"

"It's a medical condition," Spit conceded.

"Would you quit trying to poke holes in my plan! Do you want to be Polo? Seriously, you'd look cute in these clothes. Or would you rather have the truth come out that I'm a murderer and an arsonist? I'm sure you'd like to see that! Me rotting in prison for the rest of my life because you're too stupid to realize my brilliance!"

"Okay, okay. I'm sorry, Rufus."

"Polo!" Rufus corrected, plugging his nose again.

"Fine, Pufus, I mean Polo. I'll have the *Reader* run the story. But you are sure he's dead, right?"

"Of course he's dead! I don't leave things half done like some people," he said, glaring at the Mayor.

"None of this is getting traced back to me," Spit warned. "If you get caught, you're on your own."

"Naturally," Rufus said. "You're a true gentleman, Mr. Mayor. Shall we schedule the treaty signing for a few days hence?"

"Book it with my secretary on your way out."

VERY IMPORTANT RESEARCH

Rufus changed back into his own clothes and rejoined Hamilton and Satch on the steps outside. They were interviewing the librarians, who continued to chant "No pay, no work!" with quiet, inside voices. The women generally looked the part, their cardigans and hair buns tending to confirm the bookish stereotype.

When the two men approached the first lady in line, Hamilton held his hat in hand like a gentlemanly suitor. He tried to bow, but his gut limited his motion to little more than a nod.

"Excuse me, my dear saucy bitch," he said. "I'm three-time Hollander Prize winner Jay Hudson Hamilton, and this is my protégé Satch."

In an incredible display of dexterity and coordination, the old lady slapped them both simultaneously with one hand each.

"Sleazeball," she said, adding insult to injury.

The pair moved down the line. "What's with these homely dames?" Hamilton asked.

Next, they stopped in front of a plump matron with a waxy complexion. She looked as randy as a mathematics text.

"Good afternoon, sweet tits. I'm conducting some very important research for my latest novel and I'd like to ask you a few questions."

She replied softly. "Well, if it's for research..."

Hamilton posed the question as if he were reading off a survey. "If you were to compare the shape and consistency of your breasts with that of foodstuffs, would you say that they most resemble: a) bananas, b) melons, c) flapjacks, or d) rotten bologna?"

Satch braced for another slap.

"Flapjacks," she said with a sly wink.

"Hot dog!" cried Hamilton. "Now that's honesty!"

"What a relief," added Satch. He turned back and sneered at the lady who smacked him.

Their confidence bolstered, the researchers moved on to contestant number three, another rotund antediluvian with hips so wide she could have given birth to the entire protest.

"Now you, doxy. Quit hanging on the hook and come on down. Satch, lay it on her."

Satch balanced a pair of reading glasses on the tip of his nose and thumbed to a page in his notepad. He cleared his throat several times before beginning.

"Would you say, miss," he began, enunciating every syllable with impeccable diction, "that your, um, this is, do your, you know, nipples most resemble: a) raspberry nips, b) silver dollar nips, or c) taco nips?"

The woman growled with the viciousness of a starved mutt whose tail has been stomped on. She bunched up the bolt of fabric that comprised her circus tent of a dress, revealing thick, powerful-looking ankles. Satch knew what was coming, but was helpless to stop it.

Rufus arrived in time to see the swift and decisive blow. The woman jammed her knee so far into Satch's groin that Rufus feared it might come out the other side. Yet Satch managed somehow to stay upright. His feet remained fixed to the sidewalk, as the pain seemed to radiate outward through his entire body.

"We'll put her down for taco nips," said Hamilton, concluding their research.

Rufus came to Satch's aid, lending a shoulder to prevent the ailing drummer's collapse. Satch whimpered pathetically.

He labored to speak. "Let's get outta here."

"Where should we go?" Rufus asked.

"I know a real swinging grind joint on the other side of Academy Park," Hamilton proposed. "All the rotgut you can drink for a buck."

"I'm in," said Satch, still shielding his crotch with his hands.

Rufus ignored them. He was considering his next move. He needed to prepare himself to face the *Droit Moral* as Polo Younger. Yet he had no place to go, no place to sit down and absorb the events of the day. He couldn't imagine much thinking would get done drinking moonshine inside of a tent, so he blurted out the only thing that came to mind: "Satch, do you know where Ashleigh is?"

Startled by the non sequitur, Satch replied, "Last I heard, she moved back in with her folks."

"Can you get us there?"

"Um...Maybe?"

"Good enough! Lead us thither and I'll swear to find an icepack for your ailing knackers on the way."

THE HOUSE ON SANDY CREST

Ashleigh's parents lived in the faceless subdivisions of New Urbania, the sprawling suburb where Hamilton and Satch once played dog-catchers. Originally known as Cabbage Town, the large population of Irish and German immigrants that first lived in the area were later encouraged out so that it could be redeveloped to accommodate (that is, cash in on) white flight. The only trolley stop in New Urbania was the old Cabbage Town depot, just down the road from the slaughter house where thousands of chickens, cows, and pigs had been condemned to a delicious fate. Located at the southern corner of the area, the stop was inconveniently placed for accessing the endless miles of identical housing and pedestrian-unfriendly roads.

It had been designed to look nice. New Urbania was bucolic in a non-threatening, pre-fabricated, family-friendly way. Cold calculation had determined the location of every tree, and every hedge was kept meticulously landscaped. The houses were arranged according to the same rigid formula: a one-story ranch with a one-car garage; a split-level raised ranch with a two-car garage; repeat *ad nauseum*. The old Cabbage Town street names had been long forgotten. Now they reflected the pastoral dreams of the upwardly mobile: Hog's Head Road was Deer Crest; Swindle Street was Morning Crest; Tramp Alley was Forest Crest.

Needless to say, it was easy to get lost in such an antiseptic milieu. With Satch as their navigator, the trio wandered the streets until evening, making wrong turn after wrong turn and ringing random doorbells. Rufus rolled the barrel, first with his hands then with his feet, preferring to remain a few yards behind the others. After what was probably their fifth pass down Sandy Crest they finally found the correct one-story ranch with a one-car garage at the end of a cul-de-sac.

Herb Spalmino, the family patriarch, welcomed the young wayfarers inside. He was affable and shared with his daughter a narrow physique and startlingly straight hair. Rufus found this comforting.

"Hey Satch!" Herb said. "Good to see ya again! Still banging away on those drums?"

"Not lately, Mr. Spalmino," Satch admitted.

"That's a shame," Herb replied. "Ash hasn't been playing much either. But she's drawing a lot – working on some big project, she says – so that's good." He turned to the rest of the group. "So, what's your name old-timer?"

Jay Hudson Hamilton replied proudly.

"Well, what do ya know? A famous writer at my house! Greta's not going to believe it! Terrific! What about you?" he said to Rufus.

"Rufus Wiggin, sir," he said, taking the man's hand.

"A pleasure," Herb replied. "Now come on in. You boys look tired!"

Rufus took in the Spalmino home with the same awe and wonder that Ashleigh had experienced inside Alistair's Asshat. The style was simple yet cozy, lived-in yet orderly, countrypolitan and unpretentious. Rufus loved it. He loved it all: the Laz-E-Boy; the old TV; the hand-knitted quilts; the folksy sayings cross-stitched and framed; the family portraits; the bowling trophies; the magazine subscriptions; the porcelain figurines; the commemorative plates; the mismatched silverware. It was a house with only four rooms and a finished basement, but it seemed practically to burst with everything good in life. Rufus believed that anything anyone would ever need was contained within its modest walls.

"Hungry?" Herb asked in the warm, rich baritone that Kody inherited.

"Yes, Mr. Spalmino," Satch replied politely.

"Famished," answered Rufus.

Hamilton mumbled something unintelligible.

Herb made them each a quick ham sandwich on white bread, served with a side of potato chips and a can of store-brand cola.

The food here is simple and hearty, Rufus thought. He looked at the paper plate and realized he couldn't be certain that he had ever eaten off one, or drank soda out of a can, or used a paper towel as a napkin before. With every bite he thought of how it was way better than anything Angelo had ever made.

Herb fetched Ashleigh from the basement. She bounded up the stairs two at a time to greet her guests. She looked well-rested in her baggy clothes, blending in well with the subdued beauty of her home.

"What brings you all to my neck of the woods?" she asked, cautiously. She was sure their unannounced visit could only mean trouble.

"Today, my house fell victim to the war," Rufus said cryptically. "We were lucky to escape with our lives."

Ashleigh's face grew grim. She offered hugs to the refugees. "That's awful," she said. "I'm so sorry."

"What's done is done," Rufus replied.

"Are you okay?"

"We are in much better shape than what's left of my house," Rufus said. He would have liked to come clean and tell her everything, but for the time being he decided to keep the truth to himself.

"They're all a buncha animals!" Herb cried. "I swear this city has gone crazy. I remember it used to be such a nice place. A shame." He looked thoughtful for a moment and then turned to his visitors. "Anyway, you're more than welcome to stay here 'til you get back on your feet. We haven't got much room, but I'm sure we can squeeze you in somewhere."

"That's very kind of you, Mr. Spalmino," Rufus said, thinking Yes! Yes! Yes! "Thank you."

Ashleigh was quick to add, "But you can't stay forever." She was somewhat skittish about the idea.

"So, Rufus, what is it that you do?" Herb spoke with the same curious intonation Ashleigh had used when she asked Rufus the same question. "I mean, how does a guy raise the ire of the *Droit Moral?*"

Rufus had no easy answer. On one hand, he was a privileged trust-fund baby (though he questioned his financial virility at the moment). On the other hand, he had never worked a day in his life. Not wanting to flaunt his wealth inside this lovely home, with its paper plates and frog-shaped cookie jar, Rufus simply admitted,

"I'm unemployed presently," choking on the words as he said them.

"Nothing to be embarrassed about, son," Herb said. Rufus was cheered up by being called son. "A lot of good folks are outta work these days. I'll tell ya what, the garage has needed to be swept for months. Do it and I'll pay ya twenty bucks."

"Dad, stop," Ashleigh protested.

"I'll do it!" said Rufus enthusiastically, much to Ashleigh's surprise.

"You don't have to, Rufus," she said, giving him a hard stare. "Don't feel obligated."

"I'd love to, Herb," he repeated, as if he'd been offered his dream job.

While Rufus was dazed with visions of sweeping the garage, Herb turned to his daughter. "What about you, dear? What are your plans for the evening?"

"Well, Kody's throwing himself a birthday party later tonight."

"Geez, I wish your mother and I had known. We could have made plans."

"It's not that kind of party, Dad," Ashleigh sighed.

"Would it kill that boy just to call us every once and awhile? We haven't heard from him in weeks."

"Work keeps him pretty busy," Ashleigh deflected. She couldn't bring herself to tell her parents that Kody was the leader of a resistance movement plotting to overthrow the *Droit Moral* and constantly on the run. Instead, she had opted for a half-truth, telling them that Kody made deliveries for a copy shop.

"Hey, we're his parents, we worry. There's a lot of dangerous stuff going on in the city right now. Look at poor Rufus here."

Ashleigh looked at Rufus. "Kody's fine, Dad. Don't worry."

"Can you at least remind him to get in touch once in a while? And give him his birthday present for us?" Herb asked. He took out a box from the cupboard. Its silver wrapping paper reminded them all of Marie St. Alban.

HAIL, HAIL
IT IS GOOD, INDEED

Rufus took hold of the broom with a firm grip and awkwardly pulled its bristles across the concrete floor with a swoosh and a swish and a swoosh and a swish, until there was nary a dust bunny to be found. He took great pleasure in the task, and as he swept he sang an old Iroquois folk song he remembered learning in his youth:

> *Hail, hail*
> *It is good, indeed*
> *That a broom,*
> *A great wing,*
> *Is given to me*
> *As my sweeping tool*

Rufus worked as if he was expecting extra credit, sweeping around boxes, under the work bench, and behind the tool cabinet.

Rufus thought of how foolish he had been all this time to pay others to have such fun. It saddened him slightly that he had fired his house rather than his staff; otherwise, he could have usurped the estate's menial chores for his own enjoyment.

When Ashleigh came in, Rufus was making a terrible mess trying to empty the dustbin into the rubber garbage pail.

"You're a natural," she said, smiling. "My mom's been nagging Herb to clean up in here at least since I've been back."

"It's the least I can do," Rufus said humbly. Although he looked away, he couldn't help but notice her radiance. "It's actually rather pleasant."

For several moments, they stood together in silence. Finally, Ashleigh said, "I'm sorry I haven't been in touch since the party."

Rufus didn't know whether he should play it cool, admit his undying love, or confess how obsessively he thought of her. He chose none of the above.

"I was afraid you encountered some unfortunate fate," he said, relaying one constant thought.

"I just thought I should stay low-key. Moving back in with your parents isn't exactly the coolest thing to do."

Unable to think of a better question, Rufus asked, "How's life treating you these days?"

"Relaxed and hectic at the same time. Do you ever feel that way?"

Rufus imagined taking her in his arms and telling her everything. "Quite a bit, actually."

"Of course. Look who I'm asking," she laughed. Then she added conspiratorially, "I've been working on a big project, very hush-hush."

"For Kody?" Rufus asked.

"He wishes. This is my own thing. Remember when you said big statements are needed right now?"

"Of course," he replied, remembering all too well what he had said.

"Well, you'll see. I promise if the war ever ends, I'll put it on display for the whole city."

"Sounds terrific," Rufus said briefly. "Let's hope that day comes soon."

Ashleigh could barely contain her excitement. "It's big, Rufus. I mean *big*."

Rufus had his mind on something else. "So I have to ask," he began abruptly, "and I hope it's not awkward, but did you get my letters?"

Ashleigh sighed. "About that, Rufus."

Uh-oh, he thought.

"I did get them, and I read them, and they were really sweet, and you're really sweet, in an odd way, but I wasn't really sure I ever wanted to talk to you again. But, hey, here you are."

Rufus' heart sank. He was hearing his worst suspicions confirmed.

"May I ask why?" he asked sadly.

"Honestly, I was embarrassed. I don't sleep with guys I just met. I'm not one of those skanks Satch hooks up with, you know – I just got wrapped up in the moment. It was a crazy night, that's all."

"It happens," Rufus said. In fact, he wished that sex on a ping-pong table would happen more often. Or sex on a shuffleboard. Sex on a tennis court. Sex on the putting green. Sex in an elevator. Sex on an escalator. Sex on a yacht. Sex on a sailboat. Sex on a rowboat. Sex in a hammock. Sex in a sand castle. Sex in a cave. Sex in a bungalow.

Sex on a commuter train. Sex in a hot air balloon. Sex on a bearskin rug. Sex on the ceiling. Sex in zero gravity. Sex in space.

Ashleigh broke Rufus from his reverie. "Not for me it doesn't. Here's the thing, Rufus. I really do like you, but I don't want you thinking of me as some easy lay you can just have your way with."

"I never thought that at all," Rufus replied, though he recalled how easy it had been.

"Look, man, I get it. You're smart, you're handsome, you have a ton of dough, so don't try to act like you haven't had a million girls coming to your door. I'm not going to be the latest on some scorecard of conquests. If you want me, you have to be with me, straight up. No sappy letters, no drunken hook-ups, just you and me."

Rufus pictured it. Then what will be left? he wondered. My breast days are behind me.

"No funny business, Wiggin. I mean it. And we have to take things slow."

"I agree," Rufus said. He was not sure that he did.

"Man, I feel so much better now," Ashleigh said, resting her head on Rufus' shoulder. "I've been holding that in for weeks."

"Well, I'm glad you got it out," Rufus said, feeling oddly displeased.

She looked up at him with interest. "Now tell me what happened to you."

Rufus stared far away, thinking about what had happened to him. "This morning my house was reduced to rubble. I only had time to pack a few things. The rest went up in smoke."

"What happened to your insurance policy?" Ashleigh recalled. "Your gentleman's agreement?"

"The terms changed," he replied.

"Well, at least can you tell me what it was now?"

"I could, but what's the point? What's done is done."

Ashleigh pouted. "Why do I feel like there's more to this story?"

"I think it's still unfolding," was Rufus' response.

MAKING PIZZA TAKES DOUGH

Kody's party was held inside a dingy concrete cube, one of many cold storage lockers that lined this sullen stretch of the Flats. In a city built to support a much larger population, places like this were everywhere, cities within a city where abandoned treasure awaited those brave enough to venture inside.

Where do they find these dreadful places? Rufus thought. The vents exhaled a frosty breeze, reminding him of a mid-October kegger he once attended at Dartmouth.

Red balloons clung to the gray ceiling; their strings, hanging at eye level, created an irritating polypropylene jungle that one had to brush aside in order to walk around. Rufus popped one of the balloons by accident.

"It's fucking freezing," said Satch, making a beeline for the keg. "The beer's gonna have to warm me up."

The room was nearing capacity, but Kody was still nowhere to be found. The consummate rock star, he would make his fans wait before making an appearance.

What kind of pompous narcissist throws a birthday party for himself? Rufus wondered. He wished he still owned a coat.

Predictably enough, Kody made a flamboyant entrance: dressed in a gray linen suit, bright bow tie, fur coat, and bowler, he arrived with a crowd-doubling entourage. The new faces were unfamiliar to the rest of the guests; they were hard, menacing, Kody's own gang of glue-huffing child soldiers. They eyed the party nervously, suspiciously, wearing scowls inappropriate for a happy celebration.

Also there, of course, were the same young radicals who drew Rufus into this whole mess to begin with: the girls always ready to hug or scream, who would be unable to tear themselves away if they ever got a good grip of Kody's sleeve; the guys all handshakes and backslaps. One girl fainted when Kody arrived, though the whippets being passed around probably played a part in that.

A guitar was passed from person to person, through the balloon strings, until it landed in Kody's lap. The birthday boy graciously favored the crowd with a couple verses of 'Leningrad' (one of Rufus' favorites), and a truncated cover of 'All Things Must Pass'. Rufus sang along quietly, head down, always keeping a few bodies between him and the man of honor. He had never cleared the air with Kody after dressing him in puke, and didn't know whether he would find Rufus' attendance acceptable. So he sat in a corner, shivering with a cold beer in his hand, feeling miserable and unwelcome.

The party was nothing like Rufus had imagined, though something told him he should have known better. To be fair, the clandestine, dark and musty setting was appropriate and the attendees were all fashionably dressed and beautiful, but Rufus was bothered by the complete lack of social engagement among them. The disciples had broken off into clusters and closed ranks, occasionally butting up against each other with a caustic word and purposefully ignoring anyone on the periphery. Ashleigh was able to float between the cliques effortlessly, but when Rufus tried to tag along, the conversation turned out to consist of inside jokes in a pidgin dialect that he couldn't understand. No one showed the slightest bit of interest in who he was or why he was there. No one even asked his name.

The only society left to him was Hamilton and Satch, who were both fully engaged in the jolly pursuit of drunken oblivion. Satch's new clothes, which were Rufus' old clothes, were a big topic of conversation among the guests. Satch was happy to preen and vamp in his own self-effacing way.

He's not even wearing the ascot right, Rufus observed.

Nonetheless, he had to admit that Satch was amusing to watch. His affinity for mimicry became more pronounced with every drink. He would drop his shoulders and crane his neck like a giraffe, curl up his arms and hop around like a T-Rex, swivel his head like an owl as far around as he could. To everyone's delight, he growled and hooted, knocked hats off heads and licked faces.

Even old Hamilton was having a good time, chatting up feisty lasses, probably about something foul. Rufus watched him pocket no less than five phone numbers.

Tramps, Rufus thought, arms crossed tightly across his chest.

The whole scene bummed him out. He realized begrudgingly that Polo had been right, though he never liked to admit that Polo could be right about anything, ever. The clothes don't make the man. This party had finally proved it. Tonight, though he wore their uniform and had become indistinguishable from the pack, Rufus was still just another face to ignore.

It isn't so simple to change who you are, he realized. In fact, he had a hard time remembering why he had wanted to change in the first place. Why had he scorned the ascot and blazer? It seemed to be serving Satch just fine. Once again, he had thrown himself completely into some grand idea, only to become suffocated by the foolishness of it. What would come of his half-baked plan to impersonate Polo? It was obvious there was no one here who could advise him, or would even care to.

The more Rufus thought about being ignored, the more his bile rose. Had he not survived a harrowing ordeal? Did he not hate the *Droit Moral* as vehemently as anyone here? How can these self-absorbed dilettantes fancy themselves revolutionaries? He saw no activism, no passion, no outrage! Everyone seemed content to make vapid small talk until the keg was drained and then call it a night.

Just then Kody noticed Rufus sitting alone and came over to say hi. The swagger of his approach and the shadow of one of his new disciples behind him made Rufus tense up.

"Thanks for coming out, man," Kody said, taking a seat on an adjacent crate. "I really appreciate it."

"Happy birthday," said Rufus softly.

"Rufus, right?" Kody asked, extending his hand. "I'm Kody Spalmino. I don't think we've officially met."

Rufus shook Kody's hand tentatively. "Not unless you count the time – well, you know."

"Water under the bridge, my friend," Kody said. In fact, he'd never forgiven Rufus for what he'd done. "It was really cool of you to find those copies of our album. I can't thank you enough for that."

Rufus perked up at this sign of appreciation. "That's not all," he said. He took the canister of two-inch tape he had destroyed his entire life acquiring out of his pocket and handed it to Kody. "Happy birthday."

"Are you shittin' me?" Kody asked, his face lighting up with genuine gratitude for a moment. "How? Where?"

"I have a guy who finds things, all things."

"Is this for real? These are really the tapes?"

"So I'm told. Unfortunately, I have been unable to confirm this independently, as the *Droit Moral* destroyed my audio equipment along with the several thousand square feet of house that surrounded it. You're sitting next to a fugitive, my friend."

"Join the club, comrade," Kody reassured him.

"That's why I'm here," Rufus replied. "I want to pitch in. I want to do my part." At the moment he was not particularly thinking of his plan to imitate Polo Younger; he would have been happy with any guidance at all.

"Good, great, fantastic. I know just how you can help."

Rufus gave Kody his undivided attention.

"Here's the deal, Rufus. I've been thinking a lot about things lately. What else is there to do, you know what I mean? And I realized we've had the whole thing backwards. You can't fight art with art. You can't win a war of ideas against mindless thugs, am I right? I figure the only way to defeat the *Droit Moral*, is to start acting like the *Droit Moral*. Do you feel me?"

"Uh-huh," Rufus nodded. He was surprised Kody had drawn the same conclusion.

"We haven't posed a threat. Who cares if we sit around writing songs? Crying into our beers, scurrying around trying not to get busted? If it hasn't worked by now, it never will, and it's only a matter of time until they find us. They found you, right?" Rufus did not want to mention that until recently he had lived in the most conspicuous house in the city. "But now you're here! It's serendipitous, if you think about it. I admit, I would've strung you up myself if you tried to come around a week ago, but now I got a good feeling about you. We're all in this together, man.

"So, anyway, watching you sit here, it occurred to me just now that the only logical step forward is to take up arms."

Rufus didn't know if he could take that step with Kody. "That's a bit of a leap, no?" he asked skeptically.

"Hey, no one is more of a dyed-in-the-wool pacifist than I am. I believe in live and let live, all you need is love, all that crap. But we need to stop playing defense and get active."

"Don't you think that's what they'd want you to do?" Rufus asked. "You could be playing into their hands."

"Look man, in the language of the *Droit Moral*, peace just means you're not doing anything at all. Force is the only thing they understand."

"I'm not a violent person," Rufus said, preferring to consider the day's events an anomaly. "I'm not sure I can help you."

"Well, Ashleigh tells me you're some sort of rich guy," Kody replied, making Rufus wonder if those had been her exact words. "And I think she mentioned you know Polo Younger, right?"

"We went to school together," Rufus repeated by rote. "Grades six through twelve."

"That could be useful in the future, but what we need right now is weapons. A full arsenal. Handguns, rifles, shotguns, grenades, rocket launchers, anti-tank artillery, anything you can get your hands on."

"That's a tall order," Rufus admitted. Spit would surely throw a fit.

"If your guy could find our master tapes, I can't believe a few guns would be a problem."

"I suppose not," Rufus replied. He didn't think this was a very good idea.

"That brings us to the awkward part, Rufus. Thinking about pizza is free, but making pizza takes dough. I think you realize right now we have a taste for steak and a hamburger budget. If we're going to move on this, we'll need a fat wallet behind us."

"Let's not worry over the money yet, Kody. You haven't even said what's in it for me."

Kody considered. "I can promise you the peace of mind that comes from knowing you're on the right side of history."

"That is not going to suffice," Rufus replied. He finished his beer. "I want something else that is in your power to give me."

"Name it."

"I have it on good authority that Polo Younger is currently in truce talks with the mayor."

"Where did you hear this?" Kody asked, looking genuinely shocked.

"I have my sources."

"What's your point?"

"I want The Going Out of Business Sale to play at the treaty signing."

When Kody heard that this is what Rufus was expecting, he laughed out loud. "I'd be honored," he assured Rufus. "But you know what that means, right?"

"What?"

"If we're going to stop the mayor from agreeing to that douchebag's demands, we're gonna need a lot of guns, really fast."

"I suppose you will," Rufus said, sealing the deal with a firm handshake.

With that, Rufus Wiggin, already playing the role of Polo Younger impersonator, also became the chief financier of the resistance. The way of the wallet. An embarrassment of riches. Rufus had no idea why he agreed to such a dangerous plan or what he thought it would solve or how it could possibly end well, but for a long time he had been nagged by the thought that he was somehow responsible for what happened, and the lingering guilt he felt from doing nothing for so long now led him to believe that he could not overdo the destruction of Polo Younger. Kody was the only other person left who still had any influence. He was Rufus' latest hope if not his best. Besides, Rufus still associated Kody with his own salvation in some obscure way, so somehow not saying no was an apology and a debt repaid.

Kody rose to make an announcement. "Listen up everyone!" he shouted.

"Happy Birthday, Kody!" one girl yelled.

"I love you, Kody!" yelled another.

"This is Rufus, a good friend of mine, and a great friend of our struggle. As many of you know, tonight marks the launch of a new offensive, different from anything we've tried in the past. In support of the cause, Rufus has graciously offered to finance our mission, ensuring the defeat of the *Droit Moral* once and for all!"

Rufus scanned the room as the crowd of disciples erupted into a wave of applause that, inside the dank locker, was quite frankly unpleasant. At last he found Ashleigh, skulking in the corner. She was apparently not impressed.

"There have been rumors," Kody continued, "that Mayor Shyne and Polo Younger will soon be signing a peace accord. Even if – especially if this is the case, we must remember that the war, our war, won't be over until every last person involved with the *Droit Moral* is dead or in prison."

Kody's congregation was overcome by a mindless rapture. Rufus was suddenly the most interesting person in that frigid room. The clusters that ignored him earlier were now clamoring to chat. They were eager to hear his story, and Rufus was happy to oblige, adding further embellishment with every telling.

Ashleigh wanted nothing to do with Rufus and his new found fame. When she saw him collecting phone numbers from a gaggle of groupies, she left. Rufus could have Jay Hamilton's sloppy seconds by the thousands for all she cared.

Rufus didn't see Ashleigh go. He was thinking, These guys aren't so bad. I just needed a proper introduction. *Viva la revolución*!

SPOOF

After their night of revelry, the gang ended up back at the Spalmino residence to sleep it off. Rufus insisted, so Ashleigh reluctantly agreed to share her bed with him. She laid a row of pillows and a big stuffed panda down between their respective sides, creating a barricade designed to stifle Rufus' errant desires.

Before they fell asleep they sat together in silence, watching late night television and smoking weed. They expelled their tokes through a spoof: a cardboard tube stuffed with dryer sheets designed to mask the scent from Ashleigh's parents. The room grew eerie and dank with filtered smoke, as a subtle synthetic floral bouquet lingered in the air.

Rufus had never vegged out in front of a television while using a homemade contraption to hide the smell of weed. It was yet another new experience in a day of firsts. The first day of the rest of my life, he thought, finding comfort in the old cliché.

As Ashleigh's breathing grew slow and shallow, Rufus leaned over the pillows to watch her sleep. Her hair was sweet and smoky; her hands moved in concert with some distant dream. To Rufus she was the very model of bliss. He recalled her touch, the taste of her mouth, qualities that still seemed attainable, yet were strangely elusive. Peeking through cracks in the barricade, an interloper longing to breach the divide while the guard slept at her post, he was as close as he could get to what he truly wanted.

SATCH'S MIDNIGHT STROLL,
AND ITS AFTERMATH

Greta Spalmino came home from her overnight shift at the hospital early the next morning. Greta was a good-natured soul, so despite her perpetual fatigue she always ready for whatever her family could dish out. She was certainly accustomed to sleepovers, and normally she would have thought nothing of Satch, Rufus, and their surly old friend staying the night. After all, Satch had been a frequent visitor over the years, and as far as Greta was concerned a friend of Kody and Ashleigh was a friend of hers. She had, however, never encountered his sleepwalking before.

Satch tended toward somnambulism whenever he had tied on a few too many, and he also preferred to sleep in the buff. After getting properly sloshed at Kody's party, Satch passed out in the Spalmino's bathtub, but at some point in the night, he arose and ambled out to the kitchen. There, he ate a plate of leftover chicken and drank a beer. Leaving his scraps on the table, he nevertheless felt compelled to wash a load of dishes. He performed this task competently, although the finished load was left to dry in the microwave. Thence he retreated to the living room, curled up on the wicker loveseat sans blanket or pillow, and settled in until morning.

This was how Greta found him. After eight hours of helping the ill and infirm, instead of the comforting familiarity of her home, the first thing she found as she opened her door was this: Satch – snoring, shivering, and hopelessly afflicted with that male malady commonly known as morning wood – in all his glory.

The sight of Satch's member throbbing like a metronome precipitated a peal of screams so loud, so blood-curdling, that you'd think a Were-Mummy or The Swamp Ghoul was ravishing the women of the town.

Satch awoke in a panic. He didn't know where he was, but was not surprised to discover he was naked. Due to his position, he could hear the screams, but had no idea who or what was yelling.

Herb hurried out in his bathrobe to see what the fuss was about. He found his wife mesmerized by the sight of Satch's ticking cock.

"What the hell's going on in here?" Herb asked as he tightened the knot around his bathrobe. There was a gleam of amusement on his face.

Satch finally saw Mrs. Spalmino in her nurse's habit (white cap, pinafore, stockings, orthopedic tennis shoes) staring at him. He felt truly violated. Led by his divining rod, he bolted from the room. He rampaged through the kitchen like *Homo Erectus* chased by a velociraptor, knocking over everything in his path. Arriving at the basement door, he booked it down the stairs, tripped over a loafer, and tumbled headfirst into Ashleigh's room.

"Your mom saw my boner!" He yelled as loud as Greta, who could still be heard wailing upstairs. "Your mom saw my boner!"

"I can see your boner right now," Ashleigh said, peeking out from under the covers. Rufus tried to hide behind the panda.

Satch tore a Frida Kahlo poster off the wall and wrapped it around his body. "I think your dad saw it too," he added.

Upstairs, Greta had gone to the bathroom to calm down. There she found Hamilton on the john, having dozed off mid-bowel movement. She began to scream again.

Rufus knew that all this meant his stay at the Hotel Spalmino was coming to an end. He bade his middle class dream home farewell. Rufus recognized it as a place content with what it was and not trying to be anything more; he wondered if he would ever be able say the same about himself.

A LITTLE ONE-SIDED,
AND NOT VERY FUNNY

"I wish you'd come with me," Rufus pleaded. Ashleigh shoved him into the street.

"What makes you think I want anything to do with you after what you did?" she shouted.

"What I did? I'm not the naked noctambulist who provoked your mother's inner banshee!" he objected.

"A lot of people sleepwalk naked, Ash," Satch chimed in.

Ashleigh had something else on her mind. "What was that shit last night about you buying guns for Kody?"

"I don't know," Rufus admitted. "He just started talking! As you know, he can be very convincing. I didn't technically say yes, but I couldn't say no. I don't see why it should upset you so much."

"He's manipulating you," she said. She knew Kody's appeal all too well. "All you're doing is feeding his ego."

Rufus tried to explain. "I assure you that was never my intention."

"Is anything ever your intention? I know you love to talk all this shit about how you saved Kody's life. But now it's obvious that you don't care whether he dies or not. Rufus the almighty, basing life and death decisions on how he can make a few new friends!"

Rufus kept his eyes fixed on the suburban sidewalk. "I never planned on going through with it."

"Oh, that makes it better!" Ashleigh shouted. Neighbors curious about the commotion at the Spalmino house peeked through their blinds. "Have you told Kody? I doubt it, and who knows what crazy schemes he can dream up with visions of a blank check dancing in his head. How is this your business anyway? Who the hell do you think you are? Things were already out of control, but at least they were stable. Now here comes Rufus the Doofus to make things worse."

Rufus winced. "I was swept up in the spirit of the night." He looked up at her pleadingly. "You, better than anyone, should know what it's like to get caught up in the moment."

Ashleigh denied his gaze. "I can't believe how selfish you are! You think you can get whatever you want, whenever you want it, because you want it. It's just so easy, isn't it, when you can buy your way into people's lives and talk your way into and out of any situation?"

"How is that a bad thing? To long for more, rather than settle for what is?"

"There's a difference between settling and being grounded in reality, Rufus. You've never had to face any consequences so you think you're invincible. Why not go to eight colleges? Why get a job when you can 'long for more' while wasting your father's money? No need to look before you leap when you know you'll always land on your feet."

Rufus pouted. "I didn't choose my station in life, and I most certainly didn't choose my parents!"

"Well, as great as it must be for you to have my family to ruin instead, I have a choice. It doesn't include you."

"But you're all I have left," he begged.

Ashleigh was furious and beautiful. "Oh, poor little sad and lonely Rufus. Why should you have to be so alone? Did you ever think it's because you're just not that interesting? Under that shiny veneer, what is there?"

Rufus looked down at his soiled new clothes and shrugged.

"Heaven help anyone who says no to Rufus Wiggin! He'll throw a temper tantrum like a child! He'll berate everything he finds inferior to himself, which is, absurdly, everything! No need to worry about hurt feelings, because the magic of an insincere apology will make it all better! Right?"

Rufus tried to remain composed. "I'm just trying to find my way through this world like everyone else," he said. He had no idea what had gotten into Ashleigh. He was overwhelmed; he had never imagined that she harbored such anger and resentment towards him.

"You don't give a fuck about anyone else," she continued. "You don't care if your actions hurt others."

"That's simply not true," he maintained.

"Did you consider whether I would be hurt when you told Kody that shit last night?"

"Of course," he lied. "I care about you, Ashleigh."

"How can you say that? You don't even know me."

"I know that I want to get to know you. I know that I can't stop thinking about you. I know I'd run away with you today."

Ashleigh was taken aback by his suggestion. "I'm done running," she told him.

"We could go anywhere," Rufus insisted. "We could start a new life together."

"God, I have had too many new lives already!"

"Then what's one more?" Rufus asked. He knew he was running out of arguments.

Ashleigh sighed. "I moved back here to get away from all that, Rufus. Not you or Kody or anyone else can pull me back in."

Rufus' confidence grew as he realized that Ashleigh was cursing out her brother as much as she was him. "I can take care of you," he said.

Ashleigh's ire, which had begun to subside, flared again. "How dare you? You think I need you to take care of me? You think you *can* take care of me! You can't even take care of yourself!"

Rufus made a final appeal. "But what about the greater good?"

Ashleigh laughed. "When all else fails, invoke The Cause. Isn't that right, Kody Junior? What the hell do you know about the greater good? What were you contributing while I threw away two years of my life?"

"But...we're so close," Rufus said. He realized his words he sounded just like Kody's.

Ashleigh stepped up to Rufus. "You're close to getting punched in the face. And, thanks to you, Kody's one step closer to the grave. I say fuck you both! You and Kody ought to run away together."

Rufus attempted a charming grin. "He's not my type," he said.

Ashleigh just shook her head. "There you go again. It's like everything is a joke to you. Is this conversation a joke?"

"Actually, I find it a little one-sided," Rufus replied gruffly, "and not very funny."

"I give up," Ashleigh said, turning around. "Have a nice life, Rufus."

Trying at least to reassure her, Rufus shouted at her back, "Listen Ashleigh, I promise you I won't let anything happen to Kody!" He came off more like a bellicose preacher.

"Um, thanks? Do you think that means anything to me? Why do you guys think it's so cool to play outlaw, anyway? I've already played that game, Rufus. There's no future in it. Eventually, you just want to go home."

"But I have no home!" Rufus screamed. As soon as Ashleigh, unnerved by Rufus' callousness, began sobbing uncontrollably, he regretted his tone.

"Goodbye, Rufus," Ashleigh said, storming back inside.

A SUBAQUEOUS SANCTUARY

Hamilton and Satch watched Rufus and Ashleigh's discussion for a little while, but once they realized it would yield no new insights for their research, they went back to The Drawing Board. This was a grind joint in Academy Park where they could throw some bones and drink their weight in rot gut. Rufus was left to fend for himself. Finding that the trolley would only take him west to his past in Lindsay Park, or east to his future as Polo Younger, he decided to walk.

Rufus rolled his barrel out of the subdivisions and back towards the deserted city streets. Only trash accompanied them, blowing up and swirling as if stirred by some apparition. He followed his feet for hours until he came upon the Cahoos Falls, The Place of the Falling Canoe. Here the Van Schaick and Beverwyck Rivers would eternally converge, before continuing miles downstream on their tireless trek towards the infinite ocean.

The falls were dry that day, as they were 363 days of the year. They had the appearance of a glistening lump of coal seventy-five feet high and a thousand feet wide. Rufus lingered around the official viewing area, a little space enclosed within a rusty balustrade that was paved with faux cobblestones for tourists who never came. The circular platform was ringed with benches that had been decorated with spray-painted vulgarities and other markers of teenage boredom. At the center, a rostrum that was possibly made of marble was topped by a plaque commemorating the founding of the Iroquois Confederacy. The quote was attributed to Deganawida himself:

"Persevere onward to the place where the Creator dwells in peace. Let not your earthly things hinder you in life. Let not the events of your day hinder you in death."

The viewfinders on the quarter-fed binoculars had been busted out, and the lenses scratched beyond hope. Rufus tried his luck on the least-trashed device, gambling two bits for a chance to see the lump of coal up close. The machine, once capable of revealing the sweeping vistas of the entire valley, was now rusted in place. Its gaze was permanently fixed on the substation that diverted the falls: water in, electricity out. Rufus watched the thrashing turbines churning the current into a choppy bubblebath, ignorantly shredding schools of trout as they attempted to migrate downstream.

Rufus eased his way down to a bluff just below the viewing area, positioning himself to view the scene exactly as Louis Blanc saw it in his painting, directly above the plunge pool with the falls to his left. In the distance, where the two rivers began to flow together, he could see Arrowhead Point, the triangular islet where Deganawida was said to have planted the Great Tree of Peace. Now it was just a lonely outpost, barren and rocky. On a day like today, one could easily walk to the Point across the damp riverbed. For a lack of anything better to do, Rufus considered the idea. He decided against it.

What's the use? he thought. I'm already stranded.

Stepping to the edge of the bluff, Rufus looked down into the murky waters a hundred feet below. His face was distorted by the darkly shining mirror of the stagnant pool. He couldn't quite accept the idea that he was a murderer. Yet it wasn't the act itself that disturbed him, though it was quite disturbing. Rather, he was upset by the fact that he had somehow formed the requisite *mens rea* to take another life. He wanted Polo dead. No — he wanted *to kill* Polo! It didn't matter that Polo was a thoroughly unlikable person. Polo had done nothing to provoke such cruel treatment; Rufus' thin skin had been pierced by sharp words before, but he had never considered them enough to justify such a gruesome end.

"What's become of me?" he asked his muddy reflection.

He had never even been in a fight before. Although he had provoked his fair share of shouting matches, never had he personally inspired fisticuffs. Rufus had always considered himself better than that, and certainly better than Polo Younger. Yet he wondered now if he had been suppressing all of his own insecurities and perceived failures by projecting them onto Polo. Had Polo become a symbol of all that Rufus deemed unfair in life? Had Rufus really been trying to kill himself, by proxy this time, in the person of Polo?

Rufus allowed himself the shameful consolation that he didn't actually see Polo die, as he had Marie St. Alban. He didn't have to picture Polo's inevitable suffering: how it felt to bleed from the knife wound, or to have his lungs overpowered with smoke, or to be consumed by the flames or crushed by the collapsing roof. Every potential scenario chilled Rufus to his core.

At some point he had decided that the only way to be cleansed of his sins was a baptism in the mythical Cahoos, as it was a sacred ground steeped in legends of rebirth and renewal. Yet every sign warned against it: the area was littered with notices using words like

DANGER and TOXIC and CANCER that featured a swimming stick person imprisoned behind a slashed circle; frequently, statutes were cited. Nevertheless, this was the place Rufus had chosen to wash off his shameful stink.

Rufus scoured the area until he found a rubbery branch that was twice his height and tolerably heavy, and then counted off twenty paces from the edge of the bluff. He held the stick parallel to his body with both hands, left below his waist, right at his chest. In front of him, there was no bar to clear and no cushion to break his fall, just an expanse of gray sky, a giant lump of coal, and a filthy stagnant puddle.

He was off! As the turbines over the falls chugged out a steady rhythm, Rufus increased his trot to a sprint and slowly raised the branch in an overhand grip. He kept his eyes on the sweet spot, a worn patch of earth between two roots. Nearing full speed five steps from the edge, Rufus swung the branch around, lifted his hands above his head, planted his left foot, raised his right foot, and brought the stick down with all his strength, dead on target. The branch bowed as Rufus pulled it towards him. He was running out of land, so he kicked up and out while his feet continued to run, and then he was airborne. He was that starling in Blanc's painting, that warbler taking flight.

The moment, however, was short-lived.

The branch snapped in two, Rufus tumbled off the cliff, his head narrowly cleared some rusty drain pipes, and he performed spastic aerial acrobatics while trying to right himself, managing only to contort himself into ever-clumsier knots. At this point, a belly flop was the best he could hope for. The dark mirror of the pool shattered on impact.

Rufus quickly sank through the caliginous depths to the basin's litter-strewn bed. At first the water felt refreshing, but it quickly grew heavy, coarse, and oppressive. What had once been clean, freshly fallen snow high up in the mountains of the North Country had gradually melted down into the valleys, where it had been subjected to a gauntlet of human waste that contaminated its purity. At last, the murky remains settled into this icy crevasse at the base of the Cahoos.

When Rufus tried to open his eyes, the water burned. He could see nothing but a nebulous brown cloud, dull and shadowy, varying in hue where the sunlight was able to trickle in. Gritty sediment, kicked up in the wake of Rufus' fall, formed turbid shapes that faintly twinkled, like stars on a stormy night. Deeply ensconced within this subaqueous sanctuary, Rufus thought of Ashleigh.

He turned her words over and over in his mind. They continued to sting worse than the unknown toxins now punishing his skin.

How was she able to see right through me? he wondered. How did she know me so well when I hardly knew her at all? Am I so lonely that I can no longer distinguish between love and infatuation, or friendliness and flirtation, or even affection and contempt? Did I push away the one person who was willing to accept me for who I was with my pathetic need to be liked by everyone?

As his mind and body became mired in the muck, Rufus didn't find himself feeling any more enlightened. A lifetime of rash and impulsive decisions had brought him here, and at last this once brazen and cocksure gadabout had been baptized by life's torrential shit storm.

He was now no different than anyone and only better, perhaps, than these dismembered schools of fish sharing this polluted purgatory. Even here he was an unwelcome intruder, an uninvited guest. Even misery wanted none of his company. He sat in the filth until he was ready to improve his condition, and then he swam to the top. Then, at least, he was treading water.

UNTENABLE DEBTS

Night fell on the Cahoos. Rufus unpacked his barrel and curled up inside it. From his cradle he could see across the river to the ruins of the Schuyler Manufacturing Company, the industrial giant that first seized the falls, enslaved the river, and built a city in the name of progress. The abandoned complex was once the nation's largest textile mill, but now it was just a towering brick and mortar shell. A bust of Dudley Schuyler loomed omnisciently atop the last remaining turret, evermore casting a disapproving frown upon his former fiefdom.

Schuyler emerged from humble beginnings. For years he worked as an errand boy and junior apprentice, diligently saving until he could achieve his fondest dream of owning a textile mill. At last he bought a failing concern and through grit and gusto grew the smallest manufacturer in the region into a monolithic compound where eight factories churned out a million yards of cloth per day. This feat took years of hardship and triumph to accomplish, though the viewfinder of history now only showed how rapidly a sleepy cow town was transformed into a bustling metropolis. Today, a low-rent neighborhood, a crime-plagued avenue, a weather-worn marina, a fire-bombed museum, and a silenced opera house all bore his name. His most venerable namesake was Rufus' esteemed alma mater, Schuyler Academy, where the children of elites from all over the world were taught how to act like future noblemen and magistrates.

Everything the city was or would be could be traced to those dilapidated remnants across the river. Rufus eyed the ruins, rebuilding in his mind Schuyler's cathedral to progress. Having once spent six weeks enamored with the subject of industrial mills, he could imagine all of the mechanized tools and instruments – jennys, mules, spindles, looms, presses, dye vats, sewing machines – which had been cast to resemble medieval torture devices. The tired souls who worked the machines had no choice but to keep pace with them. He saw the spinners spinning, the piercers piercing, the bobbins bobbing. Rufus pictured the horizon lined with belching chimneys rising like spires or minarets, staining the sky with a frightful ashy hue. He imagined he could hear the 120 decibel racket abuse his eardrums, feel the 120 degree heat sear his flesh, taste the sweat as it rolled off his brow twelve hours a day, six days a week. He had been there all evening.

He thought about the tiny hands of children gobbled up in the gears just as those trout, swimming blindly to their destiny, were massacred by the turbines. He imagined the workers who survived each day only to return home to a bleak tenement, a worried wife, and one or more crying babies. Rufus calculated the untenable debts accrued to the company store, redeemable only with company scrip – with the paper of their bodies and the ink of their blood – debts only a lifetime of servitude could repay.

His own family had made its wealth in textiles. Though Alistair had run his factories halfway around the world, Rufus imagined that the streets of Karachi were just as crowded with miserable workers, and that the rivers of Lahore were just as irrevocably mucked. To Rufus, Alistair had been generous and caring, nurturing his son's every ambition, no matter how frivolous. Had he been the same man in his professional life? Rufus wondered. Or was he as callous and greedy as Dudley Schuyler? In giving his family a carefree life, had he ignored the burden of the men, women, and children whose industry he exploited? Was their misery Rufus' only true inheritance?

Unfortunately, Alistair was gone and could not dispel his son's fears. Schuyler, too, had departed before he could be held accountable: after a bloody strike, Schuyler found places where labor laws were lax and union organizers nonexistent, and left the city to fend for itself. The sudden loss of Schuyler Manufacturing precipitated waves of failure that rippled through every life, business, and institution that the company and the man had been supporting for decades.

When Alistair's large heart gave out during a tennis match one day, young Rufus found himself in a tailspin of his own. His mother was unable to cope and killed herself. For many years, Rufus had been naught but a ward – of nannies, servants, friends and lovers – surrounded by an ever-fattening donut of well-wishers and sycophants, the center of which was always a hole.

Rufus peered out his barrel downriver to the city's skyline. It was only a mass of miscellaneous gray rectangles. He pondered his and the city's collective future. Unprepared for the loss of their progenitors, they had both been thrust into adulthood too soon, and so they never finished growing up. Rufus saw his city as he saw himself: as an orphan in need of saving.

[SIC]

The next morning, there was a picture of Rufus on the front page of the *Daily Reader*. It was an old photo taken at the Red & Green Christmas Ball, in which he was three sheets to the wind, wearing an unbuttoned shirt and a crooked smile. There were three girls distributed across his two arms.

My best days are behind me, Rufus sighed.

He had always pictured his first day of work much differently: three-piece suit, freshly shaved, newspaper under his arm, office on the fiftieth floor. Instead, he was pretending to be Polo Younger. Well, at least he had the newspaper.

Nevertheless, he was starting to understand how the rest of us feel before each workday. After a night sleeping like a square peg inside the round barrel, Rufus was irritable and cranky. Had his spirits not been lifted by the shocking expose he had planted on the front page of the paper, he probably wouldn't even have got out of bed.

POLO'S NO-NO: DEAR LEADER A SORE LOSER
A DAILY READER EXCLUSIVE!

Rufus Wiggin, local socialite and son of the late textile magnate and amateur architect Alistair Wiggin, became the latest victim of the war yesterday, as a violent struggle with Polo Younger left Wiggin's mansion in flames, and his present whereabouts unknown.

Little could be done to save the five acre, twelve bedroom estate, once dubbed the Ugliest House in America by *Architectural Digest*. Due to an ongoing strike by the fire department over back pay, the landmark residence was allowed to burn to the ground.

The fight began after Younger arrived at the Wiggin home to confiscate a collection of artwork he had reportedly made as a student at Schuyler Academy, where Wiggin was his classmate. Our sources have revealed that Wiggin fended off the leader of the *Droit Moral* with a flurry of kicks, punches, leg locks, choke holds, noogies and wedgies, until Younger ran away crying. Making a hasty retreat, Younger is said to have tripped over a gas can, igniting the epic blaze. Preliminary estimates suggest that it was the largest conflagration in the city since the destruction of Marie St. Alban's Highway Project fifteen years ago.

Upon hearing the tragic news, Mayor Shyne issued a written statement. The executive wasted no words in excoriating Younger for the crime. "This is another example of the *Droit Moral*'s dicktatorial [sic] crusade to suppress all potentially embarrassing information," said Mayor Shyne. "As for Rufus Wiggin, it's safe to say the city has lost yet another of its best and brightest."

The artwork in question has been obtained exclusively by the *Reader*. As even an uncultivated slob could see, they reveal Younger as a talentless hack, unable to grasp even the most basic principles of drawing.

"This stuff is terrible," said Professor Willoughby Patterne, chair of the Art Department of Schuyler State College. "This man isn't fit to instruct kindergarten, much less lead a revolution, but you know, opinions are like *(expletive deleted)* and Polo is an *(expletive deleted)*, so there you go."

Younger could not be reached for comment. His spokesman, Mortimer Gout, called the news "fabricated propaganda by a desperate debutante and a corrupt city government."

For our Art Critic's full review of Younger's work, read *Sanctimonious Bullshit, or Just Plain Bad?* on page B2. Also, check out our sneak preview of Jay Hudson Hamilton's new novel, *The Banana-Boob Republic*, page B6.

Rufus found the story to be poorly written. He was upset that he had not been cast in a more heroic light. Overall, though, he considered it a miracle that Spit hadn't screwed the whole thing up.

He stopped to look at himself in the smeary window of an abandoned storefront. Rufus held the newspaper's composite sketch of Polo next to his reflection and compared the likenesses. Both men were roughly the same height and build; Polo's stupid clothes made the whole ridiculous scheme slightly more convincing. In order to make the masquerade passable, if not wholly believable, Rufus had donned a pair of gloves he had found among the debris of his campsite, and stolen a clothespin from an abandoned laundry line to slip over his nose. Giving himself one final look, he took a deep breath and thought, "Here goes nothing."

PICKLES ON PUMPERNICKEL

The *Droit Moral* was headquartered in the old Schuyler Brush Factory. This hulking brick structure had an expansively flat roof and bar-like metal window frames, making it look equal parts reform school and lunatic asylum. Polo had acquired it, along with the rest of the dilapidated factories along the waterfront, by having himself named head of the zoning board and invoking eminent domain. He sent his enforcers to negotiate a fair market price with the owners, snatching up the properties, sometimes literally, for a song. Once his pilfered kingdom was complete, Polo ordered a 50-foot wall built around his riverside domain. Then he declared the entire eastern half of the city as his own.

Rufus never ventured into this part of town. As a child, his nanny had permanently scared him off with stories of surly longshoremen and women of ill repute. He walked along Polo's makeshift rampart for several blocks. Occasionally he had to dodge a crushed beer can as it fell from on high, dropped by bored snipers stationed between gaps in the ribbon wire.

The aura surrounding the compound was authentically menacing. It was, perhaps, the most genuine thing Polo had ever accomplished, and Rufus began to reconsider the buffoonish caricature he had attached to the movement. He thought of turning back, retreating to his barrel, buying a bus ticket to Siberia, making a public admission of guilt via telegram. Instead, he lingered outside the only entrance he had seen, kicking rocks, examining crumpled discards, and otherwise delaying the inevitable.

With every moment, Rufus grew more convinced that he was being watched keenly by suspicious sentries. In fact, the guards kept their pistols holstered and patiently ignored his presence; occasionally their knees would twitch, but in general they acted like they were used to this sort of thing. I must act decisively! Rufus thought. He had brought this upon himself and there was no use in shirking his responsibility.

Mustering every bit of courage out of the cluttered catacombs of his soul, Rufus straightened his hunch, lifted his chin, and strode surefootedly over to the dark side. He tried to think like Polo. His sweatpants billowed.

Of course I'm supposed to be here, Rufus mumbled for practice. Don't you know who I am?

"Hold it right there," the guard said, blocking his path.

Busted, Rufus thought with some relief. So much for that idea. He cocked his head to the side, waiting to see what the sentry would say next.

"You forgot to say good morning, Dear Leader." The guard's voice cracked as he looked at Rufus with puppydog eyes. "We always good morning."

He had to go through with it after all. "Not today shitbird! Get out of my face," he began. With the clip on his nose, Rufus' impersonation was spot on in pitch and timbre. "Who are you, anyway? What's your name?"

"Agent Birdsong, sir."

"That's a stupid name. How did you get such a stupid name?"

"You gave it to me, sir."

"I hate it! From now on, you're Agent Shitbird."

"Yes, sir."

Rufus was surprised at how naturally acting like this came to him. "And if you ever stop me again, or try to talk to me, or think you're my friend, I'll – I'll have you crocheting potholders for the rest of your life! Got it?"

"Yes, sir."

"Not a peep."

"Ye..."

"Shhh, little Shitbird."

"Good morning, Dear Leader," another guard said, waving him inside.

"Shut up, kiss ass," Rufus said over his shoulder. The two sentries looked at each other with confused, disappointed expressions.

And so, Rufus entered the compound. Really? he thought. That's it? If they're all such idiots, this won't be so hard.

Between the imposing facades of some dozen factory buildings, a cobblestone courtyard was bustling with activity. El Caminos were being soaped up in anticipation of the next patrol for art crimes; *plein air* painters were dabbing images of brick walls, dappled in sunlight, on their canvasses; clipboard-toting functionaries ferried messages back and forth; workers were shaking out drop cloths. Amidst it all, a sixty foot replica of a Cao Cao mask was being welded together by a team of metal sculptors.

Rufus scanned the group for women. He was disappointed not to find any.

He also discovered that all of Polo's hustling, scurrying, shouting minions shared another trait in common with their Dear Leader. Their faces were covered – by Bauta masks, Columbina masks, Gnaga masks, Noh masks, Otoko masks, drab masks, colorful masks, stark and expressive masks, even latex halloween masks. Polo's dysmorphia had apparently infected his entire flock.

Unsure where to go, Rufus cut a path to the nearest building with an important looking entrance. His every step was followed by hundreds of pairs of eyes peering through hundreds of masks. Rufus had no way of knowing whether they were paying their respects or discerning an imposter. To test them, he took an abrupt step forward, waving with a particular flourish. Sure enough, they made the same motion. When he took a step back and made a showy bow, they – well, imitation may be the sincerest form of flattery, but Rufus found this particular routine a little creepy. Worse, his stratagem had left him none the wiser. He decided to seek a private place, wherever that may be, to lay low until he had enough confidence in his presumptive Polo.

When he saw the closest door was labeled ADMINISTRATION, he reasoned that would be as good a place as any to look.

"Get back to work, you creeps!" he shouted brusquely as he made his way up the steps.

Once inside, Rufus looked over the decaying factory. He was surprised to see how little Polo had done with the place. Despite the vast reservoir of funds at his command, not to mention the enormity of his own personal wealth, Polo had apparently not considered sprucing up the old plant a worthy expenditure. If anything, the handymen, all dressed in green jumpsuits and Yi Li masks, seemed to be gutting the interior haphazardly. As Rufus passed, they were in the middle of knocking a hole in the wall. They paused to bow.

"Oh my god, Mr. Younger, where have you been?" said a frantic little voice that squirreled up beside him. "I've been trying to reach you all night."

"I was where I was," Rufus barked. He hoped the clothespin would stay in place. "Now leave me alone!"

"Polo," said the lackey sincerely. "I was worried."

"Never call me Polo!" Rufus proclaimed.

The man seemed taken aback. "What shall I call you then?"

Rufus believed that he could not overdo the destruction of Polo Younger. "PuPu Bunghole," he said. "Sir PuPu Bunghole."

"Seriously?"

"Don't question me, you little man! Who do you think you are?" Rufus sneered.

"It's me, Mortimer. Mortimer Gout," he said. Behind his Jiang Gan mask, Mortimer was noticeably hurt. "Are you feeling okay? You look, seem, and smell different somehow."

"If you must know, I had a very stressful day and I was bathing in the cool, refreshing waters of the Cahoos."

"That explains the smell," said Mortimer. He too was pinching his nose.

"How do I know you're really Mortimer Gout? You could be an imposter, a flim-flam artist. Give me proof."

"What—what kind of proof?" he asked, looking away and shifting from foot to foot.

Rufus, pleased to see his desperate ploy was working, decided to run with it. "Show me where my office is."

"But you know where your office is."

"Yes, but I don't know if you know, do I?"

"Um, yes, of..."

"What is your job?"

"Excuse me?"

"Explain to me the work you do for me. And the work I do, while you're at it."

"Your work is my work, sir," Mortimer reminded him. "My work is your work."

"Then why are we standing here and not working?" Rufus demanded, realizing that imitating Polo was going to involve work, after all. "And quit pinching your nose, you look ridiculous."

"Yes, sir."

Mortimer led Rufus to a basement corridor. At the end of the hallway, Mortimer opened an unlabeled door. It was a broom closet. Not a converted broom closet, or a secret espionage broom closet; just a drab, functioning broom closet full of cleaning utensils, damp rags, and brightly colored solutions.

Rufus thought that this might be a trick. "This is my office?" he asked tentatively. Apparently his desk was a card table and an overturned bucket was his chair.

Mortimer closed the door.

"I was so worried," he said. He grabbed Rufus in an embrace, gently caressing him with one hand. The other gave his butt cheek a firm squeeze.

"Now, really..." Rufus said as he extracted himself from the advance. He knocked over the card table in the process. A pile of papers scattered across the floor.

Rufus thought of the Droit's foot patrol, staffed by capable-looking Adonises; the absence of women in Polo's concept of utopia and the vehement dismissal of women artists in his newspaper; Polo, his classmate, the sycophant and lover of theatrics. He could see it. He couldn't see, however, what Polo saw in this squat man with a weak jaw and a receding hairline. He would have expected Polo, with all his power, to keep a harem of patrolmen and skinny little artists.

"I know I shouldn't be so warm at work, but I'm just so happy to see that you're okay," Mortimer said. He tapped his mask to Rufus' in the gesture of a porcelain kiss.

It's only weird if I get a boner, Rufus thought.

"Did you see the lies written about you in the *Reader* today?" Mortimer asked, his affectionate tones turning grave.

"Those were no lies," Rufus admitted, feigning defeat. "It's all true."

"It can't be! All true? Not half true? Not even somewhat true? But actually completely true? You made those—those things?"

"Yes, and they're terrible. I'm a terrible artist. You see Mort, I've been a fraud this whole time." He put his arm around Mort. "You don't mind if I call you Mort, do you?"

"Of course not," he said, wishing Polo would be this familiar more often.

"I've been found out, Mort. It's all over, jack."

Mort attempted to cheer the spirits of his Dear Leader. "It does look bad, but we can cover it up. We've done it before."

"Don't tell what me what to do!" Rufus yelled petulantly. A mop clattered to the floor. "I'm going public and that's final!"

"Why would you throw it all away?" he pleaded. "After all we've done to get you this far?"

"What's this 'we' business? You haven't done shit! If you want to do something, get me a sandwich. I'm starving."

"Yes, sir," Mortimer said, running anxiously out of the room. He returned immediately with Polo's favorite lunchtime treat, hoping it would cheer up his grumpy mood.

Rufus looked at a soggy booger of a sandwich with dismay. "What is this shit?" he asked, poking it gingerly.

"Pickles on pumpernickel, extra mayo," said Mortimer. He peered between the slices of bread, afraid he had somehow gotten it wrong. "It's your favorite."

"So it is," Rufus sighed. He took a bite of the sandwich, pondering the kinds of things that only Polo could love. Mortimer watched Rufus' mouth as he ate, vicariously savoring the disgusting concoction. Rufus pushed the sandwich aside after a few bites. At last he demanded, "Show me my kingdom!"

WHOLESALE DOLPHIN SLAUGHTER

Their first stop was Art Re-Education. Housed in a long, narrow room crammed with easels ordered in perfectly symmetrical rows, the nominal students here were taught shoulder-to-shoulder, shackled together at the ankles, wearing on their faces that peculiar expression of aesthetic despondence.

What Rufus saw was education of the assembly line sort. Canvasses were passed down the rows; at each station, a student mechanically added their single dab or stroke to the picture, handing it off just quickly enough to receive a new image to amend. They worked at an alarming speed, producing a finished piece in as little as two minutes. Painting by numbers, each student learned his role as an artist.

"Beautiful, isn't it?" Mort asked with satisfaction.

Looking over the scene, Rufus was dumbfounded. "What are they in for?" he asked.

"Don't you remember—"

"I knew you were an imposter!"

"No, of course not, I never meant," Mortimer stammered. He collected himself and cleared his throat. "This is a first offenders program, mostly for the least significant violations."

"How long are they kept here?"

"Until they are rehabilitated," he answered studiously.

"I see. And this is all they do?"

"As per your guidelines," Mort recited, "the students are to work twelve hours a day, seven days a week, until they have learned that their old habits are futile and anti-social. Our research has shown this is the best way to teach the virtue of working under pressure and constraint, which is the only way to make truly great art."

"Very good," Rufus said, patting him on the head.

'Very good' could not have been said about the art, however, and Rufus had seen nothing 'truly great' since he got here. The canvasses were faintly pre-printed with a design that featured, almost exclusively, dolphins and spaceships, removing any chance that someone might be personally inspired. After each student had made his tiny contribution, the finished piece was handed to a foreman, who promptly tossed it into a furnace.

In this class the teachers were all armed with batons and, as could be expected, quick to wallop anyone slacking off, or sneezing, or sweating too much, or painting outside the lines, or collapsing from sheer exhaustion, or requesting a bathroom break, or taking an unauthorized bathroom break in their pants.

"How many do they produce in a day?" Rufus asked.

"Collectively, they must complete five thousand per day. Should they fail, the quotas will be increased and they could subsequently face additional physical discipline or expulsion to the work camp. Any flaw in the composition, no matter how trivial or individual, merits punishment for the group as a whole. Once they recognize their true role, their work will set them free."

"You burn five thousand paintings a day?" Rufus asked. Under the mask he was sweating profusely from the heat of the furnace where a wholesale dolphin slaughter was currently occurring.

"*We* burn them," Mortimer corrected.

"Yes, right. That's what I said. We."

"As you know, it teaches them the disposable nature of art. Our students learn that true greatness comes from the labor of the creative process, not the end result."

"Art for art's sake," Rufus said, wanting to shout out the rest his favorite phrase. He remained silent.

"Exactly," Mort boasted.

"Is there a reason that there's nothing remotely creative or educational about this whole process?" Rufus posed finally.

Mort was all ready with the answer. "The prisoners must be stripped of their bourgeois tendencies before they can be forged into the kind of artist that will embrace our exacting standards for quality and excellence."

As if on cue, another painting was shoveled into the furnace.

A FAINT YEARNING

Next they visited the Art/Work Camp, home of the *Droit*'s most incorrigible prisoners. Rufus knew that, like the students of Art Re-Education, these people were guilty only of an unwillingness to conform and the audacity to challenge the absurd. Undoubtedly, among the restive souls consigned to the work camp were Kody's followers, Ashleigh's friends, Satch's drug buddies. Thoroughly degraded by brute work, having drawn from their reserves of spirit until they had been bankrupted, these alleged criminals were suffering a much grosser fate than Rufus had ever imagined. Though they had the expressions of old men, Rufus realized that they were younger than he was.

Polo, mostly because he was cheap, had resurrected the brush factory's ancient equipment and put it to work for the cause; the recidivists thus acted out some nauseating parody of Dudley Schuyler's nineteenth-century dystopia. Rufus saw his gloom-induced vision of spinning flywheels and chugging conveyor belts, spewing plumes of dust and smoke, come to life before his very eyes.

The prisoners were lacking certain safety equipment, such as helmets, goggles, ear plugs and, in some cases, shoes. Their chains clanked inaudibly beneath the roaring din of the machines, which was so loud that even when Rufus jammed his thumbs into his ears *a la* Spit, it did little to arrest the noise. The thick stench of old machinery and human labor was so overwhelming that not even the clothespin on his nose could stifle it.

"This is where we keep the worst of the worst," Mort continued to report over the racket. "All the agitators and anyone associated with the resistance will eventually make their way here."

"What?" Rufus yelled. He knew that this was the fate that Polo would have consigned Kody, Satch, and Ashleigh to if he had ever caught them. Rufus almost imagined he could see Ashleigh among the prisoners, with hair slicked down, covered in grease and reduced to nothing but an enduring steel skeleton and a few rusty gestures. What did it matter if this widget was wispy and had a delightful laugh, while that cog was gruff and short tempered? All were forced to work together inside the broken machine.

Rufus pictured Kody assigned to the dunking vats. Live hogs squirmed futilely on hooks above these giant tubs of scalding water, their corkscrew tails still wiggling as they waited to be drowned. It was Kody who would hold them underwater as they boiled, soaking the struggle out of them until their loosened bristles could be pried off by hand. As a bonus, the carcass was now fit to be prepared for supper.

A man of nimble limbs, Satch would be forced to make the paintbrush handles. Bear-hugging barrels of molten plastic and carrying them across a series of molds, he would pour out the neon magma, high-five the machines shut, and press down with all his strength. He'd transfer the white-hot sludge into a sweltering cooler, a contraption with sharp fangs and an endless thirst, belching steam into the face of whoever fed it. After that the bristles would be crimped into place. The finished tool was worth far less than the labor expended in its creation, but Polo had argued that it would be wrong to think of the paintbrush as the final product. These were the brushes used in the Art Re-Education classes.

There was an unnatural acceptance to the way these young men and women labored. A faint yearning for their old desultory ways would occasionally cross their eyes, but those moments quickly faded, the capacity to entertain them long since sweated away. They simply were far too exhausted to indulge a crisis of conscience. At the mixing machine that sorted bristles by size and taper, Rufus saw it in those using nothing but hope and determination to keep the rusty device from jamming so they wouldn't have to stick their arms inside it. A faint yearning.

Rufus read a faint yearning on the faces of those hammering tin scraps into ferrules and of those coating the rings with toxic epoxy; everywhere on the line, it lurked just below the surface. In the shadow of the grinding drums, where a man sanded down handles in a flurry of sparks, Rufus could see it in the brief memory of satisfaction that occasionally flickered across his face, fading as soon as he was passed another piece to finish. There goes one now. And another.

Yet for the most part they toiled together mindlessly, sharing the same catatonic stare and mechanized movements. Their submission to the brutality of the routine was secured by the ominous patrols of the foremen. Rufus was not sure if the surreal cruelty of the situation made it feel less or more like a school field trip, one of those yellow-bussed voyages into history or science. He felt ill. He stared at his shoes, deliberately trying to ignore the terror that had been purchased by that fortune to which he was the illegitimate heir and which he now was hoping to bankrupt. Rufus was determined to erase these ill-gotten gains the only way he knew how: self-sabotage.

Now it was up to Rufus Wiggin to shut it down. It was his duty to open those windows, stop those machines, get that man some shoes, and unhook those poor squealing piggies – he would free them all, no matter what personal humiliation he had to endure!

"Sure is something, isn't it?" Mort said.

"What?" Rufus yelled again.

"Sure is something, I said."

"It sure is something," Rufus said to his shoes.

For some reason he couldn't bring himself to look up. He couldn't find the words to shut it down.

It's only my first day, he thought weakly.

And so it was that Rufus, now in possession of all the power there was to possess (all the power in *this* world, anyway) and confronted firsthand by the grinding misery inflicted upon the innocent, proved himself a coward. He told himself that in a city once abandoned by its powerful Daddy, Polo was simply playing from the same deck of cards that Dudley Schuyler first brought to the table so long ago. Polo had succeeded in getting what he wanted by recognizing that longing for a stern but ubiquitous caretaker in others, and knowing how to fill it. People had been used to the cruelty and duplicity for so long, they must have started to mistake it for affection.

The next day, Rufus arrived at work more sore than he had ever been. He was coming to the conclusion that there was simply no practical way to get a proper night's sleep inside a barrel.

The alternative had been to spend the night in Polo's bed. As soon as he pictured himself spooning Mortimer, he decided it was more of a commitment to The Cause than he was willing to make. He was not sure he wanted to know what he might learn between those sheets.

All night Rufus had been beset by nightmares about those poor hogs being thrust towards their watery end simply to harvest their unique facial hair. When a back spasm awakened him briefly, he scolded himself for not dreaming about the prisoners.

Still, he couldn't stop thinking about those pigs.

Rufus had grown his own unique whiskers during his time in the wild, a patchy beard with a mustache and goatee that refused to connect. Rufus looked more like a hipster than he ever had, yet never had he been less able to enjoy it. Instead, he had to spend eight hours behind a mask, pinching his nose in order to do what he needed to do.

The new day brought the same routine. Bows and curtseys. Underlings attaching themselves at the hip at every turn, asking, "Can you look this over?", "Any thoughts on this?" It was essentially impossible to take a casual stroll through the compound, yet hiding away in his office just subjected Rufus to a different set of unreasonable demands. On the card table, forms, applications, memos on cultural figures to be investigated, reports that had been rubber-stamped without a second glance, old receipts, manifestos and other tedious administrative tasks had been piled haphazardly into a mountain that was slowly becoming too daunting to approach.

Every fifteen minutes, Mortimer faithfully checked in.

The excitement of yesterday's expose had faded but nothing seemed to have changed. Rufus sat idly, thinking only about how time dragged at the office. The second hand struggled to tick. The faint essence of bleach lingered in the air, making him feel lightheaded. He could not understand why there was all this fuss about working.

Briefly he considered rolling up his sleeves and getting his hands dirty with the prisoners in the brush factory but, realizing it would be an empty gesture, he decided to do nothing instead.

Moreover, he thought the smell of pickles might drive him crazy. Rufus dreaded the idea that he would have to choke down another pickle sandwich ever again. Delivered dutifully three times a day, there was already a pile of them mostly or completely uneaten rotting away behind a washbasin. By lunchtime, he longed for nothing more than a beer and a cigarette. Yet he knew he must keep up appearances. Being Polo Younger unfortunately meant *being* Polo Younger, warts, Mort, pickles and all.

Towards the end of the day, Mortimer returned holding a pad and a pencil at the ready.

"What now?" Rufus growled. He had hardly put a dent in the mass of ministerial minutiae.

"I need your edicts for tomorrow's paper."

Polo was known for his edicts. They were a forum for the asinine and capricious, the dippy and the banal, for every lame idea Polo felt compelled to inflict on society. Here, he would divinely command, frequently in contradiction of prior decrees, new acceptable forms of dress, acceptable lengths of hair, the adoption of inventive new masks. Rufus was eager to see if Polo truly had the power to declare whatever he pleased.

"Well, Mort," Rufus began, as his right hand man earnestly transcribed every word. "I will begin by declaring that marshmallows will no longer be called marshmallows."

"Brilliant," Mortimer suggested.

"They will be now called pillows, and pillows will be called clouds."

"And clouds, sir?"

"Sky diapers," Rufus replied with a straight face. "Clouds are now sky diapers."

"Good, amazing," Mort said, scribbling away. "I love marshmallows. I mean pillows. I think."

"Secondly, I declare that cashews are no longer a seed."

"No, sir?"

"Henceforth, they will take their rightful place, once and for all, as a nut, fully endowed with all the rights and privileges of their nutty brethren."

"Cashews now a nut, simply inspired."

"Furthermore, I declare an end to the tyranny of socks and shoes! From now on, it's bare feet or bust around here."

Mort sought clarification. "What about the welders and iron workers, sir?" he asked.

"Fuck 'em. One's feet must have sole," Rufus said, choosing the moment to repeat a joke that truly did not need repeating.

"Consider it done. I'll have all the shoes burned in the furnace."

"That reminds me," Rufus continued. "Quit burning shit. It's bad for my lungs."

"You're absolutely right. I'll dump them in the river myself."

"That will be fine. This week, on the question of art, I make but one proclamation."

"Whatever you please, sir."

"Danceramics is hereby and henceforth placed at or near the top of any list concerning the worthiest of worthy artistic pursuits."

Mort paused mid-word as he wrote. "Dancer—I'm sorry, sir?"

"It doesn't surprise me that an uncultured nincompoop like yourself hasn't heard of Danceramics. Just write it down."

"I'm trying my best," Mort replied, attempting several spellings. "Is there anything else?"

At that moment, a loud crash, a cry of pain and some shouting came down to the office from the factory floor. Looking at Mortimer standing there with an expectant posture, Rufus suddenly wondered what he was doing. Using Polo's power to have a laugh while he let those brushes continue to roll off the line? Everything *was* a joke to him, wasn't it?

"No, Mort. That will be all," he sighed.

"Very good. Your 2:30 is waiting outside." It was 4:15. "Should I bring him in?"

Rufus felt he had enough of appointments for the day. "Who is it?" he asked.

"He says his name is Agent Butterknife. I don't recognize him."

"Then why didn't you tell him to get bent?" Rufus wondered.

"He says it's urgent."

"Of course it is." Rufus slumped further on the bucket. "What isn't around here?"

"I can tell him to come back later, if you'd like."

"No, I'll see him," Rufus groaned. "Send him in."

The caller entered the broom closet with a mop in hand, wearing a blue jumpsuit and a bandit mask. As this was the fashion among Polo's visitors, no one had considered this suspicious. He was short and lean, with dark ringlets of hair tied up in a bandana.

"You?" Rufus exclaimed.

"Me?" his guest rejoined. "You!"

Rufus explained. "I know who you are, Agent Butterknife."

"You should," Kody replied, taking off his mask.

Will he be able to tell who I am? Rufus wondered. What did he already know?

"Who let you in?" he asked. "How did you get past Mortimer?" Had his cover been blown?

"I made an appointment. You let me in. I overheard you."

"Semantics," replied Rufus dismissively. "What do you want?"

"You know what I want, Polo."

Rufus had never been so relieved to be mistaken for Polo. "I haven't the foggiest," he replied, determined to stay in character.

"We had a deal," Kody said. "I did everything you asked me to do, but so far you haven't done shit for me."

"Perhaps we're remembering things differently," Rufus suggested. "Please jog my memory. The strain of reforming society can make it hard to recall every detail sometimes."

"You said you would make me rich and famous."

"*I* said that?" Rufus said. "I mean, yes, I said that."

"I had a good thing going before I got involved with you. But you insisted. Come on, Kody, you said, join the winning team. You said no one would know, that you'd make it worth my while. Like an idiot I decided I could believe you. Let's look what happened. I played the game. I kept writing songs, printing S.M.E.A.R., doing shows, all the while ratting my friends out to you. You told me it was good business. You said once my album was banned, rich suckers would pay a fortune for it. I haven't seen a penny of that money."

Nuts, Rufus thought. "Have you checked with the accounting department?" he asked.

"I'm done, Polo. I'm out. You wanted a resistance, so now you have one. I even got an old friend of yours to bankroll me."

"Who?" Rufus wondered.

"Rufus Wiggin."

Rufus laughed. "Wiggin? That guy doesn't know his ass from his elbow. He's a clown. Rufus the Doofus, we all used to call him. You shouldn't believe a word he's told you."

"I believe that he doesn't like you very much," Kody sneered.

Rufus shrugged. "What's to like? Look at me."

"Really it just makes me sad. I remember believing in you, Polo. You had the chance to be part of something great, and you pissed it away for this," Kody exclaimed, waving at the bottles of floor cleaner. "I was just stupid enough to buy it."

"Caveat emptor," Rufus replied. He found himself agreeing with this opinion.

"I set myself on fire for you!" Kody whined.

Rufus was becoming seriously disillusioned by this encounter. "So that's how it is," he derided. "Committed to the Cause just as long as the art of dying for your art doesn't get too real for you? When it does, it's Rufus the Doofus to the rescue?"

Kody had the pained expression common to every confirmed asshole's jilted lover. "You're just as bad as everyone says," he shrieked.

"Worse, actually."

"Everything's a joke to you, isn't it? You couldn't care less about me."

"That is more or less correct," Rufus responded.

His face disfigured with disgust, Kody turned to leave. "Forget it. I knew I couldn't reason with you. I've always had the numbers behind me and now I have the cash, so here comes the battle you've been waiting for." In his anger, Kody stumbled over the washbasin, knocking it over and revealing a colony of dead rats curled up among the nibbled remains of the pickle sandwiches.

"Looks like I'm not the only one who wants you dead. Pick your poison, Polo."

Nuts, Rufus thought.

MY DEAREST BUTTERKNIFE

Rufus picked up the pen. "My Dearest Butterknife," he began.

"Or should I call you Ashleigh now? This has all been such foolishness, don't you agree? Let me start again.

"Dear Ashleigh, I know that, given our last conversation, I'm probably the last person on earth you want to hear from right now, but I would like to apologize for my unwarranted outburst in your driveway, as well as for the thoughtless manner in which I acted at Kody's party. You are absolutely right to point out that I take the wrong things seriously (though might I humbly suggest that you too are not entirely innocent of this flaw). I am indeed a spoiled brat, and have behaved as a holy terror lashed to the mast of my own vanity.

"These last few days have been the strangest of my life. I hope that few have experienced stranger. They have made me realize that power, whether it's financial, artistic, intellectual or otherwise, and even when it is unwanted or deserved, must be used responsibly. Above all, one must manage priorities and expectations.

"Plato writes that Socrates once said that to know the good is to do the good. I'll admit that I don't know you as well as I would like, so perhaps that quote will sound a little presumptuous in this situation. Anyway, what I'm trying to say is that I know you're good, therefore I should do good by you and therefore I should do good. I don't know if that makes sense.

"In any event, there is no Scene worth all this senselessness. Or would it make more sense to say there is nothing noble about this nihilism? Am I rambling?

"In short, I believe a new table will inevitably present itself. Isn't it weird how just now I meant to write tableau but wrote table instead. Regardless, this new table will be far brighter than anything we've seen before.

"It all begins at the treaty signing. Haven't you heard? I hope to see you there.

"Very truly yours, Rufus Redfox Wiggin.

"P.S. Don't ask how I know, but your brother is one of Them."

After composing his heartfelt missive, Rufus hollered: "Get in here Mort!"

"Yes?" Mort said, peeking his head through the door.

"Are you sure you've never seen that man who just left before?"

Mort was insistent. "I give you my word. I think he just moved here. Why do you ask, did he say something?"

"It's none of your business what he said," Rufus frowned. "Why are you so nosy all the time? Is there something you're worried I'll find out?"

"No?"

"Good, then don't fret about things that don't concern you." Rufus recalled the reason he had summoned his assistant. "Do you still have that stupid notepad?"

Mort whipped it from its holster. "Always, sir," he replied.

Rufus pondered how he should put it.

"Write this down," he said. "From this day forward, all prisoners will work eight hours a day, five days a week, with a half-hour break for lunch. Instead of students, they will be called employees."

Rufus thought that announcing the change would make him feel better. In fact, he felt just as sick as before. There must be something wrong with me, he brooded. Why can't I bring myself to do anything that will really matter?

"But Polo—" Mort objected.

Rufus cleared his throat intently.

Mort pouted. "Why do I have to say it? It makes me uncomfortable."

"Say it. It's my name."

"PuPu."

"I've decided that just Pu will be fine," Rufus announced magnanimously. "You may proceed."

"But Pu, if we don't work them until they let go of their anti-social attachment to individual expression they will never be rehabilitated! I think you must be trying to have some fun with me. Am I right? I get it. Ha ha! Very funny, sir."

"Have you known me as the sort of person to lighten the mood with some jokes?" Rufus asked.

Mort pondered the question. "You're the most serious person I know," he replied.

"Damn right I am! And I'm the one calling the shots here! Do you think it's easy to make these decisions? I'm sure you think you can do better! Is that what you want? I'd love to see a little shrimp like you trying to run the show. Just say the word, and we'll see if you can even last a day!" Imagining it, Rufus chuckled. He had come to take a certain enjoyment in his work as Polo.

Mort realized he had spoken out of turn. He withdrew his objections and continued writing.

"In accordance with my last decree," Rufus continued, "I hereby order you to distribute helmets, ear plugs, and protective eyewear to all the factory workers."

Mort felt obliged to speak up again. "Have you decided to turn this place into a country club, sir?"

"So what if I have?" Rufus replied, growing increasingly tired of having to justify himself. "Not all country clubs are created equal. For instance, the Roost has unhealthy greens, ugly, beastly tennis pros, and the most terrible food I've ever tasted. I believe they baste their prime rib in motor oil."

"We celebrated our anniversary there, don't you remember?" Mort asked tremulously. He was increasingly worried that something was wrong with Polo.

"Yes, of course. It must not have been very memorable."

"You said it was," Mort whimpered.

"Haven't you learned by now that I say a lot of stupid shit, Mort? Now can we get back to business?"

Mort felt he needed to speak up for the virtues that Polo himself had taught him to believe in. "I just want to point out that it seems a little extreme. If you think we should ease up, of course we'll ease up. But maybe we should do so gradually." He didn't want to let Polo do anything he'd regret when he was feeling like his old self again.

"Concessions are the province of the weak!" Rufus declared. He rose from his bucket where his ass had been fixed all day; at his full height, he towered over Mort. "Change must be swift and immediate! In fact, Mort, you have inspired me to reconsider. I now command the immediate release of every prisoner heretofore incarcerated under our authority!"

Mort snapped his pencil down, letting his frustration show. "What's gotten into you, Pol—Pu?" he asked. "We're apart for a day, and you're like a different person when you come back. I feel like I don't even know you anymore."

"You don't know me, Mort, and after taking some time to think maybe I've decided that what I know of you I don't like one bit."

"You don't like me?" Mort asked, his lip quivering.

"What's to like? You're an obnoxious little shit."

Behind his small white mask, Mort's face was perceptibly red. "I don't have to take this," he shouted, turning to leave.

"You'll take it and you'll like it!" Rufus shouted. It was a line he had learned from his father.

"I'll take it," Mort whined, "but I won't like it. Will there be anything else?"

"Just one small detail. After the prisoners are released, start making preparations to close up shop. I've had it."

"You're talking about the machine shop?" Mort wondered. "It has been underperforming lately."

"No, you moron, this shop. The whole shebang. The *Droit Moral* is finished."

For a moment Mort just stared at the man he thought was Polo Younger. "Finished?"

"Done. Kaput," Rufus said coolly.

"But what about all we've built? We're so close to accomplishing something truly meaningful."

Rufus decided to level with Mort. "The time has come for us to consider all that we've destroyed in the process. Thanks to us, the world is out of balance. Order must be restored, our spoils must be returned to their proper owners, and we must make good on every debt forthwith. Difficult though it may be, we must return to our, um, normal lives!"

Mort cried. "This *is* my normal life!" he sobbed.

"Not anymore," Rufus replied. "Quit being such a baby."

"I refuse to believe it," Mort insisted.

"Believe it or not, Mort, you'll probably want to start polishing up your resume soon."

Dejected and in denial, Mort asked a final time, "Is this what you really want, sir?"

"What I really want is for you to stop asking me stupid questions I've already answered," Rufus replied.

Mort's demeanor was absolutely pitiful. "What am I going to do?" he moaned.

"I don't give a shit," Rufus replied. "Now it's up to you to discover something you care about. I've personally found knot-tying to be a fun and rewarding hobby."

"I only care about what you care about. I care about you."

"Nothing else?"

"Nope."

"Pathetic," Rufus said. "This is your greatest aspiration?"

"It's for the greater good, sir."

To hell with the greater good! Rufus thought. Being a selfish dickhead had always seemed to work for him.

"Let's consider carefully how we should announce this to the others," Mort advised. "I'd hate to cause a panic."

"Screw the others," Rufus replied. "Screw everybody."

FREE AT LAST

Rufus was hanging out with the snipers atop the compound wall, drinking beer and smoking cigarettes through the hole in his mask. A foghorn sounded from the tower, dismissing the workers inside.

"Another day down the tubes," said Agent Birdsong, taking a long pull from his cigarette and tossing the butt down on the street below.

"So true," Rufus replied.

He looked out over the empty courtyard. Rufus imagined the wagons that once rolled over these cobblestones; the horses and mules drinking at the trough; Dudley Schuyler checking his watch as a crepuscular calm fell over his kingdom. Another day down the tubes.

Polo had filtered all activity through a few major ingresses; now, Rufus ordered every door in the place to be unlocked. A pair of heavy carriage doors creaked open for the first time in years. In the moaning of their rusty hinges, Rufus heard the fear of change: they had become accustomed to inaction, to keeping people inside, to being useful only by not being used. Soon, a mass of shaggy bodies shuffled out, shielding their eyes though the daylight was almost gone. Their shift was finally over.

Before long, the prisoners began to walk, run, sprint, hop, and skip away. Manically, deliriously, a streak of emaciated bodies took to the streets. Though they were worse for the wear, they already seemed to be recovering their former strength. Eventually, they began breaking off into small groups and talking familiarly, as if this were the end of any day and they were on their way to a drink. Laughing, shouting, streaming through the gates and into the afterglow of the longest day they would ever work, they were, for the moment, free at last.

Some lingered inside, certain it was a trap and that the inevitable conclusion to their confinement had merely been moved up. These prisoners had convinced themselves that the end they were working towards was a surprise bullet to the head and burial in a mass grave. They did not expect to be kicked to the curb by a thankless boot.

"What's it all mean?" asked Birdsong.

Rufus finished his beer. Somehow, he had accomplished this, though it still made him feel no better. "Well, Shitbird, I suspect it means very little," he said, tossing the empty can onto the sidewalk. "In fact, I'm afraid it means nothing at all."

Another day down the tubes.

A FORM OF SELF-ABUSE

With the prisoners free and the reeducation program dismantled, the *Droit Moral*'s administrators were extremely agitated. An emergency meeting was called, and Rufus had no choice but to sit through a series of speeches extolling the virtues of Polo's bankrupt philosophy, hastily drafted and ineptly delivered by passionate but dull underlings. He regretted having to be present, but was wary of leaving this crowd unattended. Growing bored immediately, Rufus squirmed in his seat, stared at the cracks in the ceiling, and daydreamed.

Rufus was amazed that a single person had yet to question his identity. Were they too afraid to confront him? he wondered. What twisted punishment would Polo have meted out on a subordinate who mistakenly made such a suggestion? Had Polo somehow warped their vision so thoroughly around himself that they were even unable to fathom someone orchestrating such a coup? Or could it simply be that they all were completely incompetent? The only explanations Rufus could imagine were ridiculous, but no more ridiculous than the fact that he was getting away with it.

Rufus wondered if they would even recognize he wasn't Polo if he stopped wearing the stupid mask. Did even Mortimer know what Polo's real face looked like? He doubted it. Rufus was sick of his face itching constantly, nauseated by the re-circulated stink of his own breath. The clothespin was sharp and painful; it was leaving a permanent indentation on his nose and possibly causing irreversible sinus damage. He had become a full-time mouth-breather with a wicked sore throat.

Perhaps, ultimately, they just didn't care who was under that mask. Rufus had begun to sense that the public face of the *Droit Moral*, that crafty and knowing visage that had stoked the fears and kindled the imaginations of so many, was just another façade for just another vapid bureaucracy.

Why were these men talking about membership quotas and market segmentation and quarterly projections and forecasts and branding and awareness campaigns and cover sheets and what font best represents people's hopes? Had he known it would be this sort of organization, Rufus may never have decided to infiltrate it in the first place.

Is this the forum for my big statement? he wondered. Is this where I'll find the inspiration money can't buy?

At this table, Rufus' big idea was looking very small, very insignificant, and very far away.

He was already fed up with the bowing, the curtsies, the genuflections, of all the blind reverence and demagoguery that was so self-evidently phony. He was tired of having a broom closet for an office, tired of living out Polo's belabored point about his solidarity with the everyman. It was the nature of Polo's wit that he thought he was making an original statement by putting the top dog in the gutter, the gutter punks in the corner office, and all the money in his control.

Good one, Polo, thought Rufus.

Rufus had to admit to himself that he was disappointed by the *Droit Moral*. Strip away Polo's neurotic cruelty and aesthetic hangups, and it seemed no different than any government agency or corporate bureaucracy. Was this the future? Was this the only place to be a productive member of society? If so, Rufus would be content to languish on the margins. He had never expected that playing Polo would turn out to be so *tedious*, and it was souring him on the world in totally unexpected ways. For the first time, Rufus realized he might be a misanthrope. Perhaps he was so cross and rude to people so often because he didn't actually like them. He had to wonder if busying himself with exhausting social engagements for years had simply been a very individual form of self-abuse.

Rufus decided he would expand his barrel into a riverside shanty. He started making a mental list of improvements he would like to make, simple fixes that would transform it into a permanent residence. He recalled Beckett's Malloy, another man who sought solitary seclusion, sucking on stones for nourishment. When Rufus thought of pickle sandwiches, stones sounded practically mouth-watering.

"The next to speak," crowed Mort, snapping Rufus back to reality, "will be Brother Six, our head of security."

One of Polo's Nordic gods arose. His unmasked face was open and direct, and he stood shuffling through a stack of index cards.

"Get on with it," said Rufus grumpily.

"Dear Leader," Six began with the jarring curtness of a military officer, "on behalf of the mobile patrol, I bring some very exciting news. If you recall, a few weeks ago we raided an unapproved performance space where we seized, *inter alia*, several copies of the latest issue of S.M.E.A.R. As you know, this is the official publication of the resistance."

Six proceeded to pass around copies of the Spring Quarterly to everyone in attendance. As he droned on, Rufus read his copy cover to cover. He got caught up in trying to decipher a peculiar anagram:

O'WILLY U:

FUR SUING WIG

OVER LOTTO

"The paper is run by Kody Spalmino, who you may remember is leader of the resistance and Public Enemy Number One," Six continued. "Our reports indicate that until recently his sister, one Ashleigh Victoria Spalmino, was also actively involved, but her present whereabouts are currently unknown."

"Who cares?" Rufus said. "Everyone knows Kody's just trying to make a buck and a name for himself. He'll never be a real threat. I want to hear the latest reports on Wiggin."

"With all due respect, sir, Wiggin's a reclusive nobody likely to keep to himself," Six replied. "Spalmino's a big fish, one I've been trying to fry for months."

"Your analogy is appetizing but stupid," Rufus answered.

Six continued his report unfazed. "It seems that every issue of S.M.E.A.R. is filled with a variety of alpha-numeric ciphers," he noted. "This is how they communicate the names and current locations of everyone in the resistance. We've been trying to break the code for weeks, and we're finally getting a clear picture of what we're up against."

Mort was on the edge of his seat. "And?" he asked with anticipation.

Six replied solemnly. "It seems our enemy is much larger than we imagined. They have an extensive network throughout the city, sophisticated channels of communication and, we believe, a secret cache of weapons. Thanks to today's shortsighted decision by our Dear Leader, we can only expect their numbers to grow." The beefy enforcer tried to stare Rufus down.

Rufus tried to ignore him. "What are you trying to say?" he asked. He had a pretty good idea of what Six was trying to say.

"They're preparing a major offensive," he admitted.

Mort looked anxious. "No sweat, right Six?" he asked.

"To put it bluntly, we simply don't have the manpower to stop them. Our only hope is a surprise raid to snatch Spalmino before he can act, but time is of the essence."

"How soon?" Rufus asked.

"We've received word from one of our informants that he'll be at S.M.E.A.R. tonight."

"Don't these things need to be planned?" Rufus asked. "It sounds rash, in my opinion."

"We're planning it right now," Mort reminded him.

"Aren't there some forms for me to fill out or papers to stamp?"

"No, sir."

"And what are we planning to do with Spalmino when we catch him?" Rufus wondered.

"I suppose that's up to you," Six replied.

Recalling Six's analogy, Rufus imagined a greasy fish sandwich. "Alright then, let's fry the bastard."

INELOQUENTLY-NAMED SEABIRDS

That night, Rufus stared up at where the stars were supposed to be from the flatbed of one of the *Droit*'s El Caminos. Flickering streetlights and filmy soot obscured the celestial panorama, leaving only one star in all the murky sky dimly visible.

A convoy five cars deep rolled through the streets along a circuitous path, making sure it was as conspicuous as possible. Each car was filled with eager patrolmen fingering their revolvers nervously.

Rufus felt as distant from the moment as that lonely star. He had accompanied the mission out of curiosity. This was a chance to see the mail slot where he once deposited letters to Ashleigh from her side, to steal a glimpse of the life she once led. He briefly entertained the hope that he would find her there, back by her brother's side out of familial loyalty, if nothing else. Ultimately, he decided he was glad she was far away from this.

Rufus had no reason to let the raid go on at all. He knew if he called it off, no one would challenge his edict; just as easily, he could have warned Kody, letting him slip away to the life of a fugitive. But Rufus felt swindled, bilked, sold a bill of goods by a talented and ambitious phony. He had offered to help Kody arm his rebellion because he had believed in Kody and wanted to do something to help him; in doing so, he had given up everything. Now he understood that selfishness would always trump good intentions.

The convoy broke its formation and arranged itself in a barricade around 444 4th Street. The street was quiet. Except for a single lighted room on the fourth floor, the building was dark. With as little noise as possible, the patrolmen emerged from the cars, lining up in a loose phalanx outside the door. In the crisp silence, plastic bags whispered by like tumbleweed.

Rufus eyed the drop box, a tarnished brass slot where once his hopes, his dreams, his very desires had been ferried into a rare and alluring fantasy world. Now it was just a hole in the door, no more rare or alluring than the bum sleeping under a nearby awning.

Brother Six leaned squarely against the door, poised to kick it off its hinges. He put a finger to his lips. The brigade unholstered their weapons and crept closer.

"Me first," Rufus mouthed to Six, who nodded his assent.

Six caved in the door with a blow that reverberated down the entire block; he broke things with more style and form than any strip-mall sensei could teach. When there was no more door, a narrow passageway was revealed that painted a Cimmerian shade.

Six pointed inside. Rufus stepped through the splintered door frame, taking uncertain steps forward as he took the lead. Six motioned the others to fall in behind.

Rufus shuffled ahead slowly, touching his fingertips to a wire that ran horizontally along the corridor. It was pinned down in a few places and not quite flush with the wall, which was still sticky to the touch with fresh paint. Each step took him further into darkness than the last, while he guided the dozen muffled boots behind him to an unknown terminus.

Before Rufus could realize why the wire had been abruptly directed downward, his ankle was tripping over it. He fell face-first to the floor. From under the thin coat of paint, switches sprang loose that had been spiked with roofing nails, razor wire, and glass shards fastened to leather strips. It was a technique learned from the Viet Cong that left an intruder with no time to react or recoil.

Brother Six caught a spike through his burly neck. He choked out his final orders in a pool of blood. Two men's bellies were ripped open by the jagged tentacles; their viscera spilled out, mixing in the miasma, becoming inseparable as it was squished under panicked feet. Another, blinded by an errant chunk of glass, now had only that wire along the wall to orient him.

Rufus was fine. Having fallen to the floor, he kept his head low as the barbs swung dangerously close. A nail scraping along the back of his neck induced a wince, but barely broke the skin. He listened to the groans of the maimed and mortally wounded agents, running scared into the night; the ones that could still drive peeled out in their El Caminos terrified while the rest wandered the deserted streets moaning for help.

By my own incompetence—saved! he thought.

Either unable or unwilling to move, surrounded by carnage, Rufus' mind was unable to focus on any single thought. Why am I so lucky? Wait, *am* I lucky? Is this luck? What's so lucky about it? Haven't I been looking for destruction all along? Shouldn't I be past that by now? Where I am? Hold on! What the hell was that?

The booby trap, he remembered, was named for the snares hungry sailors set to catch those ineloquently-named sea birds. Rufus made a mental note to tell Hamilton about this piece of trivia. He hoped he might include it in his novel.

The last thing he thought about was Rufus the Doofus. Then someone whacked him over the head, knocking him out cold.

DASEIN

When Rufus came to, he found himself in a familiar place. He immediately recognized the safe house where Ashleigh brought him to recover from the hullabaloo at Smitty's.

There are the crooked boards where I slept, he recalled nostalgically. There's that rusty bouquet of nails. That Thomas Cole print.

Where there had previously been nothing, the room was filled with crates of guns and ammunition. There seemed to be an assortment of makes and models, an all-purpose guerrilla starter kit.

The jittery and sour faces that were watching him were familiar, as well. Rufus recognized Kody's child brigade; soon enough, he discerned the face of their frontman as well. There wasn't a friendly mug in the bunch. Ashleigh was nowhere to be found.

Rufus would have been considerably less concerned over his predicament were he not currently duct taped to a chair dressed as Polo Younger.

"Why hello, Polo," Kody began, his voice syrupy with presumed triumph. "What a pleasant surprise. I didn't think you were the type who would get his hands dirty with the men in the field. I guess I was wrong about you."

The disciples were taking turns poking Rufus with the butts of their guns. They snickered. If Rufus had been himself, he would have snapped at them to stop it.

"You're probably wondering how we knew about the raid," Kody said smugly. "Did you really think you were the only one with double agents?"

Rufus tested the strength of his restraints, but waited to speak. He was sure they'd discover that this was just a big misunderstanding soon enough.

"My, my, what to do with you?" Kody asked, striding the room like a victorious general, opening the floor to debate. "What-to-do-with-you?"

"Cut off his balls!" yelled one.

"Fuck him up!" suggested another.

"So many possibilities," Kody said with a devilish grin. "I feel like a little kid on a hot summer day, and the Mister Ding-a-Ling truck has just come rolling up, and I don't want to have to make up my mind, I want to choose all the options. So I sit there, enjoying the very thought of it, until I realize he's already halfway down the block and I have to run after him. Then I'm huffing and puffing, trying to catch up even though I still don't want to decide, and when I get there I'm just so flustered I pick the first thing I see. And it's not what I wanted *at all*, and I'm left so unsatisfied, and I hate it and I hate ice cream and I hate everything!"

"Kill him!"

"Torture him!"

"My point, Polo, is that I've been waiting a long time for this. But surely you've figured that out already. By now I must have thought up at least a thousand ways to kill you. Maybe more. Definitely more.

But now, at the moment of my triumph, I'm conflicted. Should I fulfill my fantasy or not? I don't know what I'll do when I have nothing left to fantasize about."

"Pull out his tongue!"

"Cut off his nose!"

"I think I might like to see you publicly humiliated first. Oh! I know! Wouldn't it be fun if you worked for me for a while? Is that something you'd be interested in?"

Rufus shook his head. He felt that all this trouble could have been avoided if they had just bothered to look under his mask while he was unconscious. He just didn't have it in him to interrupt Kody now.

"You see, Polo, I didn't need an exposé in the *Daily Reader* to tell me that you were a man driven by his own failure. What else could explain– this?" he asked derisively, gesturing to Polo's fashion. "Don't get me wrong, though, I see where you're coming from. It's not my thing, but I could see it working if you submitted yourself to my ideas. After all, if I were to treat you like you'd punish me, I'd only perpetuate this horrible, vicious cycle, reinforcing the very negative ideas we're trying to overcome. We don't want that, do we?"

Rufus shook his head again.

"To defeat you, then, I have to be better than you. Which, of course, I am. In fact, I've already won, really. But I want something more than moral satisfaction, because above all else I believe in justice. In case you forgot, again, we had a deal and you didn't honor it. It's only fair that I be made whole, don't you agree? The most equitable remedy I can think of would be for you to place your future in my hands, trusting my guidance as you redress your past abuses. That way, we'll both be made whole together! Doesn't that sound fun?

"Either way, Polo, your reign is over. The crown has inevitably been passed to me."

Rufus finally felt compelled to speak. "Fuck that, Kody."

"Cut out his heart!" rejoined one of the disciples.

"Silence!" Kody demanded. "He doesn't deserve to be made a martyr! One thing I will do, however, is see once and for all who, or what, is lurking behind this goofy mask."

Finally, Rufus thought. Kody would see that this was a big misunderstanding, that Rufus had been making his own sacrifice to The Cause, engaged in a charade not unlike The Cause itself. As Kody's surprisingly soft hands untied the mask, he tried not to laugh. He thought about how funny it would be when Kody discovered the truth. A charade of a charade of a charade. Go figure. Let's discuss over drinks.

But alas, the pleasant fantasy had to come to an end. Kody peeled off the Cao Cao mask and discovered that the human face of Polo Younger was Rufus Wiggin's.

Rufus thought, Surprise!

"I should've known," Kody said.

"It's me," said Rufus. "Have you figured it out? I killed Polo, disposed of the body, and decided to pose as him in order to infiltrate his organization! The Polo you talked to yesterday was me! A charade of a charade of a charade!"

Kody nodded. "It all makes sense," he said, paying no attention to what Rufus had to say. "It's brilliant really. Why are the biggest clichés always so true? Keep your friends close and your enemies closer. Hiding in plain sight this whole time. Pretending to be your own worst enemy."

"In more ways than you'll ever know," Rufus sighed.

"I always had my suspicions, of course, but I must say you're more clever than I thought, Polo. My sister always was the weak link, so it makes sense that you would use her to get closer to me. The tapes were a nice touch too; giving us the very thing you stole in order to earn our trust. Priceless."

Rufus was beginning to worry that Kody didn't quite have a handle on the nature of the misunderstanding. He would try to explain. "First of all, I didn't have your tapes until the Mayor got them for me. I just paid for them. I asked Spit – that's Mayor Shyne – excuse me, Spit is just what I call him. I don't think he likes it very much, actually. Not that I care what that boob thinks," he began. So far, he was failing miserably. "What I'm trying to say is Spit has gotten me all sorts of things over the years, not just your tapes, and that includes a whole new wardrobe. Not these clothes I'm wearing now, naturally. These are ridiculous. Who would wear sweatpants outdoors voluntarily? Well, athletes might have to, I suppose, though in my opinion wind pants or shorts are more agreeable. Don't you agree?" Rufus rambled on nervously. He was concerned that his point was slipping away. "Did you know I used to be a pole vaulter myself? I made the all-city team, in fact. I actually made a go of it for the first time in ages recently, using a rubbery branch instead of a pole. Long story short, it snapped and I landed in a cesspool. It wasn't as bad as it sounds. With a little practice and some better equipment, I could be back in shape in no time. Spit, by the way, is a golfer, which is a useless pastime and not even a sport in my opinion."

Kody considered this intelligence carefully. "So you're saying the mayor is in on it too?"

"No, you imbecile!" Rufus shouted, for the moment forgetting his vulnerable position, "and neither am I! Don't you get what I'm trying to tell you? I bludgeoned Polo with a ceramic soup bowl that my friend made when she died – that is, she died while making it, or maybe she died after making it, or was it that she died because she made it? I can never remember and I suppose it doesn't matter. The important thing is I cracked it over Polo's big ugly head, tied him to a Shaker chair, known for its simple, yet durable and hard to escape design, then I asked my cook Angelo to stab him because I couldn't bring myself to do it. Well, I probably could have done it but Angelo always used to make these stabbing threats so I thought he would enjoy it. To each his own, isn't that what you were saying just now? Then I doused my house in gasoline. In fact, I picked up some technical skills from the way you handled the can that night at Smitty's. This time, however, I let the whole thing go up in flames. I don't think there would have been enough vomit in the world to quell that blaze. Since then I've been pretending to be Polo so I can sign a peace treaty with the mayor and end the war."

Kody stared at Rufus blankly. "That's the dumbest thing I've ever heard," he said.

"You have to believe me," Rufus pleaded. "I know it sounds absolutely unbelievable, but it's all true."

Kody seemed more amused than anything. "Keep talking, Polo. All you can do is dig a deeper hole."

"I wish you would quit calling me that," Rufus protested. "No one realizes what a drag it is being Polo Younger. All those forms to stamp, nothing to eat but a steady diet of pickle sandwiches. Oh, and did you know that Polo's gay? Or should I say, was gay? Since he's now deceased. I'm not judging him though. Like you say, to each his own.

"Except for killing, of course. Killing people is wrong. It's hard to believe that we're both guilty of murder, isn't it Kody? I still feel sick about it. It made it worse to hear your speech about the ice cream and deciding not to kill me. That is, deciding not to kill Polo. Sorry, that came out wrong again. That is, deciding not to kill me playing Polo. Actually, could you explain the ice cream story again? I stopped listening for a second."

At this point, Rufus was reasonably certain that as long as he kept talking, Kody and his followers would remain at bay. After weeks of emotional constipation, it felt good to unload. "What I'm trying to say is, you would be shocked by what you don't know about a person. Why didn't Polo come out of the closet? He was already dictator of the city, what could anyone do?" Rufus chuckled. "Dictator."

"Just this morning I was sitting at this terribly boring meeting when Brother Six started talking about your operations. Brother Six is such a strange moniker don't you think? And according to him, you and your disciples and such outnumber us. By us I mean all the people I'm pretending to lead. What I found most interesting about this was the fact that no one seemed to realize that you were already one of them, or, I should say, one of us. Or one of you? What would be correct in this case?"

"I have no idea what you're talking about," Kody said. He looked around nervously at his crew. "I've never met you before in my life. Well, I met you as Rufus Wiggin, of course, but—Goddammit, Polo, now you've got me doing it!"

"My apologies, I must be mistaken, wink wink nudge nudge," replied Rufus. "Why are we still playing games, Kody? You've already won, so why don't you just let me go?"

Kody's laugh was humorless and mean. "I can't believe you fell for it," he said. "Look numbnuts, *this* is my army. In this room is my extensive network. Do you want introductions? I wouldn't even have these weapons if I didn't have your arsenal to raid. I've already told you about the double agents. It wasn't hard to spread a few rumors and watch them rise to the top. George Washington used the same tactic against the British: inflate the size of your army, mix things up with some espionage, and soon your enemy will be running scared."

"I'm not the enemy!" Rufus cried with exasperation. He was increasingly unnerved by the guitar player's obsession with military strategy and eager for their conversation to be concluded.

"You're crafty Polo, I'll give you that," Kody continued. "But in light of the fact that you tricked me into thinking you were someone else, and weaseled your way into my life, and tried to seduce my sister," (and succeeded! Rufus thought), "I'm rescinding my promise not to kill you. From now on, the only way to keep your life is to follow my orders."

"I'd do anything to stay alive," Rufus replied, "but who's to say I'm not already dead? Maybe I died in your stupid booby trap, or in the Cahoos, or when my house burned down, or at Smitty's. If I'm not dead, naturally we can assume I'm alive. If I'm alive after all those incidents, then I'll have to assume I'm incapable of death. I can only conclude that I've been tethered to this world by some unknown force for some unknown reason. Perhaps that reason is to discover there is no reason at all. Thus, in my own small way, I must be immortal, if not now then in the future. In fact, one cannot be immortal in the present, as inherently it can only be judged at some future moment. Otherwise, at any given time we could deem everyone living immortal, not yet having any irrefutable evidence that they would die. Yet, we know this isn't true. Smitty died. So did Marie St. Alban. He left a barrel. She left a soup bowl. Maybe in the end life and death don't really matter as much what you leave behind. It makes me sad if I have to die now because I have nothing."

"Oh my god, shut up!" Kody finally interjected. "Your relentless rambling is giving me a headache. Look, go ahead and sign the peace treaty. It's nothing but a worthless scrap of paper anyway. And since one of us has to be a man of his word, The Going out of Business Sale will perform at the event as promised – even though I agreed to your original invitation under false pretenses."

"I look forward to it," Rufus smiled. "For the record, I do want to tell you how terrific your album is. I overpaid dearly just to have it. I suppose you already know all about that."

"If I let you go, will you shut up?"

"Most likely," Rufus assured him. "Either way, you won't have to listen to me anymore."

Kody worried he was making a mistake. "I expect no funny business between now and the ceremony or the deal is off, understand?"

"It's interesting you should say that. Your sister used the same expression. Funny business. It was under different circumstances of course, but it's strange that I should be in a second predicament where it would come up. I'm inclined to say that the circumstances in which she said them were more normal, though normalcy is, you'll agree, very subjective. I suppose that's how this all began. I wanted to be normal. What I mean is, I wanted to be like the people I considered normal. What was normal for my own life was, to me, a bland lacuna, just a lot of tired rubbish. To others it was desirable; Satch, in particular. Might I add that your drummer is quite the cut-up? He and Jay Hudson Hamilton are like two peas in a pod."

Kody had a disciple cut their prisoner loose. As they left the room cross and unsatisfied, Rufus continued.

"It could be that I'm confusing normalcy for meaning, or at least conflating the two somehow. Perhaps the word I'm looking for is *Dasein*. Yet, one can't go looking for *Dasein*, because *Dasein* is always already present. It can't even be conceived of from an objective perspective, let alone defined from anywhere outside of itself. Yet perhaps simply being can be enough, and I can be content with what I've already done and will continue to do. Unless, of course, you kill me. However, you've said you won't, and we've already established that I may or may not be immortal, so this might be a futile line of inquiry.

"If you think about it in the right way, it appears that I've already found what I was looking for. Now all I have to look forward to is the day that I reject hope, decide to conform and accept the absurd. Doesn't that sound like a Cause we can all believe in?"

A charade of a charade of a charade.

THE LAST PART:

Cahoos Falling

TWO CURRENTS FLOWING TOGETHER

Somewhere deep in the bowels of the hydroelectric substation, an operations manual was plucked from the shelf, dusted off, and opened to a set of instructions entitled "Emergency Restore." The engineers set about pulling levers, reading meters, pushing buttons, turning knobs, and tweaking dials. Beeps and dings filled the room, screens lit up, and equipment hummed. The dam was released. First, a trickle emerged, followed by a stream, until at last the rivers surged again between their natural banks.

As the falls came roaring back to life, Rufus and Spit became stranded on Arrowhead Point. They had walked across the riverbed earlier in the day when it was still dry; now they were hemmed in on all sides. To serve as a podium, they had taped a microphone to Rufus' barrel and wired it to whatever speakers they had been able to carry with them. As Spit prepared to speak, Rufus, dressed as Polo for the final time, fiddled with the P.A. system.

A sculpture was being erected in the viewing area. "What's that?" Spit pointed.

"No clue," Rufus answered.

Had he bothered to notice what Spit was referring to, Rufus would have seen a dozen men struggling to raise the installation. It was Ashleigh's big statement. In the shape of a perfect arch, twenty feet high at its apogee, a human skeleton, bending backwards, had been intricately fashioned, cast first in plaster and finished with a mile of tin foil. There was a fluidity in the structured madness of its design. It captured the many ages of man, discovering fun and even some sense in the grim trend of our own inevitable arcs. To everyone engaged in the debates about art's role; about the effectiveness of art with all its flaws; about civilization's trials and errors; about the big ideas; about poor planning; about the bones thrown to the masses to keep them ignorant and apathetic; about the leveling power of loosened purse strings; in short, to everyone it spoke of triviality and glory, of the undeserving and the misunderstood. In a way its effect was broad, but it was in the details that the best and the worst of the city were revealed. When he finally looked up, Rufus was struck with wonder. He beheld the human figure, in all its awkward and imperfect majesty, realized perfectly.

Ashleigh hid in the tree overlooking Rufus' camp. She watched as people pointed, poked, stared at, and snapped pictures of her personal tribute to the first artist to inspire her as a child. The shape of Marie St. Alban's final consummated passion was now memorialized for all to see. Ashleigh heard one person call it stunning.

"It reminds me of something, but I can't place it," remarked another.

A woman wondered, "Who did it?"

The crowd looked assiduously for a maker's mark. They couldn't believe an artist would forget to sign their own work. "Doesn't say," someone acknowledged at last.

When news of the treaty spread, all the political exiles and self-proclaimed expatriates returned to the city, and the traffic jam that culminated now at Ashleigh's Arch was worse than any the city had experienced since its exemplar's roadster first baffled drivers on

Highway 27. Rufus saw many of his old friends milling about, including: Quincy Quill (President of the Third United Bank of Albany); Guy Alexander (proud owner of the Schenectady Electrics baseball club); and Ulysses Rand (Managing Partner of Troy & Associates). He was moved to see that even Penelope Trouissant, his high school sweetheart, had come looking lovelier than ever, until he remembered that as far as she knew he was still missing.

While seeing his old flames and drinking buddies again inspired some sentimental stirrings, Rufus no longer felt like one of the gang. They were nothing but a fading snapshot of a different time in a yellowing yearbook buried in the rubble of Alistair's Asshat. In fact, they had probably been bulldozed away and dumped in the river by now. Rufus had already decided that, even if he hadn't been in disguise, he would to try to slip away from the ceremony quietly, preferring to leave his whereabouts forever unknown to everyone he ever cared about, damn the rest.

Rufus continued to scan the crowd. In the crowded parking lot, a line of patient book bearers snaked through the spaces between the cars. At the front of the line, propped up against a station wagon and soused beyond all hope was that distinguished man of arts and letters, Jay Hudson Hamilton. His protege Satch sat beside him, guiding the pen in his hand through a series of loops and squiggles over every title page.

"Who should I make this out to?" Satch was asking over and over.

Across the Beverwyck River to the east, a handful of *Droit Moral* true believers paraded in protest. They wore sandwich boards scrawled with misspelled slogans, cursed the apostates, vowed to live according to every commandment that Polo Younger had once endorsed, and refused to ever wear shoes again.

Once, the *Droit Moral* had seemed like a force capable of paralyzing the entire city; now, the foundering army consisted of a few remaining dogmatists with little more than the reflections of their own silly masks to rely on, the distasteful crumbs of an unfinished pickle sandwich.

"Not a sky diaper in sight," Rufus heard one say. He looked up to confirm the clear skies for himself.

To the west, on the other side of the Van Schaick River, Kody was setting up to perform. Although it was billed as a concert by The Going out of Business Sale, for all intents and purposes it had become a solo show, holding the potential to be Kody's star turn. Ashleigh, it turned out, was the true artist of the family, and Satch, even if he never picked up his drum sticks again, was the very epitome of a rock star. Despite the presence of a growing gang of disciples, who kept a wary eye on the assembled remnants of their erstwhile enemies, Kody had never looked lonelier.

Standing at the edge of Arrowhead Point, where the two rivers came together rapidly all around his feet, Rufus watched the flowing waters mix and fold together, pick up speed, and then suddenly disappear into a mist. From his vantage point, the falls were only apparent from the sound of their churning. After gravity's brief interlude, the river continued downstream, appearing much smaller on the horizon, similar in composition but altered significantly.

The Cahoos remained more real to him as a rendering; while others enjoyed the spectacular vista, Rufus could picture it only by remembering Louis Blanc's painting. This was the sacrifice he made in order to bring the dormant majesty back to life. He tried to experience it vicariously by basking in the rapt and enamored expressions on the faces now jockeying for positions above the rusty balustrade. In this sense, Rufus had a clearer view of the event than anyone.

The shutters of countless cameras, hoping to capture the sight of hundreds of thousands of gallons of water plunging continuously over the cliff – of a fluid curtain one thousand feet wide – of a torrent of endless waves falling for seventy feet, spraying a frothy effervescence everywhere before dissolving in an instant, clicked in mindless rhythm. A tentative rainbow emerged in the mist, embracing the expectant skyline uncertainly. To returning residents, it may have been a promising omen or a disappointing reminder of everything they had left behind. Even the elusive sun, which of late had not deigned to show its face in these parts, found the scene worthy of an appearance.

"What a turnout," Spit said to Rufus, rubbing his face excessively. "It looks like the entire international press corps is here."

Rufus scanned the small mob of newsmen and camera crews. "That might be a slight exaggeration," he replied.

Spit had his mind on something else. "I'm going to be the hero!" the mayor shouted. "You better believe I'm going to milk this for all it's worth."

Rufus didn't want to picture Spit milking anything. He was growing increasingly annoyed with his treaty partner. "Cover the mic if you're going to keep making moronic statements!" he hissed.

"I can't believe this worked," Spit said, his voice booming through the speakers. "I'm sorry I ever doubted your genius, Ru–."

Rufus jumped between Spit and the barrel. "Cover the mic!" he hissed more loudly.

Spit grew quiet. "Do you think we should begin?" he asked uncertainly.

Rufus glared. "Spit, if you don't get this started, so help me God..."

"Okay, okay," he whispered. Rufus stepped out of the way and Spit addressed the crowd. "Ladies and gentlemen, as your mayor, it's my honor to welcome you to this joyous event. Today, the troubles that have divided us for far too long come to an end, and we begin a new chapter in our lives."

The crowd erupted in applause. Even when he finished second at a Pro-Am tournament in Jersey City, Spit had never received such a thunderous ovation. All the attention made his nervous ticks grow all the more pronounced. He had a thumb in each ear, holding his hands behind his head in the most casual manner he could think of.

"It's only fitting that this momentous occasion be held here at the Cahoos Falls, the most storied site in the city. Running water has graciously been provided for us today by the nice folks at Schuyler Hydroelectric."

"Boo!" yelled everyone, for obvious reasons.

"Boo!" cried the *Droit* hardliners, for reasons known only to themselves.

"It was here on Arrowhead Point," Spit continued, "that Degan, uh, Deguna..."

Rufus leaned over and quietly interrupted. "Deganawida, you idiot," he pronounced.

"Degunuwita, am I saying that right?" Spit responded as the multitudes watched.

"I *will* strangle you," Rufus warned.

"It was here," the mayor stuttered, "that a heroic leader planted the Great Tree of Peace and took a fateful leap over the falls to end the hostilities of his day and create a family-friendly public space that everyone can enjoy. An inspiration, indeed. With that, I would like to read a poem written for this occasion by our own Poet Laureate, Jay Hudson Hamilton."

Hamilton groggily tipped his cap to the raving throng while Spit read from the scrap of paper the writer had given him. The piece was entitled "A Limerick."

"This old town is a real tough bitch, I say
Legs behind her ears
Down and Out of context
Up and In the sack
On the chin, on the kisser, on her back
A real tough old bitch, I say
I loved her once
Down and Out of focus
Up and Away, goodbye
Who knew whores could fly?
A real tough old bitch, I say."

Satch clapped vehemently. Among the rest of the crowd, the excitement dissipated.

"What a terrible poem," Rufus said to himself. "Why would Jay be moved to write that?"

Hamilton had dozed off during the reading. He awoke briefly to flip everyone the bird.

The mayor kept the ceremony moving. "Now I'd like to turn it over to Polo Younger, who will say a few words," he said.

"Yay!" cried the *Droit* hardliners.

"Boo!" yelled everyone else, for obvious reasons.

"Thank you, Mayor Shyne," Rufus began, knowing this would have to be his most convincing impersonation. "As many of you know, I'm a poor, pathetic turd of a human being."

"Fuck you, Polo!" yelled one of Rufus' city-abandoning pals.

"I'm a complete and utter failure," Rufus continued. "My face is so ugly that I have no choice but to always cover it with a mask."

As he paused to look over the crowd, an uncomfortable silence hung over everyone. "Is there anything else you'd like to say?" Spit asked, nervously.

"Yes," Rufus resumed. "As founder and Dear Leader of the *Droit Moral*, a movement bereft of any coherent ideology yet full of draconian dogma, whose adherents consist of a group of boring autocrats who want to force terrible art on everyone, I hereby repudiate everything I ever told anyone to believe. That's all, folks. I quit."

"Suck my balls, Polo!" yelled Ramsey von Tromp. Another Schuyler alum, he was currently serving as Undersecretary of something or other at the World Bank.

The mayor presented Rufus with a copy of the treaty and an absurdly large fountain pen. The document had been printed with a fading inkjet printer on the back of a Chinese take-out menu. It did, however, bear the city seal, which made it official enough for Rufus.

He had, however, never been one to pass up an opportunity for insult. "You're an idiot, Spit," he reiterated quietly while forging Polo's endorsement.

Spit then added his signature. Below it, the reversed lunch specials were clearly legible.

Rufus addressed the remaining *Droit* holdouts. "Now, listen, you losers. Go home!" Then he turned to the everyone else. "And to the rest of you, I pray you remember me less than fondly, curse my existence, and burn my effigy in the streets! Turn my life into a cautionary tale; tell your kids that a small-minded asshole named Polo will get them in their sleep if they don't eat their peas; use my name as a euphemism for a person who can't get laid!"

Quincy Quill elbowed his companions playfully. "Already do!" he cracked.

"Been doing it for years!" added Guy Alexander.

"The *Droit Moral* is hereby disbanded," Rufus declared, provoking chants of "Never surrender!" and "Turncoat!" and "Sham!" and "Phony!" from the hardliners.

The mayor concluded the ceremony as pompously as possible. "With all the powers vested in me as your humble public servant –

who, by the way, is running for reelection in the fall, just remember this moment when you're in that voting booth – I formally declare that the war is over!"

At that moment, Kody launched into an acoustic version of the Schuyler Academy Fight Song. In this city, the tune was well known by alumni and alumnots alike, and Rufus had decided it would be a fitting number for the occasion. Thus began a celebration as liberated as any party thrown during the halcyon days of Alistair's Asshat. People kissed under the rainbow, groped each other against the balustrades, dry humped on Ashleigh's Arch. Champagne corks popped, joints were lit, bumps were snorted off the hoods of parked cars. Groups of strangers shared cigars. Hands disappeared up skirts and were allowed to remain missing. People laughed and danced.

Watching the happiness and knowing he had brought it all to bear, Rufus felt positively beatific. Despite his earlier resolution, he wished he could just rip off the mask and join his chums in revelry. Unfortunately, he was hopelessly marooned on Arrowhead Point. His exit would require long leaps onto slippery rocks across a perilous maelstrom. One miscalculation, one bad landing, one shoe with worn treads, and he would be dragged helplessly over the falls. His lifeless corpse, battered by the rocks, would be tossed out in the splashback, still dressed as Polo Younger. He hadn't considered this prospect when he suggested placing the podium on the island. It seemed like a good idea at the time.

Rufus was thinking about how poorly Spit would handle the explanations, should he ever manage to escape Arrowhead Point himself, when he heard a familiar voice cry out.

"Imposter!" screamed the late-arrival.

A hush grew over the crowd as a loping figure, clad in a hospital gown and bandaged from head to toe, appeared. Rufus recognized Polo immediately, wandering onto the scene along the shores of the Beverwyck towards the diminished ranks of his followers. The skin beneath his bandages seeped with a purulent ooze, and blood from Angelo's stab wound was apparent through the gown. The crowd gasped and murmured at the appearance of a real live mummy. Polo's own men shrank from the grisly sight.

"Guess what, Rufus? You can't tie a knot to save your life!" Polo yelled.

Nuts, Rufus thought.

"Oh, God," Spit muttered, doubling over to calm his panicked breathing, "a ghost!"

"Imposter!" Polo repeated.

Rufus tried to play it cool. "I've never seen this scarred freak in my life," he said.

"This is all a ruse! This peace is illegitimate!" Polo cried. "That man is not Polo Younger! I'm Polo Younger!"

Ulysses Rand, who was standing nearby, eyed the ragged creature. "He certainly looks like Polo Younger," he remarked dryly, taking a puff on his cigar.

"Shut up, Rand," the real Polo snapped. "Don't think I've forgotten all the times you locked me in the trunk of your car!"

"I have," Rand said. "Move on already, loser."

"I didn't approve this treaty!" Polo plodded ahead. "There is no ceasefire! We are still at war!"

"Get lost, jerkoff," said Ramsay von Tromp.

"Take a hike, pal," added Quincy Quill.

"Kick rocks, dickhead," reiterated Guy Alexander.

Among the crowd, Polo searched out Rufus' staff, who always came when the waterfall was turned on. He pointed to Angelo, who was crisply dressed and eating a sandwich. "That man stabbed me," he cried, "while that man watched." He nodded toward Ramon, but Ramon was too busy making out with a chubby woman in a belly shirt to notice. At last, he turned to Rufus. "And him," he said, voice trembling, pointing across the river to Arrowhead Point, "He's an arsonist and an attempted murderer! He tied me up and tried to burn me at the stake! But despite being badly burned, I escaped alive!"

"I wish someone would tie you up again," replied von Tromp. "My tee time is rapidly approaching."

"That man," said Polo, pausing dramatically, "is Rufus Wiggin!"

Some people recognized the name and gasped. For a few moments, Rufus considered keeping up the charade. Instead, he decided that after trying to change himself, after trying to be someone he was not, it was time to start being Rufus Wiggin.

"He's right," Rufus confessed. He removed the mask, shook his glorious mane free of the restraints that had bound it for too long, and took a deep breath of fresh air. "It is I, Rufus Wiggin, son of Alistair, the foremost coxswain of calamity!" he exclaimed.

To Rufus' surprise and Polo's chagrin, the announcement re-energized the mob. Among the frenzied pockets of resumed celebration, Rufus noticed someone rustling in the tree. He tried to make out a face, but Ashleigh, straining to hear as much as possible, had covered herself with a leafy branch. She leaned in closer.

"Way to go, Rufus!" yelled Quill.

"Drinks on me at the Stanwick, Wiggin!" hollered Hugo Harmon. He would have been there earlier but his flight from Prague was delayed.

Penelope Trouissant, whose curves had grown more womanly since high school, shook her derriere enticingly. "You're all mine tonight, Wiggy," she purred. "It'll be prom night all over again."

Hamilton, who had an ear for these things, shouted from the parking lot. "Hot dog!"

"Best prank ever!" exclaimed von Tromp, the World Bank administrator. He was currently straddling the binoculars like a mechanical bull.

Ulysses Rand, who was standing beside his charred classmate, blew a cloud of smoke in his face. "Up yours, Polo," he added personally.

"No one throws a party like Rufus Wiggin!" Hamilton cheered.

"Wig!" said Satch, flapping his arms like a mad man.

"Hey Satch!" replied Rufus, shouting over the river from the tip of the Arrowhead.

"Thanks again for the clothes, man," Satch called back. "You have no idea how much ass they've gotten me!"

"My pleasure, Satch. Just save some for the rest of us!"

Satch waved. "Not a chance."

Before his old nemesis could slink away to the parking lot, Rufus turned his attention to the heap of dirty unraveling bandages that was once Polo Younger. "Having walked a mile in your sweats," he admitted, "I can honestly say that there's much more to you than I gave you credit for in high school. I'm sorry for trying to kill you, but you're still a didactic boor. I've bested you once again!"

"You tell 'em, baby," said Penelope, blowing Rufus a kiss.

Kody shouted close to his mic, interrupting the love parade with a shriek of feedback. "This is bullshit! Rufus Wiggin is Polo Younger! Why can't you people see that his is all part of the act?"

Quincy asked, "Who's this asshole?"

"Shut up and play, Bob Dylan!" shouted Alexander.

"As for you, Kody," Rufus continued, "I'm not sorry I puked on you and I would do it again if I had the chance. It would have served you right if you burned, but even you ought to be protected from your own bad intentions sometimes. Is there really any difference between an artist pretending to be a revolutionary, and a revolutionary pretending to be an artist? You're both didactic boors!"

"Lies!" Kody maintained. "I saw it with my own two eyes. Rufus is Polo!"

"You're fucking insane!" Ashleigh said, hopping from her low branch to the ground near Kody's platform. Rufus could barely hide his elation upon seeing her.

Greta Spalmino, who had come out with Herb because it had been weeks since they had talked to Kody, shook her head. "Such language, Ashleigh," she scolded from her lawn chair, which was set up in front of the stage.

Ashleigh ignored her mother and confronted Kody. "You could never do what Rufus has done," she said. "You're just a scared little boy who never follows through on anything."

Kody scoffed. "*I* never follow through? You're the one who gave up and went running back home to mommy and daddy!"

That reminded Herb. "Ashleigh, did you give your brother his birthday present?" he asked.

"Not now, Dad," Ashleigh begged. She climbed onto the stage. "Kody, what great cause did I give up on? One that never existed? A scheme to advance yourself at my expense, at the expense of everyone?"

"Your sculpture sucks," Kody said petulantly.

"At least it's mine. Though I'm sure you'll try to find a way take credit for it. Besides, I've already sold it, so even by your own standards I'm already more of a success than you!"

Herb's face lit up. "Terrific!" he said. "A famous artist living at my house!"

"I'll admit I should have explained my plans to you," Kody said. "But you can't say I'm not a success, Ash! I won! I beat Polo

Younger, if you would just admit he and Rufus Wiggin are one and the same! Look at my army! Five *Droit* agents killed in a single attack."

Herb and Greta looked at each other. They decided that Kody must be speaking in some sort of code or macabre hyperbole.

"You're a monster!" Ashleigh yelled. Realizing it had been more pleasant inside the tree, she disappeared back up the branches.

"You should be nice to your brother, Ashleigh," Greta shouted behind her.

"Be careful in that tree," Herb added.

"That's it, go and hide!" exclaimed Kody.

Meanwhile, Polo, who was caught up in his own drama, shouted "Turncoat!" at the young guitar player who had always, as far as anyone else was concerned, been his enemy. The irony was not lost on Rufus.

A charade of a charade of a charade, he thought.

Polo rallied his supporters, who tore off their sandwich boards and charged the strand, hopping the rocks to Arrowhead Point, which was to the quickest route to Kody and his men. Spit looked like he might have a seizure at any moment. Rufus eyed their advance nervously, trying to figure out an escape.

Kody once again assumed the pose of a general. Herb and Greta couldn't comprehend what they were seeing. "Troops, attention!" their son ordered. His disciples, who only came because they were promised a fight, fell in line. "Charge!"

Fighters on both sides were now maneuvering from rock to rock, rapidly closing in on the island. Every determined jump brought them one step closer to Rufus. Trapped between enemies on both sides, the only way out was ahead of him. He would have to put himself at the mercy of the falls. If his streak of luck held, he'd hit an air pocket and land safely in the plunge pool. If not, he was a goner.

Rufus ripped the microphone from the barrel, pried off the lid and jumped inside. He removed Polo's garments once and for all, tossing them down the river ahead of him. Exposed from the waist up, his bare legs concealed within the round stump, Rufus once again delivered his parting speech.

"Our best days are ahead!" he shouted.

"Damn right they are," said Quill. He was slated to receive a million dollar bonus after laying off half of the workers at his bank.

"I love you, Wiggy!" added Penelope.

"Which is worse," Rufus asked, "Ignorance or apathy?"

"I don't know and I don't care!" yelled Hugo, recognizing the cue.

"I've been knuckle-deep, nay, elbow-deep in the hot-wet stink of new adventure! I've feasted on the loamy loins and succulent sides of nubile temptresses," Rufus announced, causing Ashleigh to blush. "I was conscripted into the great war of ideas, bought and sold on the marketplace of ideas!"

"You tell 'em, Rufus!" cheered von Tromp.

"I've fought valiantly for a noble cause, defending virtue from the barbarous throngs of the disenchanted."

"It sounds like we have a lot of catching up to do," suggested Rand.

"I'm no longer at war with myself," Rufus said. "And today, thanks to me, we are no longer at war among ourselves. Enjoy the peace, my friends." He turned from the crowd and looked up at the shuffling branches. "Goodbye Ashleigh," he said.

Rufus hopped the barrel over to the tip of Arrowhead Point and crouched inside.

"Seal me up, Spit," he commanded.

Instead, Spit tried to worm his way inside. "Take me with you!" he wailed.

"Get your own damn barrel!" Rufus said. He shoved the mayor away, tipping the barrel precariously. "Just seal me up."

Before Spit returned with the lid, Polo shouted for Rufus' attention. "Wait!" he screamed.

"Goddamn it, Polo. I'm busy right now!"

Polo called to Rufus feebly from the shore. "Why do you hate me so much?"

Rufus realized he had never really thought about it before.

"I guess because you hate me," he replied. "Why do you hate me so much?"

"I guess because you hate me," Polo said.

"Well, tough shit, Polo." He called again to the mayor. "Spit, get over here and seal me up! God, you're useless."

Rufus crouched down while Spit pounded the lid tight with his fist. He tried to ignore the instant claustrophobia. With a little help from the mayor, Rufus mustered some torque, got the barrel onto its side, and rolled into the river just as the marauders came ashore. He was sure Spit could fend for himself. In any event, they were too late for Rufus. He had already been swept away in the rapids.

"I'm The Going Out of Business Sale," Kody announced from the stage while his disciples fought his battle for him. He flicked on his amp. The melee raged. "This one goes out to Polo Younger. It's called 'Get with the Pogrom.' 1-2-3-4."

Inside the barrel, Kody's song was but a muted bluster accenting the watery score. The current tumbled, slapped, pushed and pulled the barrel toward the falls, tossing Rufus around just as effortlessly. He tried to inventory the few items left to his name: a few outfits; the pieces of St. Alban's shattered bowl; a hardcover edition of *All the Knots You Need to Know*; an early draft of *The Banana-Boob Republic*; a copy of The Going Out of Business Sale's *Get with the Pogrom* on vinyl.

Not such a bad haul in the end, he thought. A good record is a good record.

Given the events of the last couple months, Rufus had some success in trying to convince himself that this wasn't the stupidest thing he'd ever done. After all, at least sixteen people had gone over the Cahoos in a barrel, and eleven had survived, including Deganawida, a 63-year-old spinster who went with her cat, and a guy who went over twice.

That would be almost 69%, Rufus figured. A passing grade and, as Hamilton would surely point out, an auspicious number!

Unfortunately, as he clattered around in the confinement of his vessel, he remembered that most of those people hadn't gone over the falls on a lark. They trained for months, sometimes years. Rufus felt the barrel being pulled ever more quickly as it approached the edge. The rumbling of the falls grew louder. Rufus held his breath.

Silence fell over the valley. The crowd stood in awe, wringing their hands and waiting. The photographers forgot to snap pictures. Even the armies, on the verge of Spit's inevitable surrender, halted their attacks to watch. In this stillness, only Kody continued to play, his thin melodies the de facto soundtrack to Rufus' bold departure.

Ashleigh's eyes remained fixed on the bobbing cylinder, now teetering on the edge of oblivion. As she stood there she decided that if Rufus miraculously survived she would be sure to send flowers to the hospital before leaving town forever.

He's just a guy I slept with once, she told herself.

At last, the barrel made its date with gravity. As the cask plummeted through a narrow chute in the watery curtain, Rufus was flipped end over end over end. He had experienced this sensation of vertigo twice before: once on a boardwalk ride in Maine, and again atop this very barrel at Smitty's. It seemed determined either to be the death of him or to save him. Yet more was relying on the barrel this time than Rufus alone. It bore the shopworn and haggard dreams of an entire city that had forsaken its past for its future, only to learn that its future was dependent on its past. A gesture such as this was the only thing that could inspire them all; foolhardy and maybe even a little brave, Rufus decided it might as well be him to do it.

Rufus didn't know if he would survive the ordeal. He didn't know what the world would look like when they reopened the barrel. He could only wait to find out.

Tomorrow I will climb a tree, he thought.

At that very moment, as the assembled masses watched the barrel tumble down the falls and disappear into the frothy suds of the rocky pool below, Rufus became Deganawida, The Heavenly Messenger, Two Currents Flowing Together. He was half horse, half alligator, all man. He was a warbler, a starling, the pure cleansing waters of the Cahoos. He was a legend, freed at last from space and time. Another day down the tubes.

Without planning to, Rufus Wiggin had finally made his big statement, and finally accomplished something money couldn't buy. Thus he inspired, if for ever so briefly, The Great Peace.

THE END

About the Author

Ryan George Kittleman is a San Francisco-based arts attorney and the
founder of Colony Pictura. *The Great Peace* is his first novel.

Acknowledgments

The author wishes to thank....
Shawn Saler, Melanie Robins, Tim Segreto,
Adam Peterson, Candace Myers, Mike Jeter,
Karen Hodsdon, Carly Clark, Devin Zimmer,
Blake Henderson, and of course, my family.

CPSIA information can be obtained at www.ICGtesting.com
Printed in the USA
LVOW100646260112

265596LV00001B/1/P